BLOOD COUNT

JACK BATTEN

BLOOD COUNT

A CRANG MYSTERY

DUNDURN
TORONTO

Cover image: istock.com/simon edwards
Printer: Webcom

Library and Archives Canada Cataloguing in Publication

Batten, Jack, 1932-, author
    Blood count / Jack Batten.

(A Crang mystery)
Previously published: Toronto: Macmillan Canada, 1991.
Issued in print and electronic formats.
ISBN 978-1-4597-3534-7 (softcover).--ISBN 978-1-4597-3535-4 (PDF).--
ISBN 978-1-4597-3536-1 (EPUB)

    I. Title. II. Series: Batten, Jack, 1932- . Crang mystery.

PS8553.A833B56 2017   C813'.54   C2016-908137-0
                                            C2016-908138-9

1 2 3 4 5   21 20 19 18 17

Conseil des Arts du Canada   Canada Council for the Arts

Canada

ONTARIO ARTS COUNCIL
CONSEIL DES ARTS DE L'ONTARIO
an Ontario government agency
un organisme du gouvernement de l'Ontario

We acknowledge the support of the Canada Council for the Arts and the Ontario Arts Council for our publishing program. We also acknowledge the financial support of the Government of Ontario, through the Ontario Book Publishing Tax Credit and the Ontario Media Development Corporation, and the Government of Canada.

Care has been taken to trace the ownership of copyright material used in this book. The author and the publisher welcome any information enabling them to rectify any references or credits in subsequent editions.
    — J. Kirk Howard, President

The publisher is not responsible for websites or their content unless they are owned by the publisher.

Printed and bound in Canada.

VISIT US AT

dundurn.com | @dundurnpress | dundurnpress | dundurnpress

Dundurn
3 Church Street, Suite 500
Toronto, Ontario, Canada
M5E 1M2

CHAPTER ONE

So many people turned out for the wake that it had overflowed up the stairs of the house and into my apartment. I own the house. It's a duplex on the west side of Beverley Street across from Grange Park, behind the Art Gallery of Ontario. I live in the upper apartment and had rented the lower to two gay guys named Alex and Ian. Alex was the wake's host, if host is the proper term for the person who's left behind when his companion has died. Ian had died.

"I think Ian would have adored every minute of it," Alex said.

"Except for the food," I said. "Not up to Ian's standards, the little bitty Simpsons sandwiches and those puffy cheese things."

"Oh, he'd have been absolutely appalled if he knew I had his wake catered." Alex paused and got a reflective look. "Imagine what Ian would have done if he'd cooked for his very own wake. Pull out all the stops, I mean *heaven.*"

"Ian was divine in the kitchen," Annie said. "Divine out of it, too."

Annie is Annie B. Cooke, the woman in my life. She and I and Alex were sitting in my living room. It was about ten thirty. Everybody else had left. Plumes of cigarette smoke still floated in the air, and someone had planted a glass half full of Scotch and water on top of the stack of magazines on the pine table behind the sofa. The glass left a ring in the middle of Branford Marsalis's face. He was on the cover of *DownBeat*.

"Smells like Rick's American Café in here," I said.

I walked across the room and lifted a window higher. A light May breeze wafted through the stale cigarette residue.

"Practically every person we knew in the world came," Alex said. "Ian would have loved that part."

"Ian was a party guy," I said.

Conversation was limping along. I didn't mind. The idea was to keep Alex company, even if the company was limp.

"Who was the dramatic-looking woman?" Annie asked Alex. "In the black with all the veils?"

"His mother."

"Whose?" I said. "Ian had a *mother*?"

"She never gave up her dream that Ian would find the right girl and settle down. Old witch, she couldn't abide me."

"So that's why, all the years you guys've been tenants, what, nine years and change, I never laid eyes on his mother?"

"Listen, dears," Alex said, "we got off lucky. I was petrified Ian's grandmother might attend today."

"*Grandmother.*"

"The tongue on her. She's ninety-one. She phoned Ian at Casey House toward the end. He was all skin and bones and sores and lesions, and the call came from Grannie Argyll. Ian got on the line. I was there, and he managed some banter, you know, and Grannie said, 'Well, boy, if you'd never gone queer on us, you'd at least have died of something a person could tell her friends about.'"

"Did Ian laugh?"

"Damn near till he *did* die."

"Except," Annie said, "it isn't a laughing matter."

"No," Alex said, "AIDS definitely isn't."

I went over and took Alex's wineglass from his hand. He was sitting in the wing chair. Annie and I occupied the sofa. I carried the glass to the kitchen and topped it up from an opened bottle of Australian Chardonnay in the refrigerator.

"Stop me if it's none of our concern, Alex," Annie was saying, "but I think it is."

I handed Alex his glass.

"No, I don't have AIDS," he said, speaking past me to Annie. "There, does that take care of what's on your mind?"

"We've been worrying, Crang and I, ever since we heard about Ian." Annie wasn't flustered by Alex's direct answer. "AIDS is so virulent. I'm not an expert or anything, just what I read in magazines, but aren't you at risk?"

Alex was smiling. It wasn't a sad smile, more like an expression of resignation. I'd liked Alex's face from the first day he and Ian moved in. He was handsome in a rueful way. He had the face of a guy who might be entertaining a long-running secret joke. He was tall and slim, in his mid-sixties. Ian Argyll had been almost twenty years younger than Alex, and the opposite in build, short and chunky. Ian was a real estate agent, a natural at it, a peppy, sweet-tongued guy.

"I'm not at *risk*, as you put it," Alex said. "All I happen to be is angry, which is quite enough, thank you very much."

"A doctor's cleared you?" Annie was in her persevering-interviewer mode, something she does for pay on television. "You have no symptoms?"

"Annie, I couldn't possibly have got AIDS from Ian, not unless it's conveyed by hugs and snuggles. Now, can we agree to get off this particular topic?"

I was drinking Wyborowa on the rocks. "But what you are," I asked Alex, "is angry?"

Annie laced her fingers through mine and squeezed. The squeeze meant I should lay off and leave the interrogation to her.

"It's natural you'd feel angry," she said to Alex. "Angry at fate or whatever for taking Ian."

"Oh, screw fate." Alex flapped his hand in the air. "My rage is much more constructive than that."

"At Ian?" Annie said, persisting. "That's who you're angry at?"

"Where Ian's concerned, I never felt anger. With him, I went through a regular catalogue of wretched emotions. Devastation ... I was devastated he had AIDS, and for a time there, not too long, I felt ... betrayed. But I forgave him."

"You forgave him," Annie said, "for straying."

"Annie, dear," Alex said, "what a charmingly archaic word. *Straying.*"

"Well, having an affair."

Alex was holding up the index finger of his left hand. "Actually," he said, "one man, one time, one-night stand."

"And that's how Ian contracted AIDS?"

"One *night* is to exaggerate. More like a few nasty moments."

"That sounds so awful, so wasteful, I want to cry."

"I tried that already, Annie. Buckets. It didn't help much of anything. Not the bloody rage, anyway. It's sitting in me like some malevolent lump."

Annie's hand in mine felt damp. "Ian told you about this other man?" she asked Alex. "When? Toward the end?"

"Longer ago than that. He sat me down for a real heart-to-heart and poured it all out at once, the AIDS, the encounter, the certainty he was going to die. A real black-letter day, I tell you, last February fifth. Drank an entire bottle of Chivas between the two of us."

"Now I *am* prying," Annie said, "but I remember Ian looking very much not himself back from about late autumn on."

Alex nodded. "Flu. He kept saying he had the flu, Shanghai flu, Hong Kong flu, bloody *Mississauga* flu, whatever strain was going. It was a litany with him. 'Oh, luv, I've just come down with a touch of old devil ague and no time to bring it to its knees.' Quite gallant when you realize he knew the truth."

"Gallant, okay, but misleading."

"An outright lie. But, don't you remember, the real estate market went through the most remarkably silly boom about then? And Ian was selling a house practically every day over in

Riverdale? Those old working people's homes that yuppies go mad for?"

"Sure," I chipped in. "Ian was out most nights. Open houses on the weekends. I used to see him dragging in at crazy hours."

"Well?" Alex had a defensive challenge in his voice. "You see why I believed him about the flu? And how he was too busy to take to his bed?"

"Alex," Annie said, "nobody could have suspected AIDS, not you, not anybody in your position."

"That's what I tell myself," Alex said, "but I did go through a guilt period. The guilt is one of Ian's legacies."

Conversation slacked off. Annie seemed to have checked out of the questioning, at least temporarily.

"Plus the anger," I said to Alex. "Ian left that behind him."

"That, too."

"Maybe you ought to see somebody," I said. "You know, a professional, a shrink. Get rid of the bad stuff in your head."

"I've a more satisfying therapy planned, don't you fret about that."

"Yeah, well, a guy shouldn't practise psychiatry on himself, especially if he isn't a psychiatrist."

"Crang, think of this," Alex said, leaning forward in his chair and enunciating each word as if he was addressing a slow student. "The swine who gave Ian AIDS."

"Come again?"

"I'm going to confront him. That's my notion of therapy."

"Yeah?" I said. "Ian, in fact, supplied a name that goes with the guy?"

"The murderer." Alex's voice had an edge. "Why not call him by what he is and what he did? He *murdered* Ian."

I spent some time on my vodka, a pause to give Alex space to simmer down. "I don't know," I said, "there've been cases of guys who had AIDS, knew they had it, and went ahead and engaged in sex with other people and they got charged. Convictions registered in a couple cases for criminal assault. But murder? No way, Alex."

"Oh, *Crang*." Alex hadn't simmered down. "Stop sounding like a lawyer."

"Occupational hazard. I am one."

"I know *that*, but can't you see? I don't give a flying fuck about the law."

Sitting on the sofa, I didn't pick up any vibrations that Annie was intending to return to the fray.

"Listen, Alex," I said, "back to square one. You got a name for the guy who infected Ian or not?"

"Not."

"Okay, I'd say it's game over."

"I think Ian must have held back on his killer's name because he read my reaction. He saw how furious I was over everything."

"Does it matter now?" I raised my hand and wobbled it back and forth. "All that counts is no name, no confrontation."

"But I've got something almost as good," Alex said.

"Something Ian gave you?"

"Where he met his killer. The very *place* Ian met him."

Annie and I exchanged a fast glance.

"Oh, don't look at each another that way," Alex said. "I'm not crackers, and I don't need anybody *humouring* me."

"Well, listen to yourself," I said. "The place Ian met his killer. Even if you should go rooting after the guy, which is pointless right there, destructive really, the place by itself can't be much help."

"It can, believe me on that, my friend."

"What? Some office Ian did business in? One of his open houses? Along those lines?"

"I'm keeping the location to myself, so don't bother cross-examining."

"Helping is what I figured on."

Alex was silent for a couple of moments. "I appreciate that, honestly," he said. "I appreciate just *sitting* here with the two of you. But what I've got to do, I've got to do alone."

Alex stopped himself.

"Did you hear *that*?" he said. "I sound like John Bloody Wayne."

"Even John Wayne had a sidekick," I said. "Montgomery Clift, Katharine Hepburn, or somebody."

"Crang," Alex said, "on this, I am alone and very determined."

Alex got a look on his face that I would have called determined.

"Finding the man who murdered Ian," he said, "is a rather personal crusade, if you like."

The room seemed to have become much quieter.

"I'm going to find him," Alex said. "And when I do, pardon the drama, my dears, I am going to kill the bastard."

CHAPTER TWO

Annie asked if I was awake.

Alex had gone downstairs around eleven thirty. Annie and I sat up another half hour. We had a final drink and ate some of the bitty Simpsons sandwiches, mostly chopped egg with pimento mixed in. Annie said she didn't feel like going home. She has a flat on the third floor of a nice old house in Cabbagetown. We went to bed at my place. When she asked if I was awake, the digital clock on the VCR against the far wall of the bedroom read 2:41 a.m.

"Yeah," I said.

"I thought so. You weren't making the right noises."

I rolled over on my back. "What do you mean, noises?" I said. "You implying I snore?"

"More of a whistling sound."

"Through my nose?"

"Your mouth."

"That'd be a fantastic feat, if I whistled through my nose. Probably've got me on *The Gong Show*."

"*Crang.*"

Annie did a lot of rustling in the bed. She shifted one hundred and eighty degrees so that she faced me. She had my Greenpeace T-shirt on.

"Do you think Alex is serious?" she asked me in the dark. I could feel and smell her breath. It was still sweet. I knew mine would smell rank. All I had to do was lie down and my breath turned sour.

"I go one way, then the other," I said. "I tell myself it's an aberration of the temporary sort, what Alex was saying. But I don't know, the way he sounded, he didn't *seem* to be kidding."

"What are you going to do about it?"

"Do you think he's serious?"

"That's why I'm having trouble getting to sleep."

"What are *you* going to do about it?" I asked. "About Alex?"

"Back you up every way I can," Annie said. "But, honey, you're the one who's had experience with this sort of thing."

"With what sort of thing? A murdered person?"

"That exact sort of thing," Annie said. She reached over and laid her right hand on my chest. I didn't have on a Greenpeace T-shirt or anything else.

"Yeah," I said. "But my experience, the few times I got involved, has always been after the people were already dead. What Alex is talking about, it's before the fact. I don't know where I'd start, apart from maybe putting a lock on Alex."

"That's okay," Annie said. She withdrew her hand from my chest and sat up. "I have a plan."

"I liked it when your hand was on my chest."

"I was afraid you might be getting tumescent."

"*Getting*?"

"My plan," Annie said, "is you should beat Alex to the person he thinks he's going to kill."

"That's your complete plan?"

"Unless you've got a better one."

I propped my hands behind my head. "Another thing you should remember, toots, I didn't choose to get in on these other murders you're talking about. They were more or less thrust on me, and I had to solve them in order to get out from under. So to speak."

"*Solve* them?"

"Come on, eventually I did, after maybe a misstep or two along the way," I said. "Anyway, my point is you're suggesting I get actively involved before there's a corpse."

"My point is there won't *be* a corpse if you get actively involved."

"Let me just ponder that."

"While you're pondering," Annie said, "keep this in mind. It's Alex we're protecting, Alex our friend and your tenant and someone who is in a state of something like severe dislocation."

"Sure, but maybe when he's located again, gets over his grief and everything, he'll drop this notion of revenge and the rest of it."

Annie said nothing for a minute. The sheets rustled again. She had drawn her legs up. I thought she was resting her chin on her knees, but the bedroom was too dark to tell.

"That's a chance we shouldn't take," Annie said finally. "Alex might not come to his senses in time."

"He's a very sensible person. Got a good job in Queen's Park, never late with the rent, no loud parties unless we're invited…."

"Crang," Annie said, "quit stalling."

"Okay, I agree, we have to do something."

"That's my guy." Annie slid under the covers and sneaked her arm around my waist. "Now," she said, "we have to find out first where Alex is going to start looking for this man he thinks gave Ian the disease."

"My reading is Alex isn't about to cut us in on that piece of information."

"That's where you could be wrong," Annie said. As she spoke, she was stroking my stomach in an absentminded way, probably too caught up in the conversation to realize she was stroking.

"Why could I be wrong about that?" I asked.

"Because Alex could use your expertise. You know how to hunt down people and that sort of quasi-criminal stuff. He'll be glad of your advice."

"Alex seemed pretty steely and independent tonight."

"That might've just been bravado," Annie said. She was stroking my stomach counter-clockwise. "When he gets down to the real business of trying to locate the man he says he's going to kill, that's the time he'll need some trained help."

"And that's when I make my move?" I said. "Offer Alex the benefit of my wisdom?"

"Exactly," Annie said.

The rotations with her hand dropped lower on my stomach.

"Hey," Annie said, "what's this we have down here?"

"Tumescence."

"If we're going to make love," Annie said, "there're two matters to take care of first."

"Yeah?"

"Number one, finish talking about the plan to keep Alex out of trouble."

"We're finished," I said. "The order of action is, I offer my services to Alex, and in the process, I winkle some hints out of him about where he's going to search for the alleged guilty party, the guy who infected Ian with AIDS, and I get to this party first and tell him to move out of town pronto."

"Why are you speaking so quickly?"

"Shows you what a fast study I am."

"Well, yes, that's the plan I have in mind," Annie said. "But there has to be more detail."

"Let me talk to Alex, and later on we'll regroup for the detail."

Annie hesitated. "I guess so," she said.

"What's the other matter we have to take care of before we make love?"

"On this one, buster, you're on your own."

"I am?"

"Get into the bathroom and gargle some mouthwash."

CHAPTER THREE

Next morning, Saturday, after Annie left, I volunteered to help Alex walk the dog.

"That's sweet of you, Crang," Alex said.

The dog is an Irish Setter and getting long in the tooth. Alex and Ian had named him Genet. He wags his tail a lot and barks only with extreme provocation.

"Through the park and down to Queen," Alex said. "It's the usual route."

"Don't change on my account."

"In honour of the occasion, you can be point man."

Alex handed me Genet's leash. He carried a pooper scooper and a small brown paper bag. The three of us crossed Beverley Street and walked into the park. It had plenty of trees in orderly rows and a scattering of heavy green picnic tables.

"How's the pooch bearing up under Ian's absence?" I asked.

"He whines at eating time. Only natural, I guess. Ian was the one who opened his little tins and things. And he goes around looking rather puzzled."

"I took that for his permanent expression."

"Now that you mention it...."

Genet was a leisurely walker. No yanking on the leash, no

sudden leaps and bounds. He halted now and then to sniff trees and discarded Big Mac boxes, and he squatted to do some business on the grass. Alex went to work with the pooper scooper and the brown paper bag.

"I loathe this part," he said.

"Because Ian handled the walking detail."

Alex held the pooper scooper and brown bag at arm's length. "Speaking of which," he said, "this is the first time I remember you on one of these doggy excursions."

"How come I hear suspicion in your voice?"

"Annie put you up to it, didn't she?"

"Up to what?" Playing dumb was all the technique I could muster.

"To talking me out of my intentions."

"Sort of."

Near one of the picnic tables, an elderly Asian gent and a middle-aged white lady wearing what might have been jammies were going through a sequence of slowmo tai chi moves. Step up, deflect, parry.

"I don't want you involved," Alex said. "Not just you. I don't want *anyone* involved apart from myself."

"Annie thinks I have talent in the field."

"No doubt you do. But I'm doing splendidly for a novice."

"You don't have the guy's name."

Alex stopped and looked at me. "Ah, but I know the place."

"So you were saying last night."

"*And* I've narrowed the field."

"Of what? Suspects?"

Alex nodded.

"Since last night you've done this?" I said.

Alex had what might pass for a sly expression. "I have my contacts, Crang, and I'll say no more, so don't press me, please."

The three of us walked out of the park's south entrance. We kept going to Queen Street and turned west. Alex stuffed the brown bag into a city litter bin.

"A stop at Pages if you don't mind," he said.

"I don't."

Alex took Genet's leash and wound it around the last rung of a bicycle stand on the sidewalk. Pages is a bookstore with a nice range of magazines and a small specialty in books about jazz. I bought Mel Tormé's autobiography in paperback. Alex loaded up on magazines. *Mother Jones. Forbes. This Magazine. New Republic.*

"Magazine-wise," I said, "you just defined eclectic."

"All they ever have on the plane is last week's *Time*," Alex said. We were back on the street.

"You going away?"

"After lunch," Alex said. "Bound to be strange down there without Ian."

"Yeah," I said. Alex and Ian had a cottage in Key West a couple of blocks from the old Hemingway house. "How long do you figure you'll be gone?"

"Whatever it takes to think and plot. A few days." Alex shifted the parcel of magazines under his arm. "Feel like some caffeine?"

"What about Genet?"

"Don't fret about him. He adores the passing parade."

Genet was resting his rear end on the sidewalk. His head swung back and forth to take in the street action.

Alex and I went into the café next door to Pages. I nabbed a window table. Alex lined up at the counter and brought back two cappuccinos. I waited for mine to cool. Alex stirred his in an abstracted way.

I tried a little prompting. "Anything more you want to get off your chest?" I asked Alex.

"Perhaps something in the nature of enlightenment."

"Swell. I could stand some of that."

"Gaëtan Dugas," Alex said. "Does that name signify anything to you?"

"Who is he? One of your new suspects?"

"Gaëtan Dugas's story is about AIDS." Alex had a schoolmarm air. "About AIDS but very early on, 1980, in that general period. You see, the first people doctors spotted with this new awful virus, what turned out to be AIDS, dozens of them seemed to have one thing in common. Amazing bit of research when one dwells on it, but some medical detectives worked out that these earliest victims had all had sex with one man. Or that they'd had sex with someone *else* who had sex with this man."

"What's-his-name Dugas?"

"Gaëtan Dugas. The Typhoid Marvin of AIDS."

"He spread it? Single-handedly spread it?"

"Damn near." Alex kept nodding. "What Dugas had specifically was Kaposi's sarcoma —"

"Right," I interrupted. "Same disease Rock Hudson died of. Or maybe not died of, but he caught it."

"Oh, Crang, you straights are *so* predictable. Mention AIDS and Rock Hudson can't be far behind."

"But I'm right about Rock and Kaposi's sarcoma?"

"Yes, yes. But more key to my sad little tale is that Gaëtan Dugas was afflicted, too. The Kaposi's sarcoma was the signal he had *it*. AIDS. It meant his whole immune system was shutting down. It meant he was going to die."

"When did he die?" I asked.

"Almost four years after he was diagnosed."

"Huh," I said, "the guy seems to have lived a long time with the disease."

"Much longer than Ian, you mean?"

"Well, yeah."

"Ian, dear God, he got one of the quicker brands. Isn't that just dandy, different kinds of AIDS, slower and faster? Ian had PCP. Pneumocystis pneumonia. It can kill in a few months. Weeks even."

"That name comes trippingly off your tongue."

"Practice, Crang. I've repeated the damned words often enough in the past four months."

Alex made an impatient gesture with his hand. "But this is getting ahead of things," he said. "Just please, Crang, drink your cappuccino and listen and absorb."

"Sorry."

"Now I'll tell you what Dugas looked like. He was drop-dead gorgeous. Debonair, you know, vibrant, sensual. It was no wonder everybody wanted him."

"Pardon me, Alex, am I interpreting you correctly if I say it sounds like you personally knew Dugas?"

"Not knew. Met. At a Sunday brunch one time, and my lands, he *was* a catch."

"Too bad for the guys who caught him."

"He's supposed to have had twenty-five hundred lovers in his short life, or some such astronomical number."

"Couldn't have left much time for hobbies. Stamp collecting and whatnot."

"Indeed," Alex said. "As I told you a minute ago, some doctors tracked down Dugas, immunologists, epidemiologists, scientific people. Patient Zero, they called Dugas, and I've heard they warned him to stop having sex, *ordered* him. But he kept right on almost to the very day he died. The very month, at any rate."

"Lordy."

"Some people say he got downright callous," Alex said. "They say he'd have sex with some poor soul in a bathhouse, and afterward, after the poor soul had his brains fucked out, Dugas would turn up the lights and point out his Kaposi's sarcoma spots. 'I've got gay cancer,' he'd say. 'I'm going to die and so are you.'"

"Alex, that isn't callous. We're talking serious evil."

"And wouldn't you know it, he was one of ours."

"Not of mine."

"Canadian. He was a nice French-Canadian boy from Quebec. Better, he worked for Air Canada. A flight attendant. That's how he got around so much. San Francisco, New York, Florida, coast-to-coast.

He had hundreds of lovers in every town you could book an Air Canada flight to."

"Infection in the jet age."

"There's even a case to be made that dear Gaëtan was the initial carrier, the son of a bitch who brought AIDS to North America."

"From where?"

"Paris. The route is supposed to be from some place in central Africa to Paris and from there to us lucky folks over here."

"Possibly via Gaëtan Dugas?"

"Stunning what a job at Air Canada can do for a lad," Alex said in his most brittle tone. "Anyhow, you get the picture."

"I get the picture, and something else, I have this terrible feeling I get the punch line, too."

"Punch line?"

"Where you're going with the Gaëtan Dugas story."

"Someone," Alex said, "should have shot Dugas at the very beginning."

"That's the punch line I had the terrible feeling you were going to deliver."

"Think of the lives that would have been saved."

"And next thing, you're drawing an analogy between Dugas and the person who infected Ian."

"Don't debate numbers with me, Crang," Alex said. "Dugas might have been responsible for dozens of deaths, maybe hundreds. The bastard who killed Ian killed only Ian, as far as we know. But death is death, and a murderer is a murderer, never mind the quantity."

"Alex, come on, all this talk, the only thing's likely to happen is you'll screw up your own life."

Alex's face did funny things, as if it might crack into pieces.

"Ian is dead," he said, his voice sounding rusty. "Can you honestly imagine I have anything else to lose at my age that I care about?"

"Well, sure. Your career, friends, lots of things, little things, the Bobby Short tapes you listen to on Sunday mornings."

Alex lifted his bundle of magazines off the café table. He didn't say anything, but his body language announced that the discussion had ended.

At the counter, I bought an almond cookie and fed part of it to Genet out on the street.

"That's for your remarkable display of patience, sport," I said.

"Crang," Alex said, smiling a little, trying it out, "I think you like the beastie."

"He's no Wonder Dog, Rin Tin Tin, or *One Hundred and One Dalmatians*, that calibre, but Genet's got his fine points."

"Perhaps you'd care to keep him company while I'm gone."

"What's the alternative?"

"He's booked into a doggy haven out near the airport, which isn't his favourite resort judging by past performances. But I can cancel the reservation."

"Why not?" I said. "Feed him and trot him through the park a couple times? That's it?"

"An outing in the morning and another after his din-dins."

We started up Beverley Street.

"One question," I said to Alex. "One question about your intentions and state of mind and everything, just the one and I'll lay off."

"I doubt you will. Or Annie, for that matter. But go ahead, ask away."

"How can you be so sure you haven't got AIDS yourself? The impression I got last night, you haven't asked a doctor to run tests. So how do you know?"

Alex pulled to a halt on the sidewalk. I stopped, too. Genet, trotting out front, stayed on the move. The leash jerked me forward. I did a Stan Laurel stumble, righted myself, and reined in Genet.

"Because," Alex said, mostly in words of one syllable each, "Ian and I had no sex for the last eighteen months or more."

"Uh. I have to say that to an outsider like me, the two of you seemed as chummy as ever."

"Of *course* we were." Alex sounded cross. "We were absolutely committed to one another. It's simply ... well, I *am* sixty-four and I suppose, age and one thing or another, I got the sexual blahs. Didn't care about it. Didn't *think* about it. And so, consequently, Ian and I never got around to *having* it."

"Uh-huh, sure, but how did that sit with Ian?"

"He understood." Alex gave a look that dared me to question his answer.

"Right."

"Oh, Ian made little jokes sometimes about madam and her bedtime migraines. But as you observed, we stayed as close as we'd always been."

"Uh-huh."

"Closer."

"Sure."

"Ian understood," Alex said. "We shared the same bed, as usual. We just didn't romp in it."

"Okay, I got it."

We resumed the walk up Beverley. Neither of us spoke another word until we reached the sidewalk in front of the house.

"Ian understood," Alex said. He was facing me. "That's what I always assumed. In fact, it was beyond assumption. Sex went out of my head. I never dwelt on it, and I *assumed* — this is rather in retrospect, looking back now — Ian understood."

I nodded my head.

"But —" Alex's voice might have been close to breaking. "— But one time, I realize, he mustn't have understood and it cost him his life."

We went into the house.

CHAPTER FOUR

Genet was my excuse for stepping into Alex's quarters. I was supposed to feed the mutt. I had no excuse for what else I intended to do. I intended to conduct a search of the premises.

There was a tin half full of dog food in the refrigerator. I peeled off the Saran wrap covering the top and scooped the meat into Genet's bowl.

"Yuck, this stuff smells terrible," I said to the dog.

Genet sniffed the bowl and turned his head up to me.

"You think it stinks, too?"

I looked at my watch.

"Or maybe it's the hour? Too early for dinner?"

It was four thirty, Saturday afternoon.

"See, Genet, I'm a tad keen to get on with the search...."

What was I doing? Explaining to a *dog*!

Genet blinked his rheumy eyes and focused on the bowl's contents.

"Think of it as high tea," I said to the top of his head.

On the refrigerator door, a pair of silver magnets pinned a *New Yorker* cartoon done by the guy who draws in dots. It showed a doctor examining a patient's arm and saying, "Well, Bob, it looks like a paper cut, but just to make sure, let's do lots of tests." Two more silver magnets held up a list of things to do: "Cancel *Globe* till May 19"; "Join Winston Churchill Tennis Club"; and "Book window washer." The list was in Alex's handwriting. None of the items said: "Advise Crang where to find Ian's killer."

I walked down the hall to the living room at the front of the house. Behind me, Genet slurped his protein. I sat at the elegant little Biedermeier desk and looked at the small oil painting over it, an Albert Franck of a downtown Toronto backyard. It didn't tell me anything except that it was a clear, evocative, tough-minded piece of art. Genet padded into the room and fixed a gaze on me.

"Don't even mention it." My voice was on the loud side. "I shouldn't be doing this, but it's for a good cause, okay?"

Genet whimpered.

Alex kept orderly desk drawers. Receipts clipped together — Bell Canada, Imperial Oil, Visa, the University Club. There was a file marked "Income Tax" and another labelled "Ian's Estate." A bundle of fat documents with many official seals had to do with the ownership of the Key West cottage. I fingered through every scrap of paper and found nothing that revealed where Alex might have gone digging for the guy who gave Ian the disease.

There was a black box beside the phone. It was a memory machine — an electronic gizmo that automatically recorded the number of anyone who dialed Alex's place. I fiddled around until I located the button that lit up the machine's screen. It showed three numbers.

I dialed the first.

"You have reached the Ontario Ministry of Education," a recorded female voice said. "The offices are closed today, but if you call Monday after eight thirty in morning, we will be happy to assist you."

It was Alex's business number. He'd been provincial deputy minister of education for as long as he and Ian had lived in the house.

I dialed the second number on the memory screen.

No answer. I let the phone ring a dozen times. Definitely no answer.

I dialed the third number.

"Purple Zinnia," a pleasant male voice said. "Good afternoon."

"Have I got a flower shop?"

"No, we're still a restaurant."

"This isn't the first time you've heard the flower shop line?"

"Twice before," the voice said, still pleasant, "and that's just today."

"I'll call back later when I think of something more original."

"If you want a reservation, we don't take them. But tonight, get here before, oh, seven fifteen, and you should be okey-doke."

"Thanks."

I spent another half hour in the apartment. Genet kept me company, silent and observing. The closest I came to a clue was a ceramic bowl that held a collection of matchbooks. Maybe one from a place where Ian had met the bad guy? Where Alex had traced the same bad guy? Most of the matchbooks advertised upscale restaurants. Cibo. Centro. Bistro 990. No particular leads there. When it came to dining out, Ian and Alex had always treated themselves. I opened each matchbook, about twenty-five or thirty of them, and checked for anything jotted in handwriting on the inside. All were clean.

I ended up at the Biedermeier desk. So did Genet. I dialed the second number on the memory screen. Still no answer. I used the weighty gold pen on the desk to jot the number on the top sheet of Alex's memo pad. I tore off the sheet, folded it into my wallet, and phoned Annie at her office.

"*Flicks*." It was Annie's voice.

"I'm striking out so far."

"Oh, *hi*." Annie sounded pumped up. "I just put down the phone from calling your place."

"I'm busy ransacking Alex's apartment."

"What does Alex say about that?"

"Not much. He's winging his way to Key West."

"Fantastic." Annie's adrenaline seemed to be running on high. "Gives you more time for the project. Sorry, gives *us* more time."

"Things nifty at your end?" I asked. "I feel something like sparks emanating from the receiver."

"God, Crang, you wouldn't believe what a marvel Tavernier is, so intelligent and so articulate and so *French*."

"You got the interview taped?" I said. Bertrand Tavernier was in Toronto from Paris on a North American tour to hype the latest movie he'd directed.

"*Two* interviews already. Twelve minutes each, two different topics. And he enjoyed the interviews so much he agreed to come back tonight for a third after he's had dinner with his Canadian distributor."

"Sounds like you made an impression."

"What we'll do, we'll drop the interviews into the next three shows, starting this coming Tuesday."

Annie has a TV program about movies. She landed it after some television guys with good taste caught her in her former job, reviewing movies on the local CBC morning show, *Metro Morning*, and made her an offer. Annie's the host and the program's a syndicated deal, carried on twelve stations across the country, channel eleven out of Hamilton in the Toronto area at seven every Tuesday night. The budget is minuscule, enough to pay Annie, a producer, and a part-time researcher. The syndicate guys inflicted the frivolous title on Annie, *Flicks*, but by general consensus, the show is smart and lively, a nifty balance of reviews, interviews, and panel discussion stuff.

"You talk to Tavernier about *Round Midnight*? I asked.

"Not till the last interview."

"Best jazz movie ever made."

"I'll tell him you think so," Annie said. "Listen, sweetie, I only have two minutes. What's this about striking out?"

"Alex didn't exactly leave his apartment strewn with leads, and Genet isn't saying a thing."

I gave Annie a precis of events during my prowl through Alex's drawers and ceramic bowls.

"Bingo," Annie said.

"Which bingo?"

"The Purple Zinnia's a well-known gay restaurant. There you go, a place to start."

"It's not a well-known gay restaurant to me."

"It's the local for some CBC people. That's how I've heard about the Purple Zinnia."

I was silent.

"Does it make you nervous?" Annie asked. "The thought of going to a gay place by yourself?"

"I was considering the ramifications. For numbers of gay bars and bathhouses and hair salons and so forth, I gather it goes San Francisco, Greenwich Village, Fire Island, and then probably Toronto. I could disappear into the subculture for weeks."

"But you've got something firm that this one particular restaurant might supply some answers."

"What qualifies a restaurant as gay, anyway?" I said. "The food?"

"No, silly, the clientele and usually the ownership."

"Apart from me, the clientele."

"Don't be insecure," Annie said. "Just have a nice dinner and ask if anyone there knows Ian in a special way."

"I'm not insecure."

"Then you're going?"

"Yeah, but I won't wear my most fetching getup."

CHAPTER FIVE

The Purple Zinnia was in a large grey-brick house on the block of Carlton before you get to Parliament Street. From the outside, it didn't look like much, just the grey brick, the largeness, and a discreet wooden sign that announced the restaurant's name. But inside, past the front door and the small foyer, I had the feeling I'd been whisked by magic carpet to the shores of Malibu.

The walls were stark white, and the curtains, tablecloths, and napkins were blues, greens, and tans. The visuals spoke of sky and water and beach. Airy paintings of flowers hung on the walls. Some of the flowers were purple. Some of them may have been zinnias. Horticulture isn't my long suit. Blossom Dearie was singing on the sound system.

"Just for one?" a waiter asked me.

"I'll probably miss the Saturday dance, too," I said. "Don't get around much anymore."

The waiter was too young for Duke Ellington lyrics, but he chuckled politely. He showed me to a table against the back wall.

"Something from the bar?" the waiter asked. He was a trim guy with a tidy moustache and short hair, and he had on a summery outfit consisting of a white button-down shirt and beige pleated trousers.

"Vodka on the rocks. Wyborowa if you have it."

"Will Stolichnaya do?"

"In a pinch it will."

The drink came fast, along with a menu. The waiter recited the specials.

"Ian Argyll?" I asked when he finished. "Does that name ring any bells? Any chance you served him the last year?"

"This is only my second week here. Sorry."

"Just wondering."

I ordered an avocado salad, blackened catfish, and a half bottle of Chablis.

"I'll hold the wine till you finish your cocktail," the waiter said. His manners were wonderful.

"Do that."

The place was two-thirds full, almost all men. There were no boy-girl couples, and I was the only patron alone at a table.

Three waiters did the serving. One of the other two passed my table. I stopped him and tried out Ian Argyll's name.

"This isn't my station," he said.

"That means you can't answer a question?"

"I *am* busy, *sir*." He had short hair and a moustache, too, and the same cheery shirt and pants. But he was taller and heftier than the first waiter, and his grumpiness needed working on.

"How about Ian Argyll?" I asked. "Has he come in here?"

"I wouldn't know," the waiter answered in a tone close to a snap.

The catfish was just right, firm and moist. I made it and the Chablis last almost thirty minutes. The room filled up, and people were waiting at the door.

I had a cherry cobbler for dessert, and while I was eating it, the third waiter came by my table.

"Ian Argyll," he said. It was a statement, not a question.

"Word is spreading."

"Ask at the bar," the waiter said. He had café au lait skin and the clean good looks of the young Harry Belafonte. His speaking style was matter-of-fact.

"There's a bar?" I said.

"Downstairs."

I drank an espresso and paid the bill with my American Express card. The first waiter, the polite one, showed me the route to the downstairs bar.

Whatever serene soul designed the dining room had turned the bar over to someone more hard edged. It looked like the interior of a *Star Wars* spaceship, all chrome and glass and black leather. It had room for six or seven tables, and there was a bar along one side with a dozen high stools standing in a row. Some silver-framed David Hockney posters supplied the room's one dash of colour.

I climbed onto the stool at the near end of the bar. The bartender was right with me. I didn't have much competition for his services, three men at one table and another guy, solo, halfway down the bar.

"Quiet night," I said to the bartender.

He looked at his watch. "Give it another hour, and the place'll be abuzz."

"Abuzz?"

"We get the latish crowd," the bartender said. He was working hard on his smile. "But I bet you don't want to wait that long."

"Maybe something to sit gently on a full stomach?" I said, trying for a match to the bartender's joviality.

"An *eau de vie*?"

"I can almost taste a Poire Williams."

"In a snifter?"

"You read my mind."

The bartender reached up and slid a glass out of a horizontal metal rack over his head. He had on a long-sleeved purple shirt. His face was handsome in a squared-off way. The only trouble was his eyes. They were too close together and gave his face a faintly wily cast.

"One Poire Williams," he said, setting the snifter on a plain white coaster. "Love the flavour, myself."

"Any rule against you joining me?"

"No rules, maybe some fuddy-duddy law." The bartender gave me one of his practised smiles. "But I won't tell if you won't."

"My lips are sealed."

The bartender reached for another snifter and poured from the Poire Williams bottle. He took a sip and made a yum sound. When he put the glass down, he kept it on the silver counter below the bar.

"My name's Malcolm," he said.

"Crang."

We shook hands.

"Nice place," I said. I leaned my forearms on the bar and did my imitation of a regular fella out on the town.

"We get a fun crowd in here," Malcolm said.

"A friend recommended the food upstairs." I gave Malcolm a grin that was as aw-shucks as his own. "*And* the drinks down here."

"A regular? I probably know him."

"Stocky little guy, barrel of laughs. Ian Argyll."

Malcolm took the name in stride. "Sure. Ian's famous."

"How does a guy who sells real estate get famous, apart maybe from selling one hell of a lot of real estate?"

"Famous around here. Anybody who dies of AIDS is famous around here."

"You know about that?"

"Wait till Lesbian and Gay Pride Day next month. Ian Argyll's name'll be on the memorial they put up in the park on Church Street. Cawthra Square, y'know?"

Malcolm left to pour another drink for the customer further along the bar. He put a silver dish of nuts in front of the man and came back to me and his *eau de vie*.

"You in real estate, too?" he asked.

"Ian lived in a house I own."

"Really."

"He came here often? Was I right about that?"

"He used to drop by two or three times a week. Around ten thirty, eleven, for a nightcap."

"Alone?"

"Alone, yeah." Malcolm had eliminated the smile. Without it, he looked as devious as Snidely Whiplash.

"He meet anybody here?"

"Might've."

"Hang out with a particular crowd?"

"Possible."

I reached into my pants pocket. In a money clip, there were five tens and four twenties. Malcolm didn't strike me as a ten-dollar kind of guy. I fanned the four twenties on the bar beside my glass.

"The person or persons Ian had drinks with," I said to Malcolm, "you happen to catch a name or names?"

"Two of them're famous."

"Jeez, not so famous their names might be on the memorial next month at Cawthra Square?"

Malcolm shook his head. "Famous, famous, in the world at large."

I put a finger on one of the twenties and moved it to a spot halfway across the bar.

"Daryl Snelgrove," Malcolm said.

I hesitated. "Let me work on that one a second."

"Snellie."

"Ah, baseball. The Blue Jays. A major league *ball* player hung out in here?"

Malcolm nodded. "For a while." At the same time, Malcolm took the twenty off the bar. His hand wasn't as fast as a mongoose's, but it might rate a close second.

"That brings us to famous person number two," I said. I slid another twenty into position.

"Bart."

"First name or last?"

"That's all. Everybody calls him just Bart."

"Not I, Malcolm old pal."

"He's in the movies."

"Give me a title."

"Porno movies," Malcolm said. "Bart the Bulge."

"You wouldn't make something like that up, would you Malcolm?"

"Hardly." He scooped away the second twenty, and waited. None of the other customers in the room needed his attentions.

"Two more twenties," I said.

"I noticed."

"You got two more names?"

"David."

I positioned a third bill in the middle of the bar.

"Okay, the guy isn't famous or anything that I know of," Malcolm said. He was talking faster. "I never heard his last name. But this David, Ian Argyll had drinks with him a lot of times last summer and fall, enough that I remember them together. A tall, skinny guy, weird build on him, kind of nothing as far as looks go. Very good dresser, though, always sharp suits and silk ties and shoes that somebody's put some polish on."

"David?"

"How do you like my powers of description?"

"Impressive."

Malcolm picked up the third twenty.

"I got something else," he said.

"Another name?"

"Not of somebody Ian had drinks with," Malcolm said. "I don't *know* anybody else Ian had drinks with, not regularly, anyway."

"Who's the somebody?"

"A guy that came in and asked me the same questions you're asking."

"If you say anything except Alex, you're either a liar or you've got a real scoop."

"Alex Corcoran."

"Congratulations on your honesty, Malcolm."

Malcolm pasted the boyish smile on his face.

"Did Alex recognize the third guy from your description?" I asked. "The thin, nothing-looking guy?"

"David? I forgot about him when Alex was in here."

"So you didn't try David's name on him?"

"Sure I did. When I remembered, I phoned Alex and described the guy. Last night, I phoned late from right here."

"And?"

"You mean, did he know David?" Malcolm thought it over. "I'd say he probably did."

"Good of you to phone Alex, Malcolm. All heart."

"Why not?" Malcolm's smile widened. "He was paying me fifty a name."

I shoved my last twenty in Malcolm's direction. "For the two Poire Williams."

Malcolm carried the twenty to a cash register at the far end of the bar. The cash register was silver and miniature and resembled something from the NASA program. Malcolm laid my change on the bar, a two-dollar bill, a loonie, and some loose coins.

"I'm not gay, you know," he said to me.

"I didn't know." I picked up the two-dollar bill. "Or care."

"I just happen to work here."

"And a splendid job you do of it, Malcolm."

CHAPTER SIX

The back page of the sports section of the Sunday *Star* carried a full-length colour photograph of Daryl Snelgrove. It showed a guy whose eyes were wide, whose cheeks swelled like they had cotton stuffing in them, whose smile was ingenuous and lopsided. Daryl was gripping a baseball bat so tightly his biceps popped out of the short sleeves of his Toronto Blue Jays uniform. His chest had the proportions of a silo, and his thighs could have stood in for a pair of sturdy oaks. If this guy had AIDS, I was Ty Cobb.

A box of type in the corner supplied Daryl's stats. Twenty-six years old. Born in Emporia, Kansas. Six-foot-three, two hundred and twenty pounds. Second season with the Blue Jays, but first as the starting left fielder. Threw right-handed, swung the bat the same way. Hitting .302 through Friday, six home runs, eighteen RBIs, nine stolen bases.

The Blue Jays were in the middle of a long home stand, playing Minnesota in the SkyDome at one o'clock. Channel nine was carrying the game. I fixed a ham, cheese, and cucumber sandwich, poured a glass of Portuguese red and switched on the TV set in the bedroom.

Top of the second, Blue Jays ahead by a run.

I stuck it out till the bottom of the third, Blue Jays ahead by two. Daryl Snelgrove had a single and a run scored.

I turned off the television and read some of the Mel Tormé autobiography. When I got to the part about Mel's romance with the very young Ava Gardner, I went back to the ball game.

Top of the eighth, Blue Jays up by four.

I put on a grey tweed jacket over my dark-blue work shirt and jeans and walked down to Queen, east a block to John Street, then south. The SkyDome blocked out most of the view at the foot of John Street. Maybe that's how it got the name: you couldn't see the sky for the dome.

At one of the gates, a portly man in an official blue blazer told me that the lot where the players parked their cars was somewhere on the dome's south side. The man had an attitude that bordered on surly. Probably when a place sells out every game, fifty thousand seats, it doesn't need to test its employees on a graciousness index.

I found the players' lot and waited. So did half of Toronto's under-twelve population. The cars in the lot ran to Mercedes and BMWs and American models with low ground clearance. At around six, two Latin-looking guys came out of a double door into the lot. They wore enough gold chains around their necks to pay off a Caribbean island's national debt. The kids descended on the two guys. Both kept on the move, expressionless, scrawling fast autographs, headed for an Audi, and drove out of the lot.

Daryl Snelgrove emerged by himself a few minutes later. He was generous with the kids, signing programs, patting heads, flashing the grin. I stood back until he'd worked his way free and had the door to a black Corvette open.

"Pardon me, Daryl," I said. "Mind if I call you Daryl?"

"That's the name my dad gave me." The grin looked good on the lopsided mouth. "You got something you want me to sign on?"

"Conversation is more my preference, Daryl."

"Oh, yeah? Listen, sir, I got to be getting my supper."

"At the Purple Zinnia maybe?"

Daryl's face was too callow to have developed disguises for emotions. At the mention of the Purple Zinnia, his grin fled and his wide eyes got wider.

"No need to panic, Daryl," I said. "I'm here in everybody's best interests. That includes yours."

Daryl's mouth worked enough to get out a mumble.

"Can we talk, Daryl?" I said. "I'll do most of it until you get your vocal cords back in gear. It's about a man named Ian Argyll."

"He's dead." Daryl's voice was faint.

"Didn't see you at the funeral."

"I hardly knew him."

"It's the definition of *hardly* I'm interested in."

Daryl swivelled away from me and ducked through the Corvette's door. "I don't have to take this," he said. He stuck a key in the ignition.

"Honestly, Daryl," I said. I had both hands on the top of the open car door. "Would your teammates be happy taking a shower with a guy they know drinks at the Purple Zinnia? That's after they find out who else drinks there."

Daryl craned his head to look at me. His face had all the guile of Jiminy Cricket's.

"I knew somebody like you'd come along sooner or later," he said.

"Like whom? A blackmailer?"

"What do you want out of me? I'm not as rich as you think."

"Nothing money can buy, Daryl. All I want from you is a little straight-from-the-shoulder information. I'm trying to save a life."

Daryl contemplated what I'd said. He probably found it as melodramatic as I did. I glanced around the parking lot. Four or five players had clusters of kids surrounding them.

"This isn't the place for a chat, Daryl," I said. "What do you say I get into this slick vehicle of yours and we drive somewhere more private?"

"My apartment's in Bramalea." Daryl's voice sounded flat and morose. "There's fine, I guess."

"Suburbs do queasy things to my head, Daryl. Let me choose the locale, something closer in."

Daryl leaned across the car's interior and opened the passenger door. I went around the front of the Corvette and levered myself into a bucket seat that matched Daryl's.

"Out and to the right," I said.

Daryl did what I told him, but he wore the expression of a little kid being summoned to the principal's office. We went over to Spadina and a block north to Clarence Square. He parked the car on the square's south side.

"Who are you, anyway, mister?" Daryl slanted in my direction. I slanted in his. It was tough to face all the way around in the bucket seats. "What's your name?"

"Crang. I'm a criminal lawyer."

"Mr. Crang, first off, I want you to know I've been saved."

"So far there's nothing established you need to be saved from."

"By my lord, Jesus Christ."

"Oh, that kind of saving."

Daryl's bulging cheeks glowed pink. "Have you accepted Jesus into your heart?" he asked me.

"I know that's a metaphor, Daryl, and metaphorically speaking, the heart is about filled to capacity."

The pink in Daryl's cheeks stayed put. It was his natural colouring, not the flush of fervour.

"Jesus guided me away from the paths of sin," Daryl said.

"Are we talking business now? Is that sin as in Purple Zinnia?"

"Mr. Crang, I am not a practising homosexual." Daryl's voice tripped on the last word. "I was reaching for help, and Jesus took my hand."

"Hand isn't the piece of anatomy you need to worry about, Daryl."

We hoisted ourselves out of the Corvette and walked into the square. It had a collection of spreading maples and some benches that the city had installed. We sat on a bench that faced the line of nice, old Georgian-style buildings on the square's north side.

"Whose life is it you were talking about saving back in the parking lot?" Daryl asked.

"Maybe yours."

"Just because I might've gone to the Purple Zinnia?"

"Good start, Daryl. Is it a given you've had drinks at the Zinnia bar?"

Daryl fingered one of his earlobes with his right hand. "Another fellow on the team took me to that particular bar. The people there were awful nice, and it surely to goodness beat going back to Bramalea by myself. I'm a single person, Mr. Crang, and I didn't see anything wrong with seeking a little fellowship."

"Hold up a bit, Daryl. *Another* Blue Jay is a Purple Zinnia frequenter?"

"Not anymore. He went free agent last spring. St. Louis signed him. Five million over three years."

"Very impressive, and I'm sure you'll be in the same bracket any season now, Daryl. But onto the Zinnia, you realized it was a gay spot?"

Daryl's right hand went back to his earlobe. "I never met any homosexuals back home in Emporia, Mr. Crang," he said tentatively.

"Understood, Daryl."

"So, no, I didn't know at first that those nice men at the Purple Zinnia were homosexuals. And I pass no judgment on them now, Mr. Crang, even though I have learned from my Bible that homosexuality is a grievous sin against human nature. I admit to you here and now that those men, Ian Argyll and the rest, accepted me in friendship, and I felt very comfortable in their company. I did at the time, yes, sir."

"I take it you haven't seen much of the Zinnia crowd lately, that's the implication, Daryl?"

"I have not."

"When did you withdraw your patronage?"

"Stop going there? When the Yankees were at the SkyDome for a weekend series, the third week of last September."

"Fixed in your memory, is it, Daryl?"

Daryl started to go for his ear again, stopped, folded both hands in his lap, and leaned closer to me.

"It was that weekend, on the Sunday, I committed to Jesus, Mr. Crang." Daryl's tone wasn't unctuous, but it showed a marked Jerry Falwell influence. "The Yankees were in town, and on the morning before the game, I don't know what it was, maybe a small and blessed miracle, Mr. Crang, I joined the Christians on our team in the chapel at the SkyDome. I have not looked back since, and sorry as I am to say so, Mr. Crang, I could not reconcile my new faith with the ways of those who befriended me at the Purple Zinnia."

"It'd put you in a moral pickle, Daryl, I appreciate that."

"It surely would."

"In the meantime, though, you'd had a year of socializing with the Zinnia crowd?"

Daryl's hand made a return visit to his ear. "That is true, and no getting around it."

"And was Ian Argyll a particular bud of yours?"

"He was a friend of everybody's."

"Including yours?"

"Ian was as kind and generous as any man on earth."

"That's what might have got him dead, the kindness of a friend."

"What are you telling me, Mr. Crang?"

"You're aware of the cause of Ian's death, Daryl?"

"It was in the death notices in the papers. AIDS. Just terrible."

"Put it together, Daryl. The way most gay guys get AIDS is from other gay guys."

"You are saying from somebody else at the Purple Zinnia?"

"Could be."

Daryl's lower lip quivered.

"This brings us to the crunch question, Daryl," I said. "Sorry to be blunt, but did you and Ian, your good and kind friend Ian, did the two of you exchange bodily fluids?"

"Beg your pardon?"

"Sex, Daryl. Did you and Ian have sex together?"

"No, *sir.*" Daryl did everything to register his indignation except stamp his big foot. "We did not do such a thing."

"You see why I've got to ask?"

"Ask me? I don't see that at all."

"Because some friend of Ian's may be walking around with AIDS."

"It is not myself, Mr. Crang."

Daryl's indignation had wound down in a hurry. Again the lower lip was quivering, and he generally looked miserable.

"Ian was a fine gentleman," Daryl said with a small tremor in his voice.

"Agreed."

"I truly mourn his passing," Daryl said. The tremor in his voice was getting close to earthquake status.

"Uh, Daryl, you okay?"

Daryl looked at me. "What do you think, Mr. Crang?"

"Yeah, right." Daryl's hangdog expression, the fault in his voice, was beginning to make me feel like a heel. "Tell you what, Daryl, why don't we reschedule the rest of this chat for a later date? You know, let you get a grip on the emotions, one thing and another?"

"I'd appreciate that, Mr. Crang."

"Sure." I patted one of Daryl's massive shoulders. It felt hot. "You bet."

I stood up.

"Get back to you later, Daryl."

Daryl didn't say anything, and I walked out of the park's east side without looking back.

CHAPTER SEVEN

Bart the Bulge was in the papers, too. Annie found him.

"Where does that rate on the scale of revolting?" she asked me.

Annie was pointing at an ad in the entertainment pages of the *Sun*. The ad was for a strip club, and it showed a guy billed as Bart the Bulge. He was dressed in a garment not as small as a jockstrap but not as large as a bikini. The guy's upper body was coated in oil, and the camera had caught him in the act of grinding his pelvis.

"Think he's got a codpiece under that scrap of cloth?" I said. "Kleenex stuffed in there?"

"It's disgustingly unnatural."

"True to his billing, the bulge."

"That's something you'll find out when you visit the club, the authenticity of the bulge."

"*I'll* find out?"

"At this club, where he's doing whatever he does with whatever's under the Lilliputian panties."

"This time out, kiddo, you accompany me," I said. "And listen, if the panties are Lilliputian, how can what's under them qualify as a bulge?"

"You actually want to *take* me to a seedy joint like that?"

"With you in it, the seediness will dissolve."

According to the ad, Bart the Bulge was appearing at the Club Eroticarama. It had a Yonge Street address, and the number would put it somewhere south of Bloor. The ad promised nonstop strip action from both sexes, but Bart was the feature attraction. Showtimes on the hour from nine to one in the morning.

"We're about set, Annie," Lynne Jordan called across the room.

Lynne produces *Flicks*, Annie's show. The time was around ten-fifteen Monday night, and we were in the program's offices over a Mac's on the Danforth. *Flicks* doesn't rate the budget to afford much studio time rental, which means that Lynne and Annie have to scare up their own locales to shoot some of the program's segments in. Tonight, things were simple; Annie was going to perch on a desk in the office and say the introduction and sign-off for the next night's show into the camera. A guy named Ron had a sound camera strapped to his shoulder, and he and Lynne had been working out angles and backdrops.

"Face around this way, Annie," Lynne said, steering Annie by the waist. "So the poster for *Daddy Nostalgia* peeks into the frame over your shoulder."

"Peeks?" Ron said. "You want, like, a hint of it?"

"Peeks, hints, whatever. Just so the audience doesn't get hit over the head with the damned thing."

"Sure," Ron said, huddled into his camera.

"What're you getting?" Lynne asked him. Lynne was a big, middle-aged woman who had a whisky voice and wore dresses that fit like tents. "You showing enough poster so we can see Tavernier's name on there?"

"I got, lemme see, a Bogarde, I got a Birkin." Ron was a lanky guy in his mid-twenties, not movie-wise enough to register the names of Dirk Bogarde and Jane Birkin, but strong enough to wield the heavy camera. "What's the name you want?" he asked Lynne.

"The director, for Chrissake, Bertrand Tavernier." Lynne's voice roughened. "You need me to spell it? Starts with T as in tits …"

"Okay, got it," Ron said, not flapped by Lynne. "Looks nice. Annie in the middle, poster on the left."

"Like to run down the intro one time first, Annie?" Lynne asked.

"Let's go ahead, do a take," Annie answered. "My hair okay?"

"Perfect."

It was. Annie wore her black hair cut as close as a cap. Not even a hurricane could blow a strand out of place. Her face was shaped in an old-fashioned oval, her figure was petite. She's a smidge over five foot two and a couple of ounces heavier than 105 pounds. She was wearing a belted grey-brown jacket, matching tailored pants, and a black and white printed blouse. She was also wearing a glorious smile.

"Hi, I'm Annie B. Cooke," she said into Ron's camera, "and this is *Flicks*, the program about movies. Tonight we're concentrating on directors and on one director in particular ..."

Annie talked for about twenty-five seconds. No fluffs, no stumbles.

"A keeper," Lynne said when Annie finished. "Good by you, Ron?"

"Like it."

"Stay there, Annie," Lynne said. "I think the sign-off should be from the same angle, right? Because we're going to be talking about Tavernier some more."

Annie said yes and raised her hand to straighten hair that didn't need straightening.

The sign-off took two takes. Lynne didn't care for the way Annie's voice dropped at the end of the first take. The second time, her voice rose, and everybody made sounds of satisfaction. Ron packed off down the stairs with his camera, Lynne settled in at a desk, and Annie and I walked across Danforth Avenue. My car was parked at a meter.

"Only fair you come, too," I said.

"Couldn't we talk to him at his house or something?"

"Which name do you figure he's listed under in the phone book? Bart or Bulge?"

I went around to the passenger side of the car and opened the door for Annie. The car was a white Volkswagen Beetle Convertible, eight years old and beginning to develop a slump. I got in the driver's side.

"Okay," Annie said inside the car. "You did the Purple Zinnia on your own and the baseball player. I guess I can put up with the club with the silly name."

"Eroticarama."

"Isn't Bart supposed to be a porno star?" Annie asked. "On the word of your source?"

"Malcolm the bartender. There's a guy, Malcolm, got his eye on the main chance."

"Bart's also a stripper? The man *is* versatile."

"Guess he favours professions where he can cut down on the overhead."

"No clothing?"

"Bare essentials."

I drove across the Bloor Viaduct, down Jarvis, and poked around the side streets south of Bloor until I found a parking space on Isabella. Annie and I walked over to Yonge and went north. The Eroticarama was on the other side of Charles between a discount record store and a Burger King. Annie raised her shoulders in a what-the-hell gesture, and I pushed open the door into the club.

A rush of stale, smoky air smacked us. It was a cavernous room dominated by a bar that must have been seventy feet long. Opposite it, flush to the other wall, was a small raised stage, empty at the moment. The sound system pumped out rock that was heavy on electric bass, and people, mostly women, sat at tables between the bar and stage drinking and shouting against the din. I found a table next to three matrons in Blue Jays caps taking their beer straight from the bottle.

"Feel like I'm on the inside of a piston factory," Annie shouted at me.

"What?"

"My senses are being assaulted!"

"And this is only the aural part."

I got a waitress in a deep scoop neck blouse to bring us two white wines. She set them down, dipping low in my direction, and five minutes later, the overhead lights dimmed to darkness.

"*Showtime*, folks."

A guy's voice, professionally excited and broadcasting from some invisible source, rode over the taped rock.

"All right, ladies and gentlemen, especially you ladies, let's put our hands together and welcome our feature attraction. Club Eroticarama is proud to present Bart ... the *Bulge!*"

A bright spotlight hit the stage, and a figure in silver spun into it, a glitzy, lowlife Baryshnikov. It was Bart from the *Sun* ad, Bart in head-to-toe silver. Silver shirt, silver cowboy vest, tight silver-sequined pants, silver boots, silver eyeliner, and silver streaks like cat whiskers drawn on his cheeks.

The three matrons in the Blue Jays caps were up and screaming. So were the other women in the club, going bananas for Bart the Bulge, Bart in silver, Bart shimmying and shaking on the small stage, the spotlight catching the winking sequins, the women screeching, Bart eating it up, not a bad-looking guy in a greaseball way, probably late twenties, big smile on his silver-streaked kisser, loving the noise, the tacky glamour.

The music on the sound system changed, soaring strings, electric piano, same pounding bass. And Bart got down to the serious stuff, taking off his silver duds. The vest came off, then the boots. He took longer with the shirt, unbuttoning, dropping one sleeve, pulling it back up, teasing, the women getting off on the tease. The shirt fell into the pile of clothes collecting at the back of the stage, and Bart went into a muscle-flexing routine, shooting the biceps, rippling the muscles across his chest. He had an exaggerated build, courtesy of barbells and a Nautilus machine — manufactured muscles.

Now it was Bart and the silver sequined pants. They came off in a flash, in a single, wild flourish. The move had something to do with zippers down both pant legs. Bart stood before us, arms raised, muscles shiny with sweat, nothing on him except a pair of brief briefs in silver and black stripes. The crowd went nuts.

A new tape came on, pumping and metallic. The rhythm went *thump, thump, thump,* pause, *thump, thump, thump,* pause. At the pauses, Bart, deep into it now, concentrated expression on his face, dropped into stances that looked like variations on Rodin's *Thinker* poses. He held a pose through the thumps, struck a new arrangement of legs, arms and torso at the pauses. The thumps, pauses, and poses kept up for five minutes.

The act might have been wearing thin, in my opinion, but Bart, Mr. Show Biz, knew where he was taking the audience. He was going for it all.

He whipped off his briefs. And there was no codpiece underneath, no jockstrap, no Kleenex.

"That's what's called a throbbing member?" I shouted at Annie.

"His mighty machine."

"Instrument of pleasure."

"I wish he'd cover the damned thing up."

"Way he's whipping himself around," I shouted, "a hernia clinic will be his next destination."

Bart pranced naked along the edges of the stage. All around us and further back in the huge room, women stood on chairs and shrieked. Behind the racket, I could make out music of the Sturm und Drang sort. The pandemonium lasted three or four minutes until a skinny guy in black pants and a white shirt unbuttoned halfway down his chest entered stage right. He was holding a cloak in front of him. It was done in the same silver striped motif as Bart's long-gone knickers. Bart went into an extended bow, and the skinny guy draped the cloak over his crouched form. Bart whisked himself off stage. The skinny guy stayed behind and gathered up Bart's discarded togs.

The room had a buzz, coming down from Bart's act. At the next table, the matrons wearing the baseball caps looked hot and breathless. They ordered another round of beers.

"If Bart's gay," Annie said to me, "a heck of a lot of women in here are wasting their sexual fantasies."

"What do you say we go backstage?"

"Going to be kind of fascinating to find out."

"What's that?"

"Which is Bart's real audience," Annie said, "sexually speaking."

CHAPTER EIGHT

The busty young woman was swathed in gauze.

"No civilians are supposed to come back here," she said to Annie and me, flat-voiced.

We were in the corridor behind the Eroticarama's stage. It had a linoleum floor and pink lighting.

"On business," I said. "Bart's expecting us."

The young woman shrugged. She was chewing gum.

"Which is his dressing room?" I asked.

"With the star back there."

"You the next attraction out front?"

"Uh-huh."

"Kind of a dance of the seven veils? That your specialty?"

"Four." The young woman tightened the gauze across her bosom. "Four veils come off and I'm bare-assed."

"Right."

"Which is the point of what they want out there."

"Bare, ah, assed?"

"Yeah." The young woman parked the gum behind her ear and walked toward the stage. Her walk had a roll to it, as if she was getting herself into an Arabian Nights mode.

"Bare-assed," I said to Annie.

"Not exactly the style Salome had in mind."

The door with the star was on the right at the end of the corridor. Under the star, which was silver and frayed around the edges, someone had taped a piece of plain notepaper that had "Bart the Bulge" hand-printed in block letters.

I raised my arm to knock on the door. Annie wrapped her hand around my fist. "Wait," she said.

"But I'm geared to strike."

"Just go where I lead." Annie's voice sounded firm. "I think I got an inspiration for how to do this."

She gave the door four sharp raps.

It opened about a quarter of the way. The skinny kid who'd picked up after Bart on stage was holding the knob on the other side. Up close, he had a case of acne that might have been terminal.

"Hi, I'm Annie B. Cooke, channel eleven television." Annie spoke in a no-nonsense tone. "We're researching an in-depth item on adult films. Would Bart be available for preliminary discussions?"

Someone called from inside the room. "Let her in."

The kid swung the door wide. Inside, the dressing room had cramped dimensions and smelled like a cross between a Gold's Gym and the men's cologne counter at Holt Renfrew.

Bart was sitting at a chair in front of a table and mirror against one wall. He was still wrapped in the cloak, and he'd been wiping the silver glitter off his cheeks and eyelids. Without the stage face, the strut and poses, he looked younger, vulnerable almost.

"You're from TV?" he asked Annie. It had been his voice, an easy tenor, that ordered the opening of the door.

"Annie B. Cooke, and this is my associate, Mr. Crang."

"I knew it hadda happen, TV come to me," Bart said. "Can't pass up a star, what the hell."

There was a third man in Bart's entourage. He was probably in his early thirties and definitely weighed in the mid two hundreds. He was wearing a Hawaiian shirt in reds and yellows, and he looked like he hadn't smiled in a decade.

"Yes," Annie said, "I'm keen on exploring the mystique of adult films."

Bart grinned. "Annie you said your name is? Okay, Annie, I don't do *adult*. I do *porno,* and I do it good, and I got a lotta people, *my* audience, who take it serious."

"Well, yes, point well made. I agree the form has been with us long enough to claim a status as a semi-legitimate art."

"Since the beginning of movies practically," Bart said, nodding. "You've done, what, some research already?"

"Certainly enough to be aware of your position in the field."

"Hey, all *right*." Bart looked to the large guy, who offered no response I could detect.

Annie and I remained standing. Mainly it was a matter of the three chairs. Bart occupied one. The big guy sat in another, tipped on its back legs against the wall. And Bart's costume was stacked on the third, the silver shirt and pants, silver vest, the silver-striped briefs. The briefs rested on top, soiled and soggy.

"Listen to this," Bart said to Annie, "I made a hundred and forty-two movies already, two in one week, scripts, lighting, the whole deal."

"Remarkable."

"All porno, a hundred and forty-two of the mothers."

I spoke up. "Sounds like you're going for some kind of record."

"John Holmes, man. He made two thousand two hundred seventy-four. It's a known fact. Two thousand, two hundred and seventy-four porno flicks. Holmes had the busiest penis of all-time in the industry."

I glanced at Annie. She made an affirmative nod.

"Am I right or what?" Bart said to Annie. "You're supposed to be the big expert."

"I don't know precise numbers, like the figure you mentioned, but, yes, Holmes established the most prolific career I'm aware of in pornographic film."

"What'd I tell you?" Bart said to me.

"Holmes had sex with all the leading ladies," Annie said. "On screen I'm referring to. Marilyn Chambers, Seka, and the woman who got elected to the Italian Parliament, Cicciolina's her name. All of them. Maybe not Linda Lovelace."

"Guy was amazing." Bart was practically licking his lips. "Too bad he didn't know about taking care of business, his money, and his health, you know. And he shoulda gone for the big crossover picture. Get X rating *plus* box office."

"Came to a sad end, true enough," Annie said.

"Know what Holmes used to say about his penis?" Bart asked the room. "Bigger than a pay phone, smaller than a Cadillac."

The skinny kid, hovering behind Bart, made a cackling sound. He seemed to be Bart's designated laugher. No reaction came from the large guy.

"What's this about Holmes's sad end?" I asked.

"John Holmes died two or three years ago," Annie said. "Of AIDS."

"Guy was careless," Bart said.

"AIDS?" I repeated.

"So," Bart said, addressing himself to Annie, "you want a feature on me, that the plan?"

"Just a sec, Bart," I butted in. "AIDS. Reminds me of a nice man died the other day of the same thing. Ian Argyll? You ever run across him? Could've been at the Purple Zinnia? Bar downstairs?"

The large guy's chair hit the floor hard on the front legs. The skinny kid's head swivelled around to me. His face had a stricken expression. Annie didn't look too happy, either. If I judged the room's mood correctly, I had rushed too precipitately into the main issue.

"What's happening here?" The easy sound had left Bart's tenor.

"You knew Ian Argyll?" I said.

"Where you coming from, Jack?" Bart was definitely upset. "You and the broad?"

I hesitated, searching for an answer to calm the room's mood. The hesitation was an error in tactics. Bart motioned the big guy out of his chair. Standing up, the guy was tall as well as wide, about six foot four. He gripped my arms close to the shoulders in his two hands and slammed me against the door. My shoes were a foot off the ground.

The big guy's voice was a rumble. "Go ahead, answer the man."

Something like a gasp came out of my mouth. The posture the big guy had me in, pinned to the door a foot above the floor, made my shirt ride up my neck. It was cutting off my air intake.

"You want me to tell Axe there to hammer you?" Bart was barking at me from across the room. "How come you're asking I know the Argyll guy?"

"Hey, your turn, talk." The big guy, Axe, sprayed me with spittle. "Don't matter to me, asshole, I have to hammer you."

I got out another gasp.

Axe shook me. Over his shoulder, I glimpsed Annie in motion. She flitted out of my line of vision. Almost immediately, she was back in sight. Her hand was outstretched, and she held something in it.

"I hammer a guy," Axe spit at me, "guy stays ham —"

He didn't finish his threat. Annie's hand came around in front of Axe's face. She jammed whatever she'd been holding into the guy's open mouth. He let go of my arms. I clunked to the floor. Axe was gagging, and his hands clawed at the object in his mouth.

"*Honey*," Annie shouted, "open the *door*."

I did what I was told and at the same time reached for Annie's hand. We turned right. It was only a couple of yards to the fire exit at the end of the corridor. We covered the distance, hand in hand, banged on the metal crossbar and hit the outside air at good speed.

We were in an unpaved alley. It was the width of two cars and gritty underfoot. We lit out to the right, south toward Charles Street, weaving past a pair of parked cars.

I risked a glance to the rear.

"Nobody in hot pursuit." The words came out between puffs.

"Heck with that," Annie puffed back.

"Not even cold pursuit."

"Just *run*."

We ran across Charles, down the centre of a city parking lot, left at Isabella.

I checked behind us again.

"Nobody," I huffed.

"Not Axe?"

"'Specially not him."

"Okay."

We stopped and did some deep bending from the waist and other cooling-down stuff.

"Bart got a trifle testy when I brought up Ian's name," I said after a minute or two.

"Might have been the subtle way you slid into the topic."

"You think I was too direct?"

"Never mind, fella." Annie patted me on the back. "You showed there's a connection between Bart and Ian, and Bart'd prefer to keep it under wraps."

"About all he's keeping under wraps."

We climbed into the Volks.

"A drink?" Annie said. "At my place? Calm the nerves?"

"I agree to the three of those."

I pointed the car toward Cabbagetown.

"Loved the way you neutralized Axe," I said.

"Thank you."

"What'd you stick in his mouth? The thing that got him choking?"

"I thought that was a clever bit of improvisation."

"Me, too, but what was the thing?"

"Give you a hint."

"Yeah?"

"It had silver stripes."

CHAPTER NINE

The client who came to my office for the two o'clock Tuesday appointment was nervous. That's rare in my practice. In my practice, the clients are criminals, I'm a criminal lawyer, everybody knows his or her role, and nobody gets nervous.

"Try to relax, Mr. Shumacher," I said. "Don't talk so fast, and it'll go smooth for both of us."

"Please," the man said, "call me Cleve."

"Let it flow, Cleve."

Cleve Shumacher was a fastidious-looking guy. His black hair was beautifully trimmed and blow-dried. He had on a spiffy light brown suit, a dark brown shirt, and a deep green tie cinched with a gold tiepin. He had a rubbery face, thick nose, and fleshy lips. I would have placed him in his mid-forties. He'd phoned for an appointment that morning. Urgent, he'd said.

"Can we get some chronology going, Cleve?" I said. "You're charged with what?"

"Fraud. The police say it's fraud."

"You came to the right place." In twenty-two years of practice, I'd developed a modest specialty in fraud cases. "How much money?"

"Two hundred and forty thousand dollars supposedly, but Mrs. Mortimer, the client, approved everything I did with the money, that is, Mrs. Helen Mortimer."

"What business was she in?"

"Is. She is still my client as far as I'm concerned. The market. I'm a stockbroker."

"I've acted for many of your brethren over the years, Cleve."

"I'm sure you have, Mr. Crang, but as it happens I'm quite innocent of fraud or anything remotely like it."

"Okay, Cleve, from the top, slowly and not necessarily with feeling."

At first, as Shumacher talked, I looked at him. I got sick of that in a hurry. He was fidgety as well as fastidious, and his tics and mannerisms were distracting. I shifted to a view out the window — north side of Queen Street from the second floor, east of Spadina Avenue. I'd rented the office since the years before my strip of Queen became home to restaurants where a hundred bucks might get you a reasonable dinner for two and clothing stores where another hundred might get you a knockoff Yves Saint Laurent shirt.

"I'm very, very creative on behalf of my widow clients, Mr. Crang," Cleve Shumacher was saying. "That's because they allow me room to evolve and use space. My businessmen clients, God, they badger me to buy them something on the Vancouver exchange they heard about the night before from someone they sat next to on the plane from Montreal. Dollars to doughnuts, it's a dog and I have to tap dance for half an hour to keep them from absolutely destroying their portfolios.... Are you listening, Mr. Crang?"

"The creativity of the market, so on, so forth."

"It's just that we weren't making eye contact."

"Nothing personal, Cleve." I looked at Shumacher. His eyelids were twitching. It'd be easier to make eye contact with a June bug. "From your preamble," I said, "I take it Helen Mortimer is the widow Mortimer."

"I was coming to that."

"Sooner is better than later."

Shumacher took a deep breath and resumed. "It's her son, a despicable person named Arthur Mortimer, trust me on this, *despicable*, he's the one who says it's fraud."

"Cleve, what did you do with Mrs. Mortimer's two hundred and forty thousand dollars?"

"This is brilliant, utterly. I put her money, get this, in the *Bahamas*."

"Uh-huh. Where the banks know how to keep a secret."

"But *getting* it to the Bahamas was particularly ingenious, if I say so myself."

Shumacher's hands were dancing. I ignored them and tried to concentrate on the tale of the offshore quarter of a million.

"Mrs. Mortimer had her account in the Toronto Dominion, the branch at the TD Centre," Shumacher said, eager. "Her account, but the two of us had signing privileges, Mrs. M. and myself.... Stop me if this gets too baroque, Mr. Crang.... Well, I went to the TD, and I took out a draft in the amount of two hundred and forty thousand. I walked it across King Street to the Bank of Montreal, cashed the draft and bought another for the same amount minus charges. Walked *that* draft down King to the Royal Bank, did the same thing again. Cashed the draft, bought another, less charges, et cetera, et cetera. Cute, *n'est-ce pas*?"

"Covering the money's tracks."

"No way the money's traceable."

"Next step, you flew the draft to the Bahamas."

"You *do* know your stuff, Mr. Crang."

"Not hard, Cleve. Nassau?"

Shumacher bobbed his head. "I have a contact who's persona very much grata in banking circles down there. Clever, too. Niles Kilmer. He's close to Adnan Khashoggi, that crowd."

"If we get to court, Cleve, keep Adnan and his crowd to yourself."

"It's not really germane, anyhow."

"Load off my mind."

"The drill in Nassau," Shumacher said, "this is how Niles laid it out, I paid one percent of the two hundred and forty thousand less charges to a Bahamian charity and the rest went into a bank where it sits just piling up interest, sixteen percent American, and no taxes to nobody no how. You like?"

"Not particularly."

"Oh."

I said, "Cleve, you don't need me to tell you you're facilitating the evasion of Canadian taxes. That's what hiding the money in Nassau is all about. And the one percent charitable donation, it no doubt went to the Niles Kilmer Home for Sybaritic Living. But what I don't read in all the finagling is fraud."

"Mrs. Mortimer had a stroke," Shumacher said in a low voice.

"Too bad."

"She's a total vegetable mentally."

"Ah."

"Exactly. The despicable son I mentioned, Arthur Mortimer, it's he who is the problem. He wants his mother's two hundred and forty thousand back *tout de suite*."

"You can't comply?"

"Part of the arrangement with Nassau is the money stays on deposit for four years minimum, which is still two and a half years away."

"Now you're going to tell me the only guy who can sign the money out is good old Niles."

I could barely hear Shumacher's reply, but his lips shaped a yes.

I said, "So the son, Arthur, he's vexed at you and laid the fraud charge?"

"Yes," Shumacher whispered.

"How late-breaking are these developments? When did Arthur swear out the charge?"

Shumacher's voice was the size of a titmouse's. "Last October."

"Cleve." I drummed my fingers on the desk. "You haven't kicked around a serious charge like that for six months, the fraud squad building a case, a bail hearing for sure has come and gone, probably had a couple court appearances to set a date for the preliminary, all of that, *without* a lawyer till this afternoon?"

Shumacher cleared his throat. "Mr. Sidney Stern has been representing me."

I leaned back in my chair and spoke very slowly. "Eddie Greenspan, Clay Ruby, then probably Sid Stern. Or change the order around any way you want. Those are the three big hitters in criminal law in this city, this province, could be this *country*. My question, Cleve, how come you're sitting in *my* office?"

"I want *you* to take my case, Mr. Crang."

"You didn't stiff Sid Stern on his retainer?"

"I have plenty of money."

"Sid didn't, for some reason or other, maybe you being a difficult client, toss you out on the street?"

"I chose you over Mr. Stern, Mr. Crang."

"That's very flattering, Cleve." I didn't add it also sounded fishy. "A five-thousand dollar cheque before you leave here, that might be the persuader."

"Anything you want, Mr. Crang, honestly."

"Right." I straightened up in my chair and slid an unlined yellow pad in position for writing. "Background stuff, Cleve." I printed Cleve Shumacher's name in caps at the top of the first page on the yellow pad. "How long've you been in the brokerage game?"

"Three years."

"That all?"

"But I've followed the market from when I was in college, investing in my own stocks and for my mother very successfully."

"Before stockbroking, what kind of business."

"Real estate." Shumacher still seemed jumpy, but if I followed his emotional shifts accurately, he'd added an attitude of expectancy to the mix.

"Selling, you mean?" I asked.

"Yes."

"With a firm in the city?"

"Yes."

"Let's pick things up, Cleve. What firm?"

"Good Homes Unlimited." Shumacher had the manner of a man watching to see if the penny dropped.

The penny dropped. "Ian Argyll worked out of the same firm," I said.

"Ian and I were very close."

I put down the pencil I'd been writing with. "How close?"

"We had an affair." Shumacher's face had drained of all its colour. "I'm gay."

I spent a bit of time aligning the yellow pad with the edge of the desk and the pencil with the pad.

"Cleve," I said, "I hope you're going to tell me what I'd like to hear. I don't like hearing about this affair one teensy jot, but I'd like to hear how the affair happened three years ago when you and Ian were sales fellows at Good Homes."

Shumacher shook his head. "Last summer. Ian and I kept in touch, and the beginning of last summer, just for a little while, the affair … unfolded."

"Oh, my."

"I know. Ian's AIDS."

Shumacher was staring at me with larger, rounder eyes. The atmosphere in the room had turned tense. As Shumacher stared at me and I stared at him, mostly because I couldn't think of where else to look, his larger, rounder eyes filled with tears. He sniffled.

I said, "I don't believe this."

Shumacher dropped his head. "I'm very embarrassed, Mr. Crang, honestly," he said. His voice quavered, and a tear ran off his chin onto his nice brown shirt.

"Are you *weeping*?" I said.

"It's just Ian dying, the AIDS, everything. I've been keeping it bottled up."

"Cleve, you want Kleenex? I don't carry a handkerchief."

"I have one." He pulled a snowy-white piece of cloth out of his inside jacket pocket.

"And pats on the shoulder probably don't work," I said.

Most of Shumacher's face was covered in handkerchief. He was blubbering into it.

I stood up. "Hold tight, Cleve." I moved to the door. "Relief is on the way."

I went down the stairs and west to the Lasso Lounge.

"Murph," I called to the bartender. "Yo, Murph."

"What's happening, man?" Murph was leaning on the bar at the far end, the *Sun* sports page open in front of him, the TV set behind him, sound down, showing a tractor pull.

"Two to go, Murph," I said. "Takeout."

Murph left his newspaper. "I can dig it, man." Murph's hair reached to his shoulders, and he wore a jacket with a lot of dangling fringe. He was fifty years old, the last of the cooled-out hippies. "You want the cognac?" he asked.

"Doubles."

"Who's it for this time, man?" Murph reached for the bottle of Martell. "Another chick client's got the vapours?"

"Half right, Murph."

Murph poured generously into two plastic glasses. "A chick on a social occasion?"

"Wrong half."

"A cat with the vapours?"

"You got it"

Murph handed me the two plastic glasses. "Like, wow, man, people at your place are far fucking out."

"You're on the exotic side yourself, Murph."

"Me? Man, I haven't changed in twenty-five years."

"I rest my case."

I hurried the cognacs to the office. In my absence, Shumacher had got much of his act in order. But the handkerchief was still at his face. He blew noisily into it.

"Take a shot of this, Cleve." I handed him one plastic glass and sat in the chair behind the desk with the other.

Shumacher's sip was cautious. He swallowed, paused, and raised his head. He wore a winsome little smile.

"It isn't Rémy Martin, is it?" he said.

"The drink's for medicinal purposes, Cleve, not the high life."

Both of us took longer tastes.

"You seen a doctor?" I asked.

"Not yet."

"Seems like an idea whose time has come."

"I feel fine."

"And you look dandy. But, Cleve, you come on like a guy who's getting chewed up inside."

Shumacher had more cognac. "How is Alex taking Ian's passing?" he asked.

"You're pals with Alex, too?"

"I went to a dinner party at their house once."

"My house."

"Sorry, I knew that."

"Their apartment."

"Of course."

"Alex's bitter," I said. "That's how he's taking Ian's death."

"Who can blame him?"

"Nobody's blaming him for anything. But chances are he could blame you for something."

"For what?" Shumacher developed an alarmed expression. "For giving Ian the AIDS? No *way*, Mr. Crang."

"The timing of your affair raises the possibility."

"But I don't have AIDS."

"Why not let a doctor check you out?"

"And besides, Mr. Crang, I wasn't the only person Ian had affairs with."

"Well, possibly one other guy."

"One? That is a laugh."

"Cleve, I'm not even smiling." For the first time I drank some cognac out of need and not to keep Shumacher company. "Ian was, ah, promiscuous?" I asked. "That your implication?"

"Not promiscuous, no," Shumacher said. He crossed his legs and held the plastic glass primly on his knee. "Ian was just one of those very lovely men. Very generous. Very kind."

"So I keep hearing."

"It was far more than sex with him."

"But he slept around? Or whatever the equivalent gay expression is?"

"He was giving."

"Any idea who else he gave to? Guys named Daryl, Bart, or David?"

Shumacher frowned. "Ian mentioned those names, I *think* he did, but not *necessarily* as lovers."

"Possibly though?"

Shumacher nodded his head slowly. "Possibly."

"Cleve, all this news, you're not making my day."

"I didn't come here to disturb you, Mr. Crang." Shumacher uncrossed his legs and sat very erect. "I came here because I wanted contact with someone who knew Ian at the end. When he was in the hospital and at Casey House, I couldn't bring myself to visit. You must understand, Alex would have been there and it might've been embarrassing and I wouldn't have done anything in the world to cause Ian distress. But I thought about him constantly, just wondering and wondering.... Was it awful for him at the end, Mr. Crang?"

"He weighed ninety-two pounds, lived on some kind of machine and didn't have a single joke left in him. Anything else you need to know, Cleve?"

Shumacher turned pale again. "You don't sound happy with me, Mr. Crang."

"Ask your questions about Ian, fair enough. But, Cleve, old buddy, you didn't have to hand me the line about the fraud case.

A polite inquiry would have sufficed."

"Oh, but it's all true." Shumacher seemed to bounce in his chair. "I *am* charged and I *do* want you to defend me."

"You're pulling the case from Sid Stern?"

"I already have." Shumacher's voice rose a few notes on the scale. "It's only proper. After all, I'm asking you for something, so I brought you something else to trade. My case."

"The retainer would clinch the bargain, Cleve."

Shumacher's hand went to the inside pocket where he kept the handkerchief and came out with a leather billfold. He opened it and unfolded a chequebook. "Five thousand?" he said. I nodded. He filled in date, amount, and signature, and reached the cheque across the desk. He had beautifully manicured fingernails.

I took a moment to admire the string of zeros on the cheque. "My preliminary thought on our case, Cleve," I said, "is I go into a major-league stall, say about two and a half years, adjournments, motions, appeals. See what I'm getting at? By then, two and a half years, the money'll be sprung from the Bahamas, and we do a deal with Arthur Mortimer, two hundred and forty thousand plus the interest in return for him dropping the fraud charge."

"That's wonderful, Mr. Crang, truly." Shumacher had shaken both his nervousness and his tears. "But, first, do you think you could take just a few minutes and tell me more about Ian?"

"Let's make that second, Cleve. First, why don't *you* tell *me* more about Ian?"

"If I can."

"One of the guys in the trio Ian may or may not have been kind and generous and loving with, David, you know a last name that goes after the David?"

Shumacher's forehead wrinkled. "No, I don't think Ian ever mentioned anyone's last name. Just people he met and liked. Maybe he was protecting them, you know. Lots of people, even in this supposedly enlightened day and age, some don't want it known that they're gay. Ian was a great respecter of people's privacy."

"If you haven't any surnames, how about other first names, Christian names, nicknames?"

"Other?"

"Other guys Ian was giving with."

"Oh." Shumacher did some more deep-think frowning. "Just one, a fellow I think Ian was quite fond of. Hubert."

"Hubert."

"Old-fashioned name, isn't it?"

"So far I've got a Daryl, a Bart, a David, and a Hubert."

"I guess you do, Mr. Crang."

I didn't mention to Cleve that I was also filing away a fifth name. Cleve Shumacher.

CHAPTER TEN

I bogged down on page 163 of Mel Tormé's autobiography. Tormé was describing life on the set of a movie he made in 1948, *Words and Music*, all about Richard Rodgers and Lorenz Hart and their songs. Tormé sang "Blue Moon" in the movie. The day he recorded it, Rodgers himself showed up in the studio.

Tormé sang,

"Blue Moon,

You knew just what I was there for.

You heard me saying a prayer

For someone I really could care for."

Rodgers freaked. He told Tormé the two lines went,

"You heard me saying a prayer for (pause)

Someone I really could care for."

Tormé said his way felt more natural. Rodgers said *his* way was how the song was written. Tormé won the argument and put the "for" where he wanted it.

"Listen to this," I said to Annie, and explained the dilemma.

"So?"

"So where do you think the 'for' should go? End of the one line or beginning of the next?"

"Crang, it's some ungodly hour, I'd love to be cozy in bed, instead I'm stiffening up my back something fierce in your car, and you start asking me questions from a particularly tricky card in Trivial Pursuit."

"Think of us as being on a stakeout together. Sounds more romantic that way."

"How do we know Bart's coming out the club's back door?"

"Because I deduce that's his brown Mercedes in the alley."

"I hope he doesn't linger, autographing his fans' brassieres or something."

"What's your view? On where the 'for' should go in the song? In 'Blue Moon'?"

"Never mind me. Isn't it up to the guy who wrote the song? Roger Who's-it?"

"Richard Rodgers."

"Hey, I grew up on Lennon and McCartney."

"Nobody grows up on them."

Annie sighed. "All right, old timer, what's the answer?"

"The other consideration is Rodgers wrote the *music*. It was Lorenz Hart who wrote the *words*."

"Then why didn't somebody canvas Lorenz for an opinion?"

"He was dead."

"Crang, honey, please, end the suspense."

"I hate to admit it, but Rodgers was probably right."

"Why are you begrudging him his lightness?"

"Because 'for' sounds ridiculous at the end of the line."

"Then Mel Tormé's right"

"Only grammatically. Artistically, I like it where —"

Annie broke in. "Hit the light."

The large form of Bart the Bulge's companion, Axe, had appeared at the Eroticarama's back exit. I switched off the Volks's overhead light and tossed the Mel Tormé paperback on the backseat. Axe, Bart, and the skinny kid strolled down the alley.

Annie looked at the man's pocket watch she wears on a gold

chain around her neck. "About time," she said. It was almost two, Wednesday morning. The three men got into the brown Mercedes.

"Nice deducing, sweetie," Annie said.

"It was there the other night."

"You noticed a parked car? I was too busy fleeing."

The Mercedes, Axe driving, backed out of the alley onto Charles Street. I had the Volks parked in a lot on the south side. Axe burned some rubber and headed over to Yonge and south. I fell in right behind, minus the burning rubber.

"This isn't the most discreet car for a tail job," Annie said.

"Gee, you're getting the lingo down pat. Tail job."

"Followed by break and enter, only it isn't lingo, it's a criminal offence."

"Not immediately for the search operation, not tonight. We'll find out where Bart lives, and some other night, later in the week, when Bart's at his place of employment, go in and nose around."

"I realize this is all in the interests of saving Alex from his own foolishness, but I don't know, maybe we're getting in too deep."

"The 'we' in the search of Bart's residence isn't you and me."

"God, I *know*. You've explained that."

"Me and James Turkin."

"A professional burglar."

"Never been apprehended."

"Crang, he's only twenty-one," Annie said. "He's *due* for an apprehension."

The Mercedes stuck to Yonge. Below Gerrard, the street action picked up. Guys in windbreakers banging out of bars. Hookers along the curb dressed in miniskirts and high white boots like they were caught in a time warp of Nancy Sinatra couture. The usual assortment of punks, new wavers, and skinheads slouching in armed camps outside the Eaton Centre. The motor traffic was thick enough for me to keep a couple of cars between the Volks and the Mercedes.

"If a break-in is called for," Annie said, "you being the only one calling for it, why not practise on the baseball player or the guy who called on you today, the snake oil salesman?"

"Cleve Shumacher, stockbroker."

"More heinous than a snake oil salesman."

"Because Bart got mad. The other two, when Ian's name came up, they tended to go to pieces. Bart, I mentioned Ian, he wanted to bust *me* in pieces."

"Suspicious, I admit."

"Well, yeah, if he's got something to conceal, something about his connection to Ian, if he's the guy with AIDS, the guy Alex is in pursuit of, an examination of his personal effects, his medical records maybe, might yield answers."

In the stretch of Yonge south of Queen, traffic thinned out, and I lay further back of the Mercedes. It turned left at Front, went two blocks past the St. Lawrence Market and double-parked, the car's lights still on.

"Now what?" Annie said.

I pulled into a parking spot and killed my headlights.

Bart climbed out of the Mercedes' backseat. He smacked the car's roof, and it pulled away. More rubber burning. Bart crossed Front to the north side.

"Must be that condo," Annie said, leaning forward, looking out the front window.

The condominium was the kind that came with much greenery in the lobby and a twenty-four hour concierge. From where Annie and I were positioned, we had a mostly unobstructed view of a guy in a maroon cap and suit jacket standing behind a high, dark-wood counter at the lobby's back wall. Bart was talking to the man in maroon.

"Taking a while," Annie said, "longer than if Bart was a tenant saying 'how ya doin' tonight?'"

"May not be Bart's address."

"Late for a social call."

"Probably not in Bart's circles."

The maroon doorman was speaking into a phone on the counter.

"Ringing a resident, seeing if it's okay to send Bart up," Annie said.

"Do we want to know who Bart would visit in the middle of the night?"

"Definitely."

"To salvage something from what might otherwise be a wasted evening?"

"Feckless is the adjective springing to my mind."

Bart stepped around the counter and waited in front of a floor-to-ceiling glass door. The maroon guy's hand was under the counter.

"Buzzing Bart in," Annie said.

Bart pushed through the glass door.

Annie and I got out of the Volks and trotted over to the condo. The doorman received us with a neutral look. Close-cut grey hair showed below his maroon cap and he had a grey military moustache.

"Yes, may I assist you?" His tone was as clipped as his looks.

"As a matter of fact," I said, "we were passing by, and I was darned near positive the fellow who just came in ..."

The doorman wasn't hanging on my every word. His attention had fixed on Annie. He was raising one finger in her direction, and his mouth seemed to be working toward a significant statement.

"Hello?" I waved my hand in front of his face. "Anybody home there?"

The doorman ignored me.

"I know you." The doorman was speaking to Annie, and the clip had gone from his tone. "Annie Cooke."

"Why, yes," Annie said, dragging out the yes.

"Annie *B.* Cooke, I should say. I watch every Tuesday. You and Siskel and Ebert, you're the very best things on television. Except for the films themselves, of course."

"How sweet of you to say so. You enjoy the movies?"

"Well, I have my particular tastes."

"Don't we all."

"I might suggest, Miss Cooke ..."

"Annie, please."

"Well, *Annie.*" The guy was melting. "I might suggest you do a critical examination and appraisal of war films. Not the exploitation films, not the propaganda. True, quality war films. *The Big Red One, All Quiet on the Western Front, Paths of Glory.* I have my list. *Platoon.*"

"Isn't this fascinating, I received a letter, oh, a month ago with the same suggestion exactly."

The doorman blushed in all parts of his face that weren't covered in grey hair. "I wrote it. That was my letter, Andy Elms."

"*Andy.*" Annie reached over the counter and shook the doorman's hand. "What a pleasure."

"It's all mine."

"The idea of the war films, a survey, is definitely high priority around the office."

"You have my list?"

"Almost committed to memory. Didn't I send you a letter back?"

"I appreciated it immensely, Annie, particularly the part where you said my idea has merit."

"Oh, it *does.*"

Annie hooked her hand through my arm. "Where are my manners? Andy, this is my friend Crang. Crang, Andy."

Andy had a killer handshake.

"What I wondered —" I began.

"The young man who went up a moment ago?" Andy said, clipped again. "Not a particularly savoury person, though that's really none of my business, of course. He calls himself, uh, Bulge. That's how he asks to be announced. He visits every two weeks or so."

"It's only a thought, but would you —"

"Tell you who he's visiting? Our tenants are entitled to their privacy, you know."

"Oh, Andy, we *understand*." Annie pressed her hand over the doorman's. "We've taken *so* much of your time. But tomorrow, at the office, you can just bet I'll insist we move your war movie idea to the top of the list for discussion. The *very* top."

Andy almost swooned.

"Well, I suppose there's really no harm." He tilted his head closer to Annie's and lowered his voice. "David Rowbottom."

"Who Bar — who the young man went up to see?" I blurted.

Andy didn't acknowledge me. "An MPP," he said to Annie, a touch smug.

"Yes, and a *cabinet* minister," Annie said.

"An honour to have him in the building, though I can't say I voted for his party at the last election."

"Thanks ever so much, Andy." Annie patted his hand. "Now we must let you get back to your duties."

Annie and I headed for the door.

"Ah, Annie," Andy called after us. "*Das Boot.* I left it off my list and it should be on."

"Consider the list amended, Andy."

We crossed Front Street.

"And not just any old cabinet minister," Annie said. "Know what department the Honourable David Rowbottom pulls the purse strings for?"

"I forget."

"Culture and communications."

"So.... Oh, I get it. You think he might be steering some of his ministry's grant money Bart's way?"

"The province funding porno movies, it's a thought."

We sat in the Volks, high on the lateness of the hour and the exhilaration of coming up with a possible scoop.

"Something else juicy," I said.

"Tell me."

"Photographs of Rowbottom in the papers, I seem to remember a tall, bony gent."

"That's him."

"Okay, in description and in first name, David, he's a match for the third guy Malcolm the bartender said used to hang out at the Purple Zinnia bar."

Annie punched me lightly on the arm. "Are stakeouts always this much fun?"

CHAPTER ELEVEN

At nine fifteen the next morning, Wednesday, driving home, I felt guilty about Genet. Two nights in a row I'd slept at Annie's. I'd fed Genet, but otherwise I'd left the mutt to his own entertainment.

I drove across Wellesley and down St. George, past the university buildings. The ones on the east side were ancient and grand, the ones on the west more recent and prosaic. Genet's notion of entertainment on the nights I stayed home hadn't been much, watching me read, padding downstairs to sleep in his basket by the back door. I crossed Dundas, and from a block away, I was certain the commotion further down was centred on my place.

Three black-and-white police cruisers were parked in front. A blue van marked "Crime Scene Unit" added to the jam. So did an ambulance and satellite trucks from Citytv and CFTO. I parked on Beverley past the crush and walked to the house.

A uniformed cop stood on the porch, his thumbs jammed into a belt that sagged under the heft of a nightstick, gun and holster, handcuffs, and a walkie-talkie.

"We got a situation here, sir," he said to me. His thumbs stayed in the belt. "Nobody allowed to enter the premises."

"What about the owner of the premises?"

"Far as I know, that's who the situation happened to."

"The only situation happening to the owner is he's standing on the porch of his house and can't get past the front door."

It took the cop a few seconds to put it together.

"Wait here, sir."

He rapped on the door and talked *sotto voce* to a second uniformed cop on the other side. I looked behind me. A camera operator from Citytv was shooting footage of my back and the cop's ample rear end. I was beginning to feel antsy.

"Step in here, sir," the first cop said. The door swung wide. "The other officer's gone for the detectives in charge."

He shut the door. I was alone in the entranceway, but down the hall of Alex's apartment, there was movement and voices and muted action.

Two men in suits and ties came along the hall toward me. They introduced themselves as Rick Polaski and Jerry Mullen. Polaski had a relaxed style and a calm face, something almost priestly about him. He was built like an NBA guard, lean all over. Mullen was built like a bowling ball — bulging gut, a fat man's waddle. His chubby face was hard to read. Polaski said the two of them were from the homicide squad.

"Oh, God," I said, "who's dead?"

"Gotta establish a couple things first," Mullen said.

"We don't want to upset you, sir," Polaski said, "if it can be avoided."

"Okay, my name's Crang," I said. "This the kind of thing you need? I live in the apartment upstairs and rent out the one down here."

"This is your place of residence?" Mullen asked. "Where were you last night?"

"At a friend's place."

"The friend male or female?" Mullen asked, on the aggressive side.

"Female." I gave them Annie's name and address. "All right, *now* what's going on?"

Polaski answered. His voice was almost too soft to hear. "There's been a homicide, Mr. Crang. You probably guessed that. But we don't have an identification on the victim in there, a man. Maybe you can help us with that, if you're willing."

"I'm willing, but I'm not going to feel good about it, not if it's who I think it could be who's been murdered."

"Have you seen a homicide victim before, Mr. Crang?" Polaski asked.

"Yeah, as a matter of fact, but nobody who was a friend."

"You ready?"

"Let's do it."

Mullen walked in front, me in the middle, Polaski behind me. We went as far as Alex's living room. There were seven or eight men in the room. All of them seemed to have tasks — a fingerprint guy, a photographer. I didn't spend much time recording their activities, not with what was on the floor. It was a white sheet. Silhouettes formed in the sheet where it covered a head, a torso, and feet. There were flecks of dried blood in the white where the chest of the person underneath would be.

"I'm just going to pull this down from the face, Mr. Crang," Polaski said, almost soothingly. "You don't need to take a long look. It's enough if you can identify the man."

Polaski lowered the sheet.

I felt my breakfast start to come up my throat. I swallowed hard to keep it down.

"The man was Alex Corcoran," I said. I looked at Polaski. "Can we get out of here?"

We walked down the hall and up the stairs to my place. Polaski had his hand lightly on my back.

"Excuse me," I said.

I detoured into the bathroom and threw up. My legs went wobbly. I waited a few minutes, brushed my teeth, ran water over my face, dried it off, and decided I was as close to dealing with the world as I'd get for a while.

Mullen was on the sofa in the living room, a notebook in his hand. Polaski stood by the bookshelves. He'd been looking at the American fiction titles. I sat in the wing chair.

"Do you feel like answering some questions, Mr. Crang?" Polaski said.

"How was Alex killed?"

"Thing Rick's referring to, Crang," Mullen said, "we ask the questions, you do the answering."

"He was stabbed," Polaski said to me.

"One jab clean to the heart," Mullen said. He seemed to get a kick out of the detail. "Didn't hit no ribs or nothin'. The guy must've known what he was doing or else it was dumb luck."

"The knife was still in Alex?" I asked.

Polaski shook his head.

"Perpetrator took it with him," Mullen said.

"The victim, Mr. Corcoran, he was a tenant here, Mr. Crang?" Polaski asked.

"For more than nine years, yeah."

"What can you tell us about what he might've been doing last night? Did you see him or talk to him?"

"Alex was in Florida," I said. "He probably flew back yesterday and got here after I left the house.... Hey, how'd you people get on to the murder?"

Mullen flipped open his notebook. "A lady phoned in, Susan Wu. Call came at five thirty-seven this morning."

"Susan Wu?"

"Yeah, said a dog wouldn't quit barkin'. Patrol car investigated."

"The officer had to break the glass in the back door, Mr. Crang," Polaski said. "There was no other way he could find out the cause of the disturbance."

"Genet, jeez, where's he?"

"Who's Genet?" Mullen asked.

"The dog."

"*Him*, he never stopped with the howlin'. We hadda send him with an officer over to the Humane Society there on River Street."

"He can't handle that," I said. "I'll have to bail him out, whatever the terminology is, and lodge him at the doggy home where Ian and Alex used to put him up when they went away. The pooch loves the place. He can stay there till somebody volunteers to rescue poor old Genet from his new orphanhood."

"Where else did you expect us to stick him?" Mullen said. "The dog wasn't about to tell us who knifed the guy on the floor downstairs."

"And Susan Wu?" I looked to Polaski for the answer. "Who's Susan Wu?"

"The lady next door, on the north side."

"A little old woman, she wears black pants down to her shins?"

"She had on a dressing gown when we spoke to her."

"All these years I've been nodding hello to her, smiling, I didn't know her name till this minute."

Polaski shrugged.

"Life in the big city," I said. "And death."

"Crang, for Chrissake," Mullen said, "the old dame did what a good citizen's supposed to. Can we move it with the facts here?"

"What we'd like to know, Mr. Crang," Polaski came in, smooth, easy-voiced, "did the victim live alone? There appears to us to be two sets of clothes in the closets and drawers, suits, shirts, two sizes."

"There used to be somebody else," I said. "Until last week, but he died, a man named Ian Argyll."

"Died how?" Polaski asked. "Of natural causes?"

"Getting to be more natural every day," I said. "Ian died of AIDS."

"What'd I tell ya," Mullen said. He was speaking to Polaski, and his voice had a ring that was harsh and triumphant.

"You guys want to let me in on this?" I asked. My question, like the others, was directed at Polaski.

"The victim," Polaski said to me, "Mr. Corcoran I mean now, he was homosexual?"

"Yeah, but he didn't have AIDS, if that's a factor in where you're taking this."

"AIDS don't matter," Mullen said to Polaski. He jiggled his enormous right thigh as he talked. "It's one of those queer deals. Has to be. The guy, Corcoran, he picks up somebody, a hustler, a kid maybe, chickenhawk. Let's say it's a kid. The victim brings him back here. Idea is, have some fun, some sex, get laid. But things get rougher'n the kid counts on, or maybe the kid's on something, uppers, a little wild. Whichever, the situation's out of control in general. It only takes a bit of backing and forthing for that to develop. So, upshot of it, the kid knifes the guy and takes off."

"Alex wasn't a picking-up sort of guy," I said.

Mullen ignored me. "Add it up, Jesus, no sign of forced entry. The victim hadda of let the perpetrator inside the apartment himself."

"Do you go along with this stuff?" I asked Polaski. I felt close to throwing up again.

Mullen still had the floor. "The victim's lyin' down there in his underwear, nothin' else," he said to Polaski. "You know what that tells me? He was gettin' ready to get it on with the guy that put the knife in him."

"No sign of a struggle," Polaski said.

"So? The perpetrator was too fast, too good with the knife. Tough cheese for the victim. He was an old guy, anyway. Couldn't handle the violent stuff."

"There's a lot of money still in the victim's wallet," Polaski said, reasoning. "Nothing of value missing I can see. You usually get some robbery in these cases."

"The dog started in with the barkin'," Mullen said. "Perpetrator's got a dead guy on the floor, a dog won't shut up. He yanks his knife out and he beats it out the door."

"Is anybody going to listen to me?" I said. "Alex wouldn't *do* that, he wouldn't go cruising."

Mullen looked at me. "Lemme lay it out for you, Crang. Rick and me been on these murders before, six, seven, eight of the buggers, and this here one's got all the signs."

Polaski was leaning against the bookshelves, hands in his pockets, saying nothing.

"Jerry, you up there?" a voice called from downstairs. "The ambulance guys want to take the body out soon as you guys give the word."

Mullen stood up. "Tell them to hold it," he shouted in the direction of the stairs. "Be right back," he said to Polaski. "Something I needa ask Doc." He left the room.

Polaski moved over to the sofa.

"Is this an act, what you two perform?" I said.

"How do you mean, an act?"

"Good cop, bad cop, you and Mullen, in that sequence," I said. "If it is, it's wasted on me."

Polaski didn't say anything.

"Or," I said, "is Mullen just a natural at offending people?"

"You should make allowances, Mr. Crang." Polaski's tone was patient. "Before we got the call to come over here, Jerry and I, we'd been on another homicide until eleven thirty last night. A man slammed his eight-month-old baby against the wall. It's hard to fall asleep, get any rest, after you've been on a case like that."

"All right. I appreciate that you guys have it rough on the job."

"Something else, Mr. Crang, Jerry's run up a hell of a record on solved homicides."

"That's reassuring to us taxpayers."

Polaski was unruffled. "We've been partners for four years and there are only two homicides still on open file. The rest we made arrests on."

"What am I supposed to say?" I said. "I'm impressed."

"I'd be impressed if I were you, Mr. Crang."

Polaski crossed his legs and looked like a man right at home on my sofa, in my living room.

"What I'm coming to," he said, "if you have other ideas about Mr. Corcoran's murder, go right ahead and lay them out."

"Other ideas?"

"You don't seem enthusiastic about Jerry's scenario."

"Alex going cruising for a kid prostitute?"

"In a case like this, Mr. Crang, assuming Jerry's theory is right, we have contacts, street kids. We'll talk to them. If somebody out there has killed a man, word gets around fast. Street kids are like the rest of us, they love to gossip."

"Sure, I follow you."

"But if you want to suggest another avenue, I'd be glad to listen."

"You would?"

"Any lead might be helpful at this stage."

"But at the moment," I said, "you lean to Mullen's interpretation?"

"Well, as Jerry said, it has the merit that it matches a pattern we've seen more than once before."

"Uh-huh."

"That doesn't close us off to different approaches."

"It doesn't?"

"Maybe you've seen something we've missed. Or know something."

"Maybe I do."

Mullen's feet made a racket on the stairs. I sat, not speaking for the few seconds it took him to reach the living room. Polaski watched me, no change in his equable expression.

"Victim mighta had sex before he died is what I was thinkin'," Mullen said to Polaski. "I asked Doc about it."

"Did he?"

"Doc says no. But all it means, the perpetrator stuck his knife in the guy before they got it on."

My stomach did some more roiling. I knew I wouldn't throw up again. There was nothing left for my stomach to lose.

"Jerry," Polaski said, "I was just asking Mr. Crang if he had anything that might be helpful."

"Like what?"

"Anything about Mr. Corcoran."

Mullen turned to me. "So?"

"No," I said.

"Nothing at all?" Polaski asked.

"Nothing."

Polaski paused a moment, still watching me, letting the silence in the room stretch.

"Rick, the guys downstairs got another one out at Jane and Finch," Mullen said. "If we're gonna speak to them, we have to do it now."

"You bet." Polaski stood up. "Our people'll be in and out of the victim's apartment most of the morning, Mr. Crang, and the TV guys outside may ask you for an interview. You don't have to do it."

"I'll pass."

"Your choice," Polaski said. "And call us if you think of anything. You never know."

"You never do."

Polaski and I shook hands. Mullen was already on the stairs. Polaski followed him.

I went out to the kitchen and plugged in the electric kettle. Tea was all my stomach would welcome. I dropped a bag of Red Zinger in the teapot and poured boiling water over it. The front door downstairs opened and closed a dozen times, and voices drifted up from Alex's apartment. I sat at the kitchen table and drank the Red Zinger. It worked on my stomach but it didn't do much for the image in my head. When Polaski had rolled the sheet away from the head of the body on the floor, Alex's eyes had been wide open, and the expression on his face was that of a man who was terrified in the last few seconds of his life.

CHAPTER TWELVE

I sat at one of the Rivoli's outside tables on the sidewalk in the Saturday sun. The Rivoli has qualities I admire in a restaurant: proximity to my house and office, Stan Getz tapes on the sound system, a menu that leans to Thai dishes. I ordered a half-litre of the house red and brooded.

James Turkin showed up fifteen minutes later.

"Watched you from across the street," he said. "You don't look your usual."

"A funeral yesterday, James, another a week ago yesterday, both nice men, that's taken the usual out of me."

"Very, uh … debilitating?"

"Arranging to have a dog adopted, too, which doesn't help my morale. So yeah, debilitating is close."

James Turkin's occupation is burglary. His obsession is vocabulary. In the three years I've known him, from the day I defended James in court on his first and only crime involving a degree of violence, an assault with intent to rob, he's been building his word power. James has the appearance of a 1950s method actor — same blank face, same silent stare, and the nerves of what he is, a second-storey man.

"You're looking spruce, James," I said. "Any specific occasion for the suit and tie?"

"And the briefcase."

"That, too."

James's navy blue suit looked like the sort that came with two pairs of pants. Cheap or not, he wore it with a certain stolid panache. His shirt was light blue; his rep tie had blue and green stripes. The briefcase was top of the line, black leather, slim, and had more locks than Conrad Black's house.

"Projecting an image," James said. "Like, as if I'm organized, which I am."

"Impresses the hell out of me."

"You don't count."

"Sorry."

"It's for clients who want a commission job, obtained to order, you know, a picture, item of jewellery, something they definitely got their mind on that they want procured. That variety of client, they'll automatically think of me, the guy with the suit and the briefcase."

"I don't imagine there're many burglars around like you."

"We don't say burglar."

"We don't?"

"Commission agent."

"You should get a calling card printed with that on it. Something bold but tasteful, a no-frills typeface. 'James Turkin. Commission Agent.'"

James thought about it. "Excellent idea," he said.

"If I were you, I wouldn't put a phone number on the card."

"Clients leave the messages for me at my sister's, anyway."

"The phone number might run you afoul of the law, assuming a commission went wrong."

James told the waiter he'd like a coffee.

I said, "I have a commission for you, James."

"A minute ago I said that you don't count. The jobs you ask me to do, this is what I was getting to, they mean trouble that is, uh, inexorable. And you shouldn't be asking me, anyway, being a lawyer."

"Is this just for the record?"

"You gonna tell me it's for a good cause?"

"It's for a good cause."

"No way that justifies illegal entry."

"Want me to fill in the background or will you take my word for it that the purpose is noble?"

"Three hundred dollars plus expenses."

"What expenses?"

"I'm not in a position to apprise myself of them until you provide the minutiae of the commission."

"Minutiae? Jeez, James, this is a condo with, I assume, the usual security."

The waiter brought the coffee. James loaded it up with cream and sugar and sipped it. It apparently met his approval. He put the cup down and devoted his attention to spinning the combination locks on his briefcase. The top flipped open, and James removed a spiral notebook and a ballpoint pen. He moistened the tip of the pen on his tongue.

"May I commence?" I asked.

"All details that are …" James hesitated.

"Pertinent?" I tried.

"Uh-uh."

"Relevant?"

"Relevant, right."

I described the lobby and the doorman's counter at David Rowbottom's condominium on Front Street. James made notes, asked questions, and made additional notes. I added stuff that was neither pertinent nor relevant just to give James more to write. He seemed to be relishing the note-taking. I told him the trip into Rowbottom's apartment was more for the purposes of reconnaissance than plain theft.

"A daytime commission," James said, holding the ballpoint pen suspended over the notebook.

"That much I reasoned for myself. The guy's *in* the condo at night."

"With a truck and uniforms."

"These are the expenses?"

"Two people will be requisite, myself and an associate I highly recommend."

"The associate is also three hundred?"

"One seventy-five."

"Tell you what, James, I'll be the associate."

James got an exasperated look.

"I highly recommend me," I said. "And I come cheaper by a hundred and seventy-five dollars."

James tapped the pen against his notebook. "The thing you fail to comprehend, *you* have to go into the apartment, anyway. You're the only one knows what we're looking for. The other person, my associate, he waits outside in the truck."

"Ah, a wheelman."

"In a daytime commission such as you envision, it's preferable to prepare for every ..."

"Disaster?"

"Eventuality."

"Like a quick getaway?"

"An unforeseen departure of the location."

I refilled my wineglass.

"This associate," I asked James, "you care to assure me that I'm getting bang for the buck?"

"He and I have collaborated previously, and he is under thirty-five years old."

"What's his age matter?"

James showed me an expression that was more blank than usual, flat and categorical. "All persons of my profession over thirty-five years of age are presently in two locations: jail or rehab. That's my analysis of the statistics and from personal acquaintanceship. See, what I do for a living is stressful. The general public thinks it's maybe colourful, like in certain movies. But they don't comprehend the stress, working nights, having to be one hundred percent alert, keeping an eye out for cops, security, dogs, sometimes performing at high heights on the outside of buildings. This is stressful, which people over thirty-five are no longer of the temperament to compensate for. The people I refer to get careless in their work habits and are caught in the act of a commission. Or they resort to artificial means to stimulate their nerves, by which I mean alcohol or chemicals. You notice I, uh, disdain both of those."

"Strictly coffee. I've always applauded your personal ethic, James."

"So the older agents I speak of, they are serving sentences in Millhaven or they are attempting to terminate their alcohol or chemical dependency in rehabilitation centres, which is fruitless being as there is a high rate of remittance among them."

"Recidivism, I think that's the preferable word, James."

James turned his notebook to a blank page. "Wanta spell that?"

I spelled *recidivism*.

"How about yourself, James?" I asked. "Where do you see life taking you at age thirty-five?"

"Naples, Florida, learning to play golf."

"Nailed the future right down?"

"Already opened a bank account in Naples, Florida."

James placed the notebook and pen in the briefcase and snicked it shut.

"In the interim," he said, "my associate and I will be outside your house at ten o'clock Monday morning. Advance calculations will have been effected."

James left without a goodbye or a nod. I asked the waiter for another half-litre of red. It was twelve thirty. I told the waiter to bring two glasses this time.

CHAPTER THIRTEEN

Annie came along the sunny Queen Street sidewalk, her head fixed straight ahead, neither window-shopping nor passing judgment on the street's unceasing fashion parade. She had on a casual outfit — a buttoned cashmere sweater, top, loose skirt, and oversized sunglasses. Everything was in shades of brown that brought the word *autumnal* to mind, even in spring.

She picked her way through the Rivoli's tables, and before she sat down, she reached for the second glass of wine and drank from it.

"You never hear me say I need a drink, do you?" she said. "Today I *need* a drink."

She sat down.

"The kind of week it's been," I said, "help yourself to the whole carafe."

"The part I can't shake, what seems so damned sad," Annie said, "is Alex was wrong."

"About Ian?"

"Yes, about Ian. The poor man thought the companion of his life, or most of his life, had had one brief fling and contracted AIDS and died, and he was going to take his vengeance. And now it's turning out it wasn't that way at all with Ian."

"Ian fooled around in a rather active way," I said. "That seems to be the irresistible message I'm getting out there in the gay world."

"Poor Alex. Poor sodding, pitiful, cuckolded, *dead Alex.*"

Annie drank more wine.

"There's a list of possible guys Ian slept with," I said.

"And some probables and some for damn sures," Annie said. The wine hadn't gone far in cooling her angry mood.

"Don't overstate it," I said. "Maybe he slept with Daryl the baseball player and Bart the Bulge and David Rowbottom, though I tend to rule out Daryl. A guy named Hubert could be another of Ian's bedmates, and certainly, by admission of the second party, he had an affair with Cleve Shumacher."

"The aluminum-siding salesman."

"Cleve Shumacher, I seem to have to keep reminding you, sweetie, is a stockbroker."

"Far worse."

Annie took off her sunglasses and put them on the table.

"Ever hear of MPS Technology?" she asked.

"What's it got to do with our immediate problems?"

"Nothing," Annie said. "But as long as I'm getting my rocks off about what's upsetting me, I may as well throw in this sordid episode, too. Years ago, long before I met you, I dated a stockbroker. He said I should let him 'goose my capital.' His exact phrase. I handed over my humble savings, and he put them in a 'hot new venture' he had the 'inside track on.' Those were more of his phrases. The hot venture was MPS Technology, and overnight, it and my savings vanished down a deep, black hole."

"And this is why you've had a hate on for stockbrokers ever since?"

"There's more. Can you believe it, the unprincipled prick I'm talking about actually charged me his usual commission for investing me in this MPS Technology. While I'm *losing*, he's *earning*, and that's what's called business as usual."

"Stockbrokers wouldn't be aces with you, I can understand."

"Putting it mildly."

"Well, at the moment, all we know about Cleve Shumacher is he's charged with fraud and may be the AIDS carrier who infected Ian Argyll."

"A prince among men compared to the guy I once dated."

The waiter came. I ordered pad Thai. Annie asked for the special hamburger, the one made from meat guaranteed free of chemicals and other poisons.

"James Turkin and I had discussions of a practical nature before you got here," I said.

Annie shook her head and looked disbelieving. "Love your style, fella," she said.

"Is that a heckle I hear?"

"Three days ago now, Wednesday morning, you had a perfectly timed occasion to point two homicide officers in the direction of all the complications in Alex's life. But, no, you pass, and today you place your trust in a guy barely out of adolescence who makes a living from stealing other people's property."

"If you'd been there Wednesday," I said, "you'd have gone for the same choice."

"Just because you got sore with one of the detectives."

"His mind was made up, Mullen, the fat guy. I might've tried out my ideas on the other guy, but telling one is telling both. They're a unit, and anyway, I wasn't really sure about how far I bought Polaski's act."

"You haven't mentioned anything about an act."

"Just out of the seminary, that act."

"Give the man a break. It was probably genuine. Cops can be nice people, too, you know, honey bun."

The food arrived. Annie stacked slices of tomato and onion on top of the hamburger, added a splash of mustard, and bit into the whole pile.

"Comfort food," she said when she'd cleared her mouth.

"Yeah."

"Not yours," Annie said. "The Thai stuff you're eating is for the taste. A hamburger, even a healthy hamburger, *that's* for comfort."

Her teeth went back into the burger.

"I can come up with another rationale for excluding the two detectives," I said.

"Excluding them from all we've learned about Ian and Alex?"

"Yeah," I said. "I would've had to explain to them why I think the person killed Alex, the reason for the killing, and the reason doesn't reflect well on Alex."

"On Alex's memory, now that he's dead," Annie said. "What's the reason?"

"The guy killed Alex because Alex intended to kill the guy."

"You think that's what happened?"

"It's as solid an explanation as any right now, and I didn't feel up to revealing it to a cop like Jerry Mullen. He already has enough ammunition for his gay bashing."

"Have I got this straight?" Annie said. "Your theory is the man Alex was searching for, the man who infected Ian with AIDS, was the one who stabbed Alex?"

"Found Alex before Alex found him."

"Or perhaps knew Alex had uncovered his identity because he'd threatened the guy."

"It could've been one of the men in the bunch we were talking about, Bart, Rowbottom, any of that lot."

"I don't like it," Annie said.

"Seems neat and tidy to me, no loose ends."

"I don't like where it *leads*," Annie said. "If you're right, if you go chasing after the man Alex was hunting, you're not just getting close to someone who gives people AIDS, you're up against an authentic, certified, grade-A murderer."

"I don't plan to get *that* close."

"You better not."

"Just close enough that when I explain things to the cops, it'll be so solid Jerry Mullen won't keep yakking about kid hustlers and Alex cruising."

"Don't ask me to embrace your plan with both arms."

"The first part's already laid on," I said. "James Turkin and an associate of his are escorting me into David Rowbottom's condo on a little look-see operation."

"Rowbottom? A few nights ago, it was Bart the Bulge you targeted for the break-in."

"Rowbottom strikes me as a better first choice. A cabinet minister, guy of that stature, he must have a bit of sophistication to him. More the kind of guy Ian was likely to have socialized with in a heavy way, if you follow me."

"I do," Annie said. "Unfortunately."

She had polished off almost all of her hamburger. I had a long way to go with my plate.

"Why can't what I'm eating be comfort food?" I asked.

"Because, silly, to be comfort food, it has to be big and juicy and filling and North American and no exotic elements."

"Like a hamburger."

"Especially a hamburger." Annie used the paper napkin to give her mouth a delicate wiping. "You know," she said, "the sun's shining, food's good, the wine, we should do something this afternoon that's fun and celebratory and different and happy."

"As opposed to funerals and discussions of murder?"

"I've got it," Annie said, brightening. "We'll shop for clothes."

"What, I stand around and watch you run in and out of changing rooms?"

"No, for *you*," Annie said. She had on her biggest smile of the lunch. "We'll make it a male shopping excursion."

I had on a dark-blue crewneck sweater, blue work shirt, jeans, and Rockport Walkers on my feet.

"Right now," Annie said, "you look like a superannuated preppie."

"These are my regular Saturday duds. Other days, too."

"Who's your model? George Bush?"

"This is hurting a guy."

"All I ask," Annie said, "let me nudge you in the direction of the 1990s." She waved her arms to encompass the street. "In walking distance from right here, in spitting distance, there's Le Château and a half dozen other stores we can choose shirts and things for you of slightly more advanced fashion."

"I don't want somebody's name on my clothes, in big letters across the front or anything."

"Only on the label alongside the cleaning instructions."

"In small print?"

"I promise."

I asked the waiter for the bill.

CHAPTER FOURTEEN

I modelled one of the new outfits Annie chose in the long mirror on the back of my bathroom door — a brown single-breasted four-button wool suit with red pinstripes and buttons. I wore it with a white button-down shirt, no tie, and brown suede shoes.

"Fred Astaire, circa 1952," I said to my reflection.

I was alone in the apartment, Sunday afternoon.

The doorbell rang. I answered it, debating how many of the four buttons I should do up. I settled on the middle two.

"Mr. Ross wants to see you," the young guy at the front door said.

"Tell Mr. Ross office hours start nine thirty weekdays."

"You Crang?" The young guy had a formidable nose and a long scar along his jawline.

"Correct. So, your turn, who's Mr. Ross apart from somebody who doesn't know my office hours?"

"The person who's gonna talk to you in 'bout a half hour, he's Mr. Ross."

The young guy stepped to the side of my front porch and gestured behind him. A metal-grey Lincoln Town Car waited at the curb. Another guy sat in the driver's seat, and a woman was giving me an inconclusive little wave from behind the closed window of the back seat. The woman was Annie.

"A half hour happens to build into my schedule just about right," I said to the young guy. He had on a blue satin windbreaker and billowy white pants. He held open the Lincoln's back door for me. I got in. He sat up front. The man in the driver's seat was bald and had on a jacket and tie.

"The suit fits like a dream," Annie said.

"Wasn't sure how many buttons to do up," I said. "You okay?"

"Well, I had other plans for my Sunday, but the gentlemen were persuasive."

"A Mr. Ross, apparently."

"Yes." Annie paused. "All four on the jacket, I think."

I did up the top and bottom buttons. The Lincoln went west on Queen and turned north at Spadina. Inside, the car smelled new and felt plush. There was a little bar behind a glass panel in the rear of the front seats, and cellular phones were fitted into the armrests on either side in back.

Annie nodded to the two guys up front. "This sort of has the feel of blackened palms, know what I mean?" she said in a low voice.

"Try pig Latin, why not?" I whispered. "Atchcay my iftdray?"

"Crang, black from the tar paper, catch *my* drift."

"You want to elaborate? In a code of your own choosing?"

"Their *hands* got stained *black* by the tar paper they wrapped the *bodies* in."

"Oh." My voice rose to conversational level. "Black Hand. You think Cosa Nostra?"

The bald guy behind the wheel turned his head sideways. "Quit it with that insulting crap back there."

Annie and I sat in silence. The car cut off Spadina at Eglinton and headed north again through the Jewish community on Bathurst. Men on the sidewalk wore black suits, stringy black beards, and black hats as flat as Frisbees.

"Is that true about the Black Hand?" I whispered to Annie. "The tar paper and so on?"

"I read it in the research before my interview with Al Pacino last year."

"*The Godfather Part III*, right."

The bald guy turned sideways again. "What I tell you two before?"

"Only movie talk," I said. "We were just discussing how family-conscious the Corleones were, the kind of closeness you hardly see enough of these days."

"Don't dick with me," the bald guy said. "That crap's crap."

"Family closeness is?"

"A guy gets whacked in the movies, bet on it, Christ, the guy doing the whacking is of Italian descent."

"Not a whole lot of Icelandic mob people in film. Norwegian, Swedish … you've got a point."

"It's a liable."

Annie raised her eyebrows at me.

"As in liable and slander," I said.

The Lincoln was still pointed north on Bathurst, past Highway 7, in the exurbs. A shopping plaza the size of Luxembourg came up on the right.

"Don't do no Al Pacino talk around Mr. Ross," the bald guy said.

"What would Mr. Ross's line of endeavour be?" I asked. "Law-abiding, it goes without saying, but specifically?"

The young guy with the scar spoke up. "Lotta businesses. Garbage dumps is gonna be big."

"Recycling depots," the bald guy said.

"Oh, yeah, I forgot. Recycling depots."

Forty kilometres north of the city, the new subdivisions were divided into two-acre lots. But size was relative. The monster houses on the lots reached within a yard of the sidelines, and the trees that had covered the area when it was recently wilderness had been dispensed with. If the houses' owners had come looking for land, lots of land under starry skies above, they'd moved to the wrong prairie.

The bald guy picked up the phone in front and punched in a number.

"Tell Mr. Ross three minutes," he told the person on the other end.

The Lincoln turned right onto a road that looked like an expressway ramp. It wound up and down some low hills straight toward the only house on the property — a mansion built of cut stone and enormous slabs of dark wood.

"Your basic Sheraton probably has more rooms," I said, "but I bet not a bunch more."

"What I told you," the bald guy said, "no lip inside with Mr. Ross."

Baldy parked the car in the driveway outside a garage that had entrances for five vehicles. The house's front door stood open, held open by an Asian man in a white butler's jacket. Annie and I followed him across the entrance hall. It went up two storeys and had a deep-blue marble floor. Baldy and the young guy had dropped out of the picture, and Annie and I stuck behind the butler, down a broad carpeted stairway and around a couple of turns in a wide hall. We finished up at a room that had a bar *Arthur 2: On the Rocks* would envy, a lot of low-slung Italian furniture, and a man standing up from one of the chairs who looked like Cesar Romero.

"Paulie Ross," the guy said. It came out abruptly. The guy shook my hand and nodded at Annie. "Okay," he said, "we're gonna sit down, talk, but you want a drink first? I got anything you name, and also, before the talk, there're a couple rooms I needa show you."

I gathered Paulie Ross wasn't inclined to go in for much in the way of elaborate ceremony. He looked Annie's way.

"White wine, please," she said.

"Crang?"

"Tahitian Lady."

"Huh?"

"Just testing. White wine's fine."

Paulie Ross was a little over six feet and fit, though he might have had to put some effort into holding in his stomach. He had a long face, tanned, a full head of silver hair, and very white teeth. He was probably sixty, and he had on a perfectly pressed grey pinstripe suit with white pinstripes.

"Like your suit," I said.

"That right?" Ross gave me a funny look. "Got a good tailor."

"Red pinstripes are in this season, your tailor may not know."

"Yeah?"

"And the four buttons."

The butler handed around a silver tray holding two glasses of white wine.

"Okay," Ross said, "we're goin' this way."

He slid back a door and indicated a lighted tunnel that was about twenty-five yards long. Ross stepped in front and headed down the tunnel at a quick pace.

"Shut up about the suit," Annie hissed at me.

"First time I've been on the cutting edge of fashion. It's a chance to show off a little."

"Well, don't make the situation dicier than it already is."

The tunnel ended at a workout room done on the grand scale that seemed to be the norm chez Ross. I noted a climbing machine, rower, pair of stationary bicycles, treadmill, and line of weight machines.

"Whaddaya see, Crang?" Paulie Ross asked.

"It's a cut above the stuff Charles Atlas erected his empire on."

"Yeah. What else?"

I gave more scrutiny to the gleaming equipment.

"Looks brand new from the factory," I said. "Waiting for its first customer."

"Not bad," Ross said. "None of it's been touched, nuthin' in this whole friggin' room."

He wheeled around and set off down the tunnel, across the room we started from, and through a door next to the bar. We were in a movie theatre with a slanted floor, a screen worthy of a Cineplex, and seats for three dozen viewers. Annie made an um sound.

Ross opened a door at the rear of the theatre. "Wait'll you take a gander at back here," he said to Annie.

In the room at the back were two movie projectors and a long table that held a small computer and other machines I couldn't identify.

Annie did more umming. "The editing machine," she said, "as far as I can judge, is state of the art."

"That's what the guy said who sold it to me," Ross said.

"Looks like the stuff down the tunnel," I said. "Unused."

In the main room, the butler refilled our glasses. Two rows of framed photographs hung on the wall behind the bar. Paulie Ross and an attractive dark-haired woman were featured in all of them, decked out in tennis clothes, sitting in a cabana, leaning on a ship's railing. A teenage boy appeared in some of the photos. He looked chunky, dark, sullen, and familiar.

The three of us, Ross, Annie, and me, settled into the leather furniture.

"So you wanta know why I gave you the tour?" Ross said.

"To talk about the guy who isn't availing himself of the equipment," I said.

"What?" Ross said, surprised. "Albert and Joey B. run off at the mouth on the way up?"

"He's in the pictures over there," I said. "Behind the bar."

"Who?" Annie asked.

"Bart the Bulge."

"Tell ya this once, Crang, that's all," Paulie Ross said. "Around here, I don't care where you heard the kid gettin' called by some other name, he's Bartley. Especially when his mother happens to be present, which she won't, but you understand what I'm sayin'."

"Bartley."

"Yeah."

Ross was looking less like Cesar Romero. He wasn't showing much of the white choppers, and his eyes in the tanned face had the warmth of last year's ice.

"Are you his father?" I asked. "Bartley's?"

"Stepfather. I've known the kid since he was, I don't know, fifteen, sixteen, since I started dating his mother, my wife."

"Your wife's a bit sensitive about Bartley's chosen fields?"

"The porno movies she don't know about and she ain't gonna. The stripping, okay, there's sometimes ads in the papers and she might see them, but she don't understand what goes on in those clubs. She thinks it's artistic, whatever, modern dancin' or somethin' crazy like that."

"Your interest is in keeping her in the dark?"

"Till I get the kid to lay off with this shit. My wife's a very classy person, you follow me, Crang?"

"That's what the workout centre is all about down the tunnel and the replica of MGM's back lot in there?"

"Only two things the kid gets it up for, long as I been around, longer probably, they're bodybuildin', liftin' weights, that crap, and movies. Makin' them, I mean. So, okay, I fix it so's he can do the both of them right in his own home, and his mother's got her family together, under one roof, y'know, me and the kid."

"But Bartley's opted for independence?"

"If he stays with me, I can put him in business, he's gonna clear thirty, forty cents every dollar. Instead, he goes porno."

"His money as well as his body? You mean, besides performing in these movies, he finances them? Produces them?"

Ross hesitated. "Whadda I know? Bartley's maybe got a little money, his sources. Anyway, this is off the track of why we're talkin.'"

Behind Paulie Ross, an oil portrait of the attractive dark-haired woman hung over a fireplace. The woman's head was looking slightly down, the black hair falling like a screen over part of her face. She was wearing pearls and a pale blue sweater set.

"So now you got the picture, Crang, you and your friend," Ross said, glancing at Annie, "and now that you got it, the two of you can butt out."

"What you're requesting," I said, "is assurance nothing I do, or Annie, will lead to Bartley's mother catching a whisper of his involvement in porno movies."

"Yeah, right."

"Or in stripping."

"What she doesn't know already, the little she does."

"Or," I said, "his bisexuality."

Ross let out a long sigh. "The kid's gonna drive me nuts, but one thing, he's no faggot."

"Half a one."

"Let's keep it simple, all right, Crang? I'm not *warning* you here. I'm *telling* ya."

"That Bartley's mother learns nothing through any action of mine or Annie's?"

"You got it."

"Or else."

"Or else is somethin' Albert and Joey B. are good at."

"Except," I said, "you're leaving a murder out of the equation."

"Guy downstairs at your place?"

"It doesn't matter how much or little I mess in your stepson's sex life or his movie career. If Bartley's mixed up in Alex Corcoran's murder, they could come unravelled, anyway, get so public even his mother would catch on."

"Not Bartley. The kid's got a lotta balls, but not for killin' a guy."

"Hey, listen to you, the stepfather who doesn't think Bartley's gay, either."

"This conversation's goin' on longer'n I'd like."

"Or how about Bartley's pet piece of muscle, Axe? How about him for the killer?"

"How'd the guy get knocked off downstairs from you, remind me?"

"A knife in the chest."

"Forget about Axe. Baseball bats, axe handles, okay, but Axe knows shit about knives."

"Always a first for everybody."

"Crang, you gettin' my message or what?"

I looked at Annie.

"All clear over here," she said. "Everything Mr. Ross has explained."

"Your friend's a smart little lady," Ross said to me. "The thing that bothers me, Crang, is that I keep hearin' your name lately. Crang comin' by some club Bartley's dancin' at, Crang tailin' after Bartley another night, Crang doin' this and that. What I'm sayin' here and now, one time only, that stuff stops, understand what I'm tellin' ya?"

"Somebody spotted us following Bartley the other night?"

"Crang, all the crap I know about you, I don't need to know no more. Here on in, I don't want there to *be* no more."

Paulie Ross stood up.

"Finish the wine if you'd like," he said. "Albert and Joey B. will give you a lift downtown after."

Ross flashed us some teeth and left the room.

I swallowed a little wine. "You think I should have told him he doesn't need to wear a tie with the pinstripe suit?" I said to Annie.

"I'm sure he observed your example."

"He apparently observed everything else about me lately."

CHAPTER FIFTEEN

I dawdled at home Monday morning, taking my time over coffee and the *Globe and Mail*'s letters section, rallying from the command performance at *Palais* Ross, and waiting for James Turkin to come by. Tom Catalano phoned.

"We need to get together," he said.

"This for business or you just think it's too long since we beheld one another's smiling faces?"

"We should catch up."

"So it's business."

I've known Tom since law-school days, from the years before he proceeded ever upward to the senior ranks at Mcintosh, Brown and Crabtree. It's a King Street law factory with maybe three hundred partners and associates, specialists in mergers, takeovers, lease backs, and other machinations that have nothing to do with widows and orphans.

"Only a few minutes of business," Tom said, "and there's a treat that goes with it. How about I take you to the ball game tonight? Have some beers, a Big Mac, watch the Blue Jays."

I didn't answer.

"Well?" Tom said.

"When do we get to the part about the treat?"

"Baseball, beer …"

"I heard all that. Baseball, hours go by nothing happens. Beer gives a guy a lethal dose of halitosis. And Big Macs, leaving aside McDonald's environmental record, they're like mainlining cholesterol."

"My God, fella, what's your stand on the flag and Anne Murray? The beaver?"

"Why don't we meet in a chic bar and be civilized about it?"

"Look, the firm has a box at the SkyDome. Very congenial surroundings. You don't have to order a beer or a hamburger. You don't even have to watch the damn ball game. All I'm asking, would you meet me tonight?"

"In this box," I said, "you get to drink whatever you want?"

"Even that weird Hungarian stuff you like. I'll phone ahead and make sure."

"Polish," I said. "Wyborowa. You better write it down."

"This means you'll come?"

"Sure, I'm curious about the inside of the place. Looks absurd enough from the outside."

"The SkyDome? You're kidding, you've never been inside? It makes the city world class."

"I'm considering a move to the west coast. One of the humble Canadian-class Gulf Islands."

"Come early, six thirty," Tom said and hung up.

I went back to my coffee and dawdling. The doorbell rang at exactly ten and I hustled downstairs. James Turkin had on a pair of loose-fitting white coveralls with lots of pockets. There was a white painter's cap on his head, and across the coveralls, on the left breast pocket, a name was stitched in blue. Larry.

"Neat disguise, James," I said.

"Larry," James said. "That's my name soon as the commission commences, which it has."

"You call the shots," I said, "Larry."

James held out another set of white coveralls, folded, and another white cap.

"Wanta put these on upstairs?" he asked. "Or in the back of the truck?"

Behind James on the street was a white panel truck with Surefire Security Systems painted along the side.

I unfolded my coveralls. They had a name in blue on the breast pocket. Moe.

I looked at James. "Moe?"

"It's what they come with," James said, "Moe."

I stepped into the hallway and pulled on the coveralls over my jeans and shirt. The cap sat loosely on my head.

"Dressed and ready," I said.

James and I climbed into the truck's front seat. A third guy was at the wheel, about James's age, pudgy, a faint blond moustache on his upper lip. His white coveralls bore a name. Curly.

"Come *on*, James."

"Larry."

"That's what I'm talking about." My voice bounced around inside the truck. "The *names*."

James and his colleague, Larry and Curly, exchanged looks. The colleague's expression was as blank as James's.

"The truck and the uniforms," James said, speaking to me in a deliberate tone, "were rented from a gentleman who specializes in equipment for the commission-agent trade."

"This gentleman got a sense of humour?"

James shrugged. "He kids around."

I thought for a moment. "Okay, never mind," I said.

Curly started the truck's motor and pulled into an opening in the Beverley Street traffic.

"The names better not be an omen," I said.

"What?" James asked, impatient.

I sighed. "Let it go."

"This commission," James said, "I don't know what you're worried about, it's been researched and analyzed. Since yesterday, me and Curly have been extremely thorough."

"I'll take your word for it."

Curly drove south on York Street to Front and across Front to David Rowbottom's condominium. He pulled up on the east side of the building and parked.

"Everything synchronized?" James asked his colleague, Larry to Curly.

"The three different positions we talked about, I choose one for the truck depending on things transpiring out here."

"It's in your, ah, discretion."

James leaned into the back of the truck and came up with a clipboard and a long narrow metal toolbox. He and I got out of the truck and walked to the condo's entrance.

"Wait a sec, Larry," I said, "shouldn't you brief me?"

James handed me the toolbox. It was heavy. "Carry this and don't open your mouth apart from signifying accordance with me."

"Concordance might be a better word there."

"Oh, yeah? Remind me when I got my notebook."

James led the way into the lobby. The doorman behind the counter was a beefy, red-faced man. He wore a maroon uniform and a questioning expression.

"How ya doin'?" James said. "We got a rush job for ..." He consulted the paper on his clipboard. "Apartment 16A. Guy wants his security system checked out. Fault in the wiring, something of that nature."

The beefy doorman shook his head. "News to me. That's Rowbottom's place, and nothing here, no messages, about letting you guys in if that's what you think you're askin'."

"How ya like that?" James put one hand on his hip.

"Night man, Andy, he goes off at eight, he woulda told me if Rowbottom wanted something done about his ... what'd you say?"

"Security system. Jesus, this really pisses me off."

"Rowbottom's outa here, six thirty, seven, before I even come on."

James turned in my direction. "This always the way, Moe? Guy orders a rush job, he forgets to set it up?"

I shifted the heavy toolbox from one hand to the other. "You said it, Larry."

The doorman said, "What can I tell ya?"

"Listen," James said. He lay his clipboard on the top of the counter. "You wanta do me a favour ... What's your name?"

"Mikey," the doorman said, sounding like a man giving away something he wanted to keep.

"Okay, Mikey, you wanta just call this Rowbottom's office, ask if it's okay to pass us in, save everybody a lotta grief?"

"I don't know, he's a cabinet minister, busy man."

"Cabinet minister's exactly the reason he's in a knot about security. That's what they said down our office. State secrets in there, all that crap."

The doorman had large, suspicious eyes in his red face. "I got an office number for him." He slid open a drawer and drew out a sheet of paper in a clear plastic folder. "But that don't mean I'm gonna get a hold of the man."

"You wanta give it a shot? Means Moe, here, and myself don't have to come back a second time. Maybe you could, like, talk to somebody else in authority, his secretary, whoever?"

"'Kay," the doorman said, reluctance at the edges of his voice. "I'll dial the number, but if I don't get Rowbottom, that's it, forget it."

He picked up the receiver on the counter phone and, looking at the list of names and numbers on the paper in the clear plastic folder, he began to dial. One digit, the second digit, third ...

"Hey, what am I thinking," James said suddenly.

The doorman stopped dialing. "Yeah?"

James spoke more quickly. "You probably got just the regular office number, am I right, Mikey? Some receptionist gonna come on the line? Okay, right here on the order form, I got a number that'll put ya straight through to the man himself's office. Says right here, David Rowbottom's executive assistant, any trouble comes up."

The doorman put down the receiver and spent some time studying James's face, considering.

"Means we don't hafta screw up our schedule tomorrow, bill Rowbottom for the two trips," James said. "Don't wanta annoy the customer, know what I'm talking about?"

The doorman took a deep breath. "Read off the number from that form you got there."

James read it, and the doorman dialed.

"Hello," he said into the phone. "Yeah, this is Mr. Rowbottom's office?"

He paused.

"Yeah, sorry, lady. I heard what you said the first time when you answered. Well, thing is, this is the doorman at Mr. Rowbottom's apartment and there's two gentlemen here want —"

The doorman stopped, listened, covered the receiver with his hand and looked at James. "Surefire Security, that you?"

"Tell her yeah."

"Yes, ma'am," the doorman said into the phone. He listened again, his face going a marginally deeper red. "Well, look, I'm sorry, nobody told me — Right away.... Yeah, no problem."

He hung up the phone. "Woman's a real ball-buster, Jesus."

"Dame gets a job like that," James said, "thinks she's the Queen of England."

The doorman rummaged in his drawer. "She says to give you guys the passkey."

"Hey, Mikey, I owe ya."

The doorman handed James the key and buzzed the lock on the glass door. James and I stepped around the counter and pushed open the door.

"That key," the doorman said from behind us, "I'm the one responsible for it. Come back to me personally when you're done up there."

James waved a friendly hand. The wave didn't appear to dispel the doorman's wary look.

There were two elevators. One was waiting on the ground floor. We got on, and James pressed number sixteen.

"Don't tell me," I said. "It was your sister."

"Who the guy phoned? Yeah."

"Nice, James."

"Larry," James said. "How long's the shortest amount of time you need?"

"In Rowbottom's apartment? Hard to say. Fifteen, twenty minutes. Why?"

"The guy down there, he might give us trouble."

"Mikey?"

"Guy acts like he doesn't trust two members of the ..."

"Working class?"

"Proletariat."

The elevator stopped at sixteen. David Rowbottom's apartment was directly across the hall. James put the key in the lock and opened the door.

CHAPTER SIXTEEN

James and I stepped across the Rowbottom threshold and into a Victorian parlour.

Close to the centre of the room, two cane rocking chairs flanked a table draped in a fringed shawl. Heavy velvet curtains were drawn across the three windows. The colour of the curtains belonged in the mauve-puce range. There were two student lamps on tables at either end of a fat stuffed sofa. The shades on the lamps were crimson, and the sofa had petit point pillows tossed here and there. On another table, which was a solid mahogany piece of work with a lot of curlicues carved in the side, a stuffed owl sat under a glass jar.

I looked around the strange room, and at first, I couldn't spot doors leading off of it.

"Ah," I said.

The entrance to an adjoining room was made almost invisible by a thick curtain of beads.

"Sure we got the right apartment?" James asked.

"Positive."

"More like somebody's grandmother's place."

"Larry," I said, "would you do a fast inspection in the other rooms?"

James disappeared through the beads.

I put down the metal toolbox and made a slow tour of the parlour. Nothing caught my eye. Or rather, everything caught my eye but nothing struck a chord of recognition.

James came through the beads.

"There's what you'd expect," he said. "Dining room, kitchen, bedroom, and another bedroom that's an office."

"Show me the office."

"It might be two guys live here," James said. "Or the second guy visits some nights."

"Uh-huh?"

"The suits, jackets, stuff in the big closet are for a tall guy, not too much weight on him. There's another person's clothes, three, four items, they'd be for a guy also tall but bigger around, more of a bulky guy."

"Good sleuthing, Larry."

"All leather. The second guy wears leather pants, windbreakers."

"Noted," I said. "Now the office."

It was a real office, an office away from the province's offices for Rowbottom. File folders were stacked on chairs and on the floor. The documents in piles on the bookcases and the papers scattered across the desk carried an official look. Many of them had been stamped "For the Minister" and "Intra Office Only."

The desk provided the room's single personal touch, black lacquer with bowed legs. It had three drawers. Two were unlocked and held pens, envelopes, paper clips. The third drawer, small and on the left side, was locked.

"Larry," I said, "your trained services are required here."

James left the room. I could hear him in the parlour opening the metal toolbox. When he returned, he was carrying a large ring that held forty or fifty keys.

"The lock on the drawer's special," he said.

"Special how?"

"It didn't come with the desk. Somebody put the lock in after."

James sorted expertly through his ring of many keys, pausing two or three times to hold keys up to the lock on the drawer. He settled on one key, short and stubby, and inserted it in the lock. The drawer clicked open.

It contained photographs, about three dozen of them. I studied the photos one by one. All were the same size, probably taken on the same camera, all in colour. All were of men sitting in one of the cane chairs in the Victorian parlour. And in all, the men were content, at ease, smiling into the camera.

I shuffled through the photographs a second time. I could put names to two of the men. Ian Argyll and Bart the Bulge. I recognized the man in a third photo but couldn't name him. He was the black waiter at the Purple Zinnia, the one who resembled the young Harry Belafonte. The man in a fourth photo stirred memories, but of whom and where and when I couldn't pin down, a husky guy with a moustache and a short, neat haircut. I put the fourth photo in one of my coverall pockets and returned the rest to the drawer with the special lock.

The telephone rang.

It was on the black lacquer desk, hooked up to an answering machine.

"Answering machine'll get it," James said.

"I wasn't intending to say hello."

The phone rang again, then there was a delay of a second or two, and an authoritative male voice spoke on the machine.

"You have reached 555-3342. I am unable to take your call. If you wish, leave your name, number, and time of call after the beep."

Another delay came next, then a *beep*.

"Hubert, pick up the phone," a male voice said on the line. "It's me."

A moment of staticky silence went by.

"Hubert, for *heaven's* sake …"

The voice trailed off.

I looked at James. "Any second now the guy's going to con-
clude neither one of us is Hubert."

"If it isn't Hubert, who in hell ..."

The voice on the phone sounded further away, off the receiver.

James said, "The guy's talking to another person in the room,
wherever he is."

"Somebody better damn well ..."

The last words were fainter still. There came the click of
a hang-up, and the answering machine on the desk went into a
sequence of its own blips and buzzes before it fell quiet.

"Voices were the same," James said.

"Voices, plural?"

"Guy on the answering machine, guy who phoned, they were
the identical same voice."

"Uh-oh, David Rowbottom knows we're here."

"Knows *somebody's* here."

"I hope you professionals got an escape drill in place."

"Must've been the guy on the door downstairs, Mikey," James
said in a tone close to musing. "He phoned this Rowbottom, and
Rowbottom phoned here."

"*Larry.*"

"Anything else you need from the place?"

"What I need is my ass out of here."

"Five minutes minimum before somebody's gonna show, like
the cops. Private security, longer for them if there is any."

"You're leaving out the intrepid Mikey."

"He looked more like the type that'd phone in and leave it
there, no big hero stuff."

"Larry, ordinarily your theorizing and character analysis
would be edifying, but at the moment, I'd rather we *please* make
the getaway."

James took the lead, through the dining room and into the
parlour. He opened the apartment's front door, looked into the
corridor and let two or three beats go by.

"One elevator's on the third and coming up," he said.

I was at James's shoulder. "What've you got in mind, we stand and debate the odds it'll stop at sixteen?"

"Bring the toolbox," James said.

I leaned over to pick up the box and froze.

"Holy *mackerel*," I said. "Hold it, James. I mean, Larry."

I galloped through the apartment to the office. At the same time, my hand was reaching through a slit in my coveralls to the back pocket of my jeans, where I carried my wallet. I got out the wallet and removed the piece of paper I'd written on nine days earlier, on the Saturday afternoon after Ian's funeral, the paper with the number from Alex Corcoran's phone gizmo that recorded the numbers of incoming calls. The number on the paper was 555-3342. So was the number on David Rowbottom's telephone.

"Moe." James's voice came from the front door in a stage whisper. "Elevator's still coming. At eleven."

I hurried through the apartment, stopping to heft the heavy toolbox with one hand.

"Better if you leave the door open behind you," James said.

The lights on the floor indicators over the elevators showed that one was at the fourteenth and rising and the other was sitting, unmoving, on the top floor, the twenty-fifth.

James and I scurried down the corridor toward a hallway that turned right and out of sight. The toolbox was awkward to carry, and the tools and keys inside made threatening noises. *Chinka, chinka, chinka.* As we passed the elevators, James punched the down button. We kept moving to the security of the small hallway. I concentrated on keeping the toolbox from chinkaing. James took the observation post, up against the wall and peeking around the corner where the hall and corridor met.

I heard the slick sound of elevator doors sliding open.

"Right there," a voice said. It was Mikey's. "Looka that, front door's not even closed."

The elevator doors made a hushed gliding-shut noise.

"Hold it, sir," another voice said, deeper and louder. The voice must have been addressing Mikey. "We'll go in first."

James pulled his head back.

"We?" I mouthed at him.

James held up two fingers.

Two what? Must be two cops. Two cops and Mikey.

"Anyone in there?" The deeper, louder voice was deeper and louder. "Police officers. Identify yourself, please, you in the apartment. Nobody wants any inconvenience."

Inconvenience? Was he kidding?

James flattened against the wall again and eased his right eye into the corridor. Ten seconds passed, an eon by my own personal measurement. No voices, no sounds came from the direction of the Rowbottom apartment. I watched James's blank face, his tensed body.

His body untensed, and he beckoned me to follow him into the corridor. It was unoccupied, and the entrance to the apartment stood wide and empty. The cops and Mikey must have disappeared through the door James and I had left conveniently open to receive them. I put my attention into keeping the damn tools from rattling in the metal box.

James motioned for a halt. The doors of the descending elevator slid open. We stepped on, and James pressed the ground floor button.

"Those hadda be the cops on the beat from around here," he said when the door had closed and we were on our way. "Them coming by so fast, that was a ..."

"Fluke?"

"Happenstance."

"Yeah, well, there better not be more happenstances waiting downstairs."

The elevator stopped at the tenth floor. A stout woman got on, sixtyish, wearing a flowered dress, a beige cardigan thrown over her shoulders. She eyed James and me. It was, by and large, a friendly eyeing.

"Isn't this a coincidence," she said a little breathlessly. "Are you gentlemen painting in the building?"

"No," James said.

"Because if you are, we're having estimates done on our apartment. You're sure you're not painters?"

"Yeah."

"May I ask what you do, do?"

"Security," James said.

"Oh, *really.* Locks and buzzers and things? I said to Owen, my husband, as recently as dinner last night that we really should do something about our protection. I mean to say, the *horrors* you read in the newspapers."

The elevator arrived at the ground floor, and the three of us stepped off, four counting the damn metal toolbox. On the other side of the glass entrance, four cops were milling around the lobby looking confused. Behind them, outside the condo, their two cruisers were parked half on the sidewalk.

"I'm positive Owen could be persuaded to invest in our security, not that the building isn't first class in *that* respect," the breathless woman was saying. She pulled open the glass door and noticed the cops for the first time. "Oh," she said, very breathless.

"Anybody know where the doorman is?" one cop asked. He had puffy cheeks and tiny eyes.

"Mikey?" the woman said. "He's terribly reliable. I couldn't imagine ..."

James spoke up. "We came through here, Mikey said he had something on sixteen."

"When was this?" the piggy-eyed cop asked.

"Ten, I don't know, twelve minutes back."

"Thanks."

A woman cop, blond and trim, switched her gaze from James's coveralls to mine.

"Ed," the cop with the eyes said to one of the others, "hold the fort here. Rest of us'll try the sixteenth."

He turned toward the elevators, stopped and turned back.

"You two guys," he said to James and me, his eyes no bigger than raisins, "what floor're you working on?"

"Penthouse," James answered quickly.

"*Really?*" The breathless woman sounded thrilled. "The mysterious Mr. Palmer's apartment."

"That's the man," James said. "Doin' a job for Mr. Palmer."

"No one in the building has had so much as a *glimpse* of his place," the woman said. "We're *consumed* with curiosity."

James nodded his head vigorously. "Lotta valuables in there."

"Oh, I *imagine*."

The blond woman cop with the interest in our coveralls had developed a half grin.

"What kinda work you doing for this Palmer gentleman?" the gimlet-eyed cop asked James.

"Security," the breathless woman answered before James could open his mouth. "Oh, and if Mr. Palmer hired them, they must be the very *best*. You wouldn't believe how *lavish* Mr. Palmer can —"

"Right." The cop cut her off. "Thanks."

He turned to the elevators, apparently done with James and me. The two of us made our own turn to the front door.

"Hey, Moe and Larry." It was the woman cop. "Where's Curly?"

A small crack showed in the blank facade of James's face.

"Ah, Curly, heh, heh," I said. My voice sounded hysterically jovial. "He's out in the, heh, heh, truck."

"Sure," the blond cop said, her mouth stretched to a full grin. "Watch he doesn't poke you in the eye."

"You mind, Melissa," the cop with the currants for eyes said. "We're on a robbery in progress in case it slipped your mind."

James and I headed for the front door.

"You really must give me your card," the breathless woman called from behind us. "If you're good enough for Mr. Palmer, I *know* Owen will hire you in a minute."

"Surefire Security," James said over his shoulder. "In the phone book."

"Sure … what was that?"

"*Surefire.*" My voice was climbing toward a scream.

"Well, it *is* business I'm offering …"

James and I were out the door and galloping up the street. The toolbox banged against my thigh, and the tools and keys inside clinked and clanged. Curly had the white truck parked in a lane behind the condo, the front end facing out. James and I piled through the passenger door. I cracked the toolbox on my shin.

"*Damn!*"

"I seen the cops," Curly said to James. "I was wondering."

He swung the truck out of the lane, turned north and butted into the east-west traffic on King Street, forcing the drivers of a Volvo and a Buick to stand on their brakes. The truck shot across King and up to Adelaide. Curly managed the same butting-in manoeuvre. He drove like Mario Andretti, if Mario Andretti doubled as a fleeing break-and-enter man. At Richmond, Curly turned left and caught all the green lights as far as Bay Street.

"So," he said, "everything go okay?"

"Except for the cops," James said.

"*Except* for the cops?" I said.

Neither guy paid any attention to me.

"No problems on the outside?" James asked Curly.

"Funny thing," Curly said. He continued across Richmond and up University. "Coming down here, I thought I seen a Lincoln behind us. Two times I seen it, maybe just a coincidence. Waiting for you guys, same car, or probably the same car, came around the block."

"What kind of Lincoln?" I asked.

"Town Car," Curly answered. "Two guys in it. I had a notion they were looking the truck over."

"What colour?" I asked.

"Grey. I think I lost it back there before Adelaide. That's if they was interested in us in the first place. I coulda been mistaken."

James said nothing.

Curly turned left near Mount Sinai Hospital and picked his way through the side streets toward Beverley.

"That cop in the lobby," James said to me.

"Which of the many?"

"The woman."

"Melissa. Very attractive."

"How come she knew Curly was Curly?"

"Leave it at this, James …" I hesitated. "Are we still on the job?"

"Until Curly and me drop you off at your place."

"Okay, leave it at this, *Larry*," I said. "Melissa is a good bet to go a long way in surveillance work."

CHAPTER SEVENTEEN

I got ready for the SkyDome with a shower, a double vodka on the rocks, and another of the new outfits Annie had picked out. I pulled on a light brown turtleneck and baggy cords in an olive drab shade. A medium-brown rough leather jacket rounded out the ensemble, with two pockets cut on the bias at chest level. I looked like the hippest member in Robin Hood's band of Merry Men.

It was six o'clock. I got halfway down the stairs, came back, and checked up and down Beverley Street from the front window. What I was checking for wasn't out there. I cut through the first-floor apartment, eerie with Ian's and Alex's possessions still present but not their persons, and out the back door. There's an alley behind my house. I walked south to the first cross street, back of the Chinese church on the corner, and spotted the grey Lincoln parked further along the curb close to Beverley.

Neither of the people in the car, Baldy and the kid with the scar on his jaw, saw me coming from the rear. I rapped on the driver's window. Baldy lowered it.

"It's okay to take the evening off, guys," I said, leaning over. "Just going to the Blue Jays game and straight home to bed."

The bald guy's face had a hard, closed-off look. "Mr. Ross don't like whatever you and those clowns were doing down at the condo on Front this morning."

"Listen, let's get a rapport going. Which of you fellas is Albert and who's Joey B.?"

"I'm Joey B.," the bald guy said. He jerked his thumb at the young guy. "He's Albert."

"Funny, I thought it'd be the other way around."

"You're asking to get boffed, you know that?"

"And you, Joey B., and you, Albert —" I nodded at each "— you're just the right lads to boff me. But out here on the street, still daylight, people passing by, I'm feeling relatively boff proof."

Joey B. and Albert exchanged a look that seemed to say I might be pressing my luck.

"Next time you report in, guys," I said, "tell Mr. Ross I will personally keep him abreast of all developments as they come to my attention. A promise."

Joey B. registered disbelief. "You nuts?" he asked me.

"Joey B.," I said, "I'm too far into this thing, whatever it is, to back out now. And that, too, is a promise."

I ran the words back in my head. Just the right touch of fearless resolution, I told myself. I straightened and walked away from the grey Lincoln with what I hoped would pass for dignity and purpose in the eyes of Joey B. and Albert.

Tom Catalano had sent a courier to the house that afternoon with my ticket to the game and a map showing me how to find the box at the SkyDome. It involved a climb up a flight of outdoor stairs steeper than the Himalayas, a ride in an elevator designed more for freight than people, and a hike down a long, curving, claustrophobic corridor. It wasn't exactly like going behind the scenes at the Taj Mahal.

Doors led off one side of the corridor into the boxes. I opened the one marked "Mcintosh, Brown and Crabtree. Barristers and Solicitors" and found myself in a mini rec room. A curly-haired guy in white was setting up a bar, and two women in maids' uniforms were spreading cold cuts on a buffet table. On the other side of a chummy arrangement of armchairs and sofas covered in yellow nubby material, Tom Catalano stood with a big smile on his face and a beer in his hand.

"This spectacular or what?" he said to me.

"So far I must be missing something."

I crossed the room, and Tom, examining me up and down, made a sound like a chuckle.

"Mummy let you dress yourself, little guy?" he asked me.

"Annie," I said. "She's doing a fashion makeover on me."

"Basically a good idea, but tell her not to use the boys' section of *Seventeen* as a reference point."

Tom Catalano was a handsome guy from the school of chiselled features and glossy black hair. He radiated hormones and muscle, and usually dressed in gorgeously tailored three-piece suits. Tonight's was chocolate brown.

"Here's the real show," he said, turning me with a firm hand on the shoulder to face outward from the box and inward to the SkyDome.

Immediately below us, as part of the box, there was a short flight of stairs leading to rows of seats — four rows and sixteen seats. Beyond, spread out below, lay the rest of the fifty thousand seats and the entire field. The latter's artificial carpet was of a green that nature must abhor, and on it, players were going about their leisurely pursuits, taking batting practice, shagging flies, and tossing balls on the sidelines. Above the field, restaurants predominated — Windows, Hard Rock Café, and a slew of McDonald's outlets.

"People come to a ball game," I said, "and what? Eat?"

"Part of the grand old pastime's ritual," Tom said.

"Um, fella, you're sounding perilously like a shill."

Tom shrugged. "The firm handles the Blue Jays' legal work."

"Aha, that have anything to do with the business you and I are supposed to discuss?"

"Plus a third party."

Tom went to the bar and asked the curly-haired guy behind it for a drink. He brought the drink to me and went back to the bartender and the women at the buffet table. They listened to what he had to say, Tom speaking intently, and allowed him to usher them out the door.

I said, "What we're talking to your third party about is hush-hush?"

"How's your drink?"

I tasted it.

"Hey," I said, "Wyborowa."

"We aim to please."

"You must be wanting a *really* large favour."

Someone knocked on the door. Tom opened it and gave the severe-faced man who came in a hearty clap on the back. The man was wearing a Blue Jays uniform, cap to spikes. He looked about fifty, and he had an incipient paunch, which the tight uniform emphasized, and a ruddy complexion.

"Crang, meet Woody Alison," Tom said. "Woody, Crang's the lawyer we're dealing with."

Woody stuck out a hand of calluses for me to shake, and the three of us sat down on the yellow nubby furniture.

"Crang, you'll know Woody by reputation," Tom said. "Blue Jays' hitting coach, best in the game since Charley Lau."

"Ah, yeah, Woody, you bet."

"Not that good," Woody said. He had an accent that faintly suggested Maine or Vermont. "Charley was a legend."

"Look, guys, we going to talk hitting a baseball?" I said. "Because if we are …"

"A *hitter*," Tom interrupted. "We're going to have us a little conversation about the future of one of the most promising young hitters in the American League."

"Let me guess," I said. "Daryl Snelgrove, Snellie to some."

Tom smiled an indulgent smile. Both men seemed to be waiting for me to launch the chat.

"Well, let's see," I said, "the little I know Daryl, off the one meeting, he's a sincere young guy, religious, you know, born again."

"Hot damn," Woody said in a suddenly loud voice, "don't get me going on that one."

"Which one?" I said. "Born agains?"

"Dead truth," Woody said, "I'd rather have twenty-five drinking guys on the club than twenty-five Christians. Drinking, cussing, carousing, that's my kind of player."

"Whatever happened to a healthy mind in a healthy body?"

"Hell, yes, the healthy bodies, but they don't have to come with your healthy mind, not your normal healthy mind."

"Really?"

"I want my guys storming up and down the dugout. Know what I'm talking about? I want the war whoops and the guys that smash the water cooler to smithereens if they get caught looking at a third strike. That sure as hell isn't any healthy mind, not according to most folks' notion, but I tell you, man, it wins ball games."

"I'm beginning to get it. The born agains, the Christians on the team, they're not so passionate about winning and losing?"

"Lord's will. Goddamn, I hate those words. Win a game, lose a game, it's all the same. Lord's will."

"Got a lot of them on the Blue Jays?" I asked. "Born agains?"

"These guys know everything about the Apostle Paul and practically nothing about Willie Mays."

"That bad, is it?"

"More Bibles in the locker room than *Playboy*s, and I tell you, that's a very sick situation."

"Right, Woody," Tom broke in, "I think we're getting away from the main point."

"Snellie'd be a better hitter if he wasn't a damn born again," Woody grumped.

"Uh-huh," I said, "and how about if he wasn't gay? Would that make him a better hitter, too?"

"Hold it right there, Crang," Tom said. "Daryl's gayness remains to be proved, and frankly, I don't think it can be."

"The boy's no queer," Woody said. His ruddy face had tightened up.

"Is this a damage-control meeting?" I asked Tom. "Is that why we've convened tonight?"

"Here's the picture," Tom said, sounding like the decisive corporate lawyer he is. "A week ago Sunday night, Crang, right after Daryl apparently had a talk with you that shook him up badly, he drove straight to Woody's apartment and spilled it all out."

"Boy's been a personal project of mine since he came into the organization," Woody said, solemn.

"The whole works?" I asked. "Daryl told you about the Purple Zinnia, his buddies there, and a man named Ian Argyll?"

Tom answered. "Everything, at least as Woody and I have pieced it together."

"Including the AIDS possibility?" I asked.

"Now we're getting to the crux of the matter," Tom said.

"We sure are," I said.

"Understand out front, Crang," Tom said. "Woody brought this information concerning Daryl to me. *Directly* to me. Nobody else on the club is privy to Daryl's situation, not the manager, not the people upstairs, the directors, no one. It's confined to the three of us in this room."

"And a bunch of the boys at the Zinnia," I said.

"I don't see that as a concern." Tom paused. "Have you leaked this to anyone else?" he asked me.

"Annie, if you call her a leak."

"Jesus," Woody said, "a woman."

Tom held up his hand in a stop signal. "Not to worry, Woody. Annie's more trustworthy than even Crang here."

Woody's expression left the implication that anyone short of Benedict Arnold might be more trustworthy than I was.

"What about the AIDS?" I asked Tom.

"We moved fast on that one," Tom said. "I scooted Daryl in to see a doctor friend of mine next day, the Monday. He's a specialist, *the* blood authority in the country. My friend gave Daryl every test in the books."

"And?"

"The results came in first thing this morning."

"Go on."

"Daryl's as healthy as he looks."

"A Clydesdale."

"Excuse me?"

"What he looks like," I said. "A horse."

"Not a glimmer of AIDS or anything else," Tom said. "No way he's carrying a disease."

"I saw Ted Williams toward the end of his years with the Red Sox," Woody said. "Daryl's got a swing as natural as Ted's."

"Well," I said, ignoring Woody's non sequitur. "I never figured Daryl for the guilty party, anyway."

"Guilty of *what*?" Tom said, close to explosive.

"You really don't want to know."

Tom made an exasperated noise. "Crang, hear me out. You threw a scare into Daryl last week, into all of us. Just a second ago you heard Woody describe the kind of potential the kid has, a swing like Ted Williams's. He could lead this club to the pennant, hell, the World Series. And that's why I don't want to hear you casually tossing around a word like 'guilty' in this conversation. Guilt, for God's sake, connotes the commission of a crime."

"As a matter of fact," I said, "murder."

"You better explain that little bombshell," Tom said to me, distaste and disbelief spreading across his handsome face.

I explained. I told the two of them of the possible connections between Ian Argyll's AIDS and the gang at the Purple Zinnia, of Alex Corcoran's intentions and his subsequent murder. I left out some names and details, like Bart the Bulge's involvement and the ominous shadow of Paulie Ross, on the grounds they might unnecessarily clutter my explanation. Mostly, for clarity's sake, I stuck to Daryl Snelgrove's possible fit into the whole ugly stew.

"But," I wound up, "in view of what you people tell me, Daryl passing the medical tests with flying colours, not to mention my own doubts that Daryl is a violent sort, where murder is concerned anyway, I'm ruling him out as a possible murderer pretty much unequivocally."

I finished, and silence reigned in the room.

Woody broke it. "Better the kid's a born again than a pansy, I s'pose."

Tom turned his exasperation briefly on Woody, then switched it back to me. "Okay, fella, it's a grim story," he said, "and it reminds me again, if I ever needed reminding, why I didn't go into criminal law."

"Not as tidy as the corporate-commercial hand-holding you do," I said.

"Exactly."

"Or as lucrative," I said. "No criminal lawyers in these boxes that I can see."

"Except as guests of old friends, old friend."

"And in that category," I said, "what you're expecting of me is I keep my mouth shut about Daryl."

"Crang," Tom said, arranging himself in a summing-up posture, "I think you and I agree that Daryl Snelgrove is a naive young kid who came to the big city and fell in with the wrong crowd. But he doesn't have AIDS, probably isn't a homosexual, and certainly didn't commit a murder. Now wouldn't it be a shame, a tragedy of sorts, if rumours got out, possibly reached the ears of the press, that could irretrievably destroy a brilliant baseball career?"

"Boy gets a little more selective about his pitches," Woody said, "he'll hit .330 consistent. Forty homers."

"Don't twist my arm, guys," I said. "I made up my mind a while ago."

"Yes?" Tom said.

"Mum's the word on my end."

Tom clapped his hands. "I knew we could count on you, fella."

Woody smiled for the first time.

"Woody," Tom said, "I wish this was the time and place I could offer you a little happy-times drink, but I know they'll be needing you down on the field."

"Field?" I said. "You call that funny green stuff a *field!*"

Woody gave me his collection of calluses to shake again and left the box. Tom summoned the bartender and waitresses, and I got myself another Wyborowa on the rocks. Soon, people from Tom's law firm began arriving, some with wives and husbands, and the ball game started. I watched for a while from the seats with four lawyers. The rest of the guests stayed in the box's interior, eating, drinking, talking shop. After two innings of minimal action, the Blue Jays leading the Brewers 1–0, I left the minority of ball fans and joined the majority of eaters, drinkers, and shop talkers. Someone's wife asked me what group I was with. When I answered with a confused look, she said something about, well, um, the uniform you're wearing, and drifted off to greet a new arrival. I asked for one more vodka and began organizing a plate of soggy cold cuts and limp salad.

A roar came from the crowd below.

"Crang," Tom called across the room, "you see *that*?!"

"Not from over here by the buffet."

"Snellie just hit one up into the second deck."

"Great," I said. "I'm glad somebody's getting some good news out of this damn shemozzle."

CHAPTER EIGHTEEN

The television screen showed Annie from the shoulders up. She was looking to her left and introducing Philippe Noiret's name into the interview.

"By my count," Annie said, "you've used Noiret for major roles in six of your films. That's a remarkable relationship between an actor and a director."

The screen switched to a shoulders-up shot of Bertrand Tavernier, head looking to the right, responding to Annie.

"Philippe comes from Lille, you know, and that is a very secretive city," Tavernier said, a rumpled, middle-aged, simpatico kind of guy. "There's a saying in Lille, 'One must never lie, one must never conceal.' So, for an outsider, it takes time to enter and discover the panoply of interesting elements it offers. With Philippe, too, it takes time to get inside, and once you're there, you just don't want to leave."

"Watch this," Annie said to me, both of us sitting in white wicker chairs in front of the TV set in her living room.

The screen went to a clip from a movie, Noiret in a World War One French officer's uniform, a man with sagging cheeks and a beagle nose, slow and dignified and very sad, leading a weeping woman between lines of plain wooden caskets.

"From *La vie et rien d'autre*," Annie said, not taking her eyes from the TV set. "Noiret got a César for it, the French equivalent of the Oscar."

The clip ended, and a shot from a pulled-back camera showed Annie and Tavernier together in conversation. Annie steered Tavernier on to the use of jazz in his movies. Tavernier got off some wise words about jazz's appeal.

"You're gonna love how we go out," Annie said to me.

The screen went to another film clip, the scene near the beginning of *Round Midnight* when Dexter Gordon as Dale Turner makes his entry down the corridor of a low-down Paris hotel. This great, wonderful, dying wreck of a jazz musician. Watching it, I got a heaviness in my chest.

Annie came on the screen, speaking into the camera and telling the audience what to expect in next week's program.

"… and we'll talk to the Hollywood director Oliver Stone for the first in a series that looks at movies and war."

"How 'bout that," I said in the living room. "You weren't snowing the old guy the other night."

"Andy Elms." Annie got out of her wicker chair and switched off the TV set. "We got lucky. It happens Oliver Stone's coming up this week to talk at the Canadian Film Institute. So we got him lined up and, well, la-di-da…. Your drink okay?"

I looked at my empty glass. "Nonexistent," I said.

Annie took the glass out of my hand, and I followed her to the kitchen.

"I take it you haven't made verbal contact with the tenant in Andy's building yet?" Annie asked, her back to me, taking the ice tray out of the freezer.

"Good old 16A? No, but I left a message on Rowbottom's answering machine, and I called the ministry twice. Made it all the way up to his personal secretary or whatever the title is, and I impressed my name on her."

Annie put three ice cubes in my glass and covered them in Wyborowa.

She said, "Guess you didn't mention in any of these communications you happened to be one of the guys who burgled good old 16A yesterday morning?"

"Omitted that."

Annie handed me the drink.

"It'd have got Rowbottom's attention," she said. "Probably have also got you a trip to the hoosegow." Annie frowned and put her hand on my cheek. "Honestly, Crang, some of the antics you get up to scare the wits out of me."

I kissed Annie's forehead. "Can't let that happen," I said. "Your wits are crucial."

"Well, if you must talk to Rowbottom," Annie said, "and at this stage of the game, you being up to your hairline in it and everything, I'll grant that's necessary, it's pointless for you to wait around until he deigns to return your messages. Which could be never."

"Is that this evening's contribution from your wits?"

"Why not waylay him?" Annie said. "Catch him first thing in the morning."

"Yeah, time is becoming of the essence."

"Politicians are always having power breakfasts."

"Confront him over grapefruit?"

"Where is it cabinet ministers and their cronies plot policies in the early morning? Prince Arthur Room in the Park Plaza? I read in *Toronto Life* which place is supposed to be the current in spot, but I forgot. Victoria Room at the King Eddie?"

"Why don't I just wait for the man outside his condo at sunrise tomorrow?"

"Then I'll never find out where these big shots take their power breakfasts."

We left the kitchen and went back to the wicker chairs in the living room.

"The interview with Tavernier," I said, "was a beauty."

"Thanks." Annie had her legs curled under her in one of the

chairs. "But, listen, when you talk to Rowbottom, what are you going to talk *about*?"

"Got the wording of my first question down pat," I said. "As a professional interviewer, you'll appreciate the technique here. Catch a guy with a zinger opening and let him kind of dangle out there until —"

"Crang, the first rule of interviewing is the interviewer should make the question pithy and then get out of the way."

"What I'll ask Rowbottom, 'Well, Mr. Rowbottom, why did you telephone the late Alex Corcoran on the Friday night of the late Ian Argyll's funeral?'"

"He did?" Annie said. "Rowbottom phoned Alex that night?"

"Another piece of pure deduction on my part."

I raised the glass of vodka and ice in a toast to myself.

"I don't know how much of this I can stand," Annie said, "the patting your own back."

"I'll speed it up."

"Oh, would you, please."

"Alex got three calls that night, the Friday. They showed up on the memory machine attached to his phone. First call came from his office. We'll let that one pass. Assume it was some kind of business. The third call, Malcolm the bartender made it. It was to tell Alex about David Rowbottom being another guy Ian used to drink with at the Zinnia, though, Malcolm didn't know David's last name was Rowbottom. He just had the David part. Anyway, Malcolm told me he placed the call from the Zinnia sometime Friday night. The second call came from David Rowbottom's apartment. *Ergo*, he phoned Alex, and I want to know how come he called and why at that particular time."

"Or maybe it was somebody else phoning from Rowbottom's apartment."

"Hadn't thought of that."

"Either way, you got hot stuff to fire at Rowbottom."

"Not to mention questions about all those guys Rowbottom

has the photos of under lock and key. Ian Argyll and the waiter at the Zinnia and the other guy I can't put a name to."

I looked at the time. Almost eight. "There're other people I got questions for, we could go talk to them right now."

"On an empty stomach?"

"Dinner goes with the answers," I said. "On me."

"Where?"

"The Purple Zinnia," I said. "I recommend the blackened catfish."

Annie unfolded herself from the chair. "Now you're talking, honey bun."

She went into the bedroom. I tagged along. She stood at the mirror and touched up her lipstick. I knew what shade it was, Raspberry Glace from Clinique. She lifted her head and spritzed her neck with Chloé cologne.

We went out onto Winchester Street. The air was unmoving and relatively unpolluted. We walked hand in hand under the high old trees lining the street. When we got to Parliament Street, past the blast of beer and cigarette smoke from the open door of the Winchester Hotel's bar, I looked over my shoulder. Further south on Parliament, outside the studio where the local CBC Radio shows are broadcast from, I did another check to the rear.

"Really," Annie said, "those guys can't follow you twenty-four hours a day. They've got to break for food and sleep, too, you know."

"Yeah, maybe I'm getting a touch paranoid about Joey B. and Albert."

"*Is* there anything back there? The grey Lincoln?"

"No, but they're fairly dodgy about keeping out of sight."

"You're right about the paranoia," Annie said. "That's a serious case you're developing."

We crossed Parliament on the green light at Carlton.

"There's one thing that doesn't fit right about those guys trailing me," I said.

"Apart from the inherent creepiness?"

"It's the timing I'm talking about," I said. "Paulie Ross knew we went to see Bart do his act at the Eroticarama, right? But Ross couldn't have sicced his followers on us *before* we went. We hadn't done anything up till then to rouse his interest in us, nothing I can think of, anyway. We didn't decide we were even going to *see* Bart that night until the last minute."

"You got an answer? How did Mr. Ross get onto us so promptly?"

"Axe might be the key."

"The brute who pinned you to the wall in Bart's dressing room?"

"To the door." I said. "He pinned me to the door."

"You think it was Axe who informed Paulie Ross that you and I had arrived on the scene, in a manner of speaking?"

"One tip-off about the connection between the two, you'll remember Paulie seemed well versed on Axe's preferences in maiming and killing people."

"Uh-huh. He said Axe favours baseball bats and axe handles. Which is no doubt how he came by the nickname, axe handles and Axe and so on."

"Exactly," I said.

"But what's your theory about why Axe would do such a thing? Report to Paulie Ross? I mean, Ross and his stepson, who appears to be Axe's employer, they're supposed to be on the outs."

"That's the explanation right there, because those two *are* on the outs. Paulie wants to keep tabs on Bart, see what kind of wild stuff his wife's son is into, stay up to the minute on the latest craziness, be on guard about the developments he has to prevent the mother from discovering, all that."

"So Axe is his informant on the inside?"

"With the kind of contacts Paulie has, he probably planted Axe with Bart."

"And," Annie said, "you think among other pieces of information Axe zipped along to Mr. Ross was the call you and I made on Bart at that awful club?"

"After which Ross put Joey B. and Albert on the tailing detail."

"Well, what you say makes sense," Annie said. "A nutty sort of sense."

"Sweetie pie, these people *are* nutty."

We reached a point about halfway along Carlton between Parliament and Sherbourne. The buildings were an uneasy mix of homes and businesses, a chic hairdressing salon next to a down-at-the-heels rooming house where three guys in undershirts were sitting on a collapsing porch passing around a bottle in an LCBO brown paper bag. The Purple Zinnia was just up ahead. On the stairs leading to its front door, clusters of men in sharp clothes stood talking, smoking, and waiting.

"One thing I hate," I said, "it's lining up to get into a restaurant."

"Gee," Annie said. I could hear wheedling in her voice. "My taste buds are just primed for what you recommended."

"The blackened catfish."

"And a lovely bottle of wine." Annie sloped against me. "I'll spring for the wine."

"Tell you what," I said. "We can wait out the lineup in the bar downstairs."

"That's my sport."

Annie hooked her arm through mine.

"It'll give me a chance to pump Malcolm, anyway," I said. "Malcolm the avaricious bartender. That's one of the outing's purposes, talking to him and the black waiter."

There was an entrance directly into the bar at street level. Annie let out a small whoosh at the high-tech decor inside. Eight or nine customers sat at the tables, and two of the bar stools were taken. We took two stools at the bar's far end. Malcolm, serving one of the tables, glanced my way and delivered one of his smarmy smiles. I had the impression that visions of twenty-dollar bills might be dancing in his head.

Malcolm came down the bar. He was dressed in the same loose purple shirt he'd worn on my first visit.

"Hello again," he said to me.

I introduced Malcolm to Annie, and after pleasantries on both sides, he fetched a glass of white wine for Annie and a vodka on the rocks for me. Malcolm leaned his hip on the counter.

"We're hoping to catch a word with one of your colleagues," I said to him. "A waiter upstairs, the Black Canadian."

"Who looks like Denzel Washington, only lighter skinned?"

"Well, different generations, I guess, different comparisons. I had him down for a young Harry Belafonte."

"Another customer thinks he looks like Miles Davis."

"You *guys*," Annie said. "Could we get past the descriptives, the similes, and all the other distractions?"

"He quit," Malcolm said.

"Who quit?" I asked.

"Maybe not quit per se, but he hasn't shown up for work since the end of last week, and management's really pissed at him, so it's identical to quitting."

"The black waiter?" I said.

Malcolm nodded. "Birks Robinson. Quitting like that, he must have a screw loose. You know how much he was taking out of here a week?"

"Couldn't imagine."

"At least a thousand."

Annie made a whistling noise.

Malcolm turned his attention to her. "See, your gay customers, they know superior food, really *know* it, and when they get it, like they do here, they tip like it's going out of style. Thirty percent is nothing."

"So this waiter," Annie said, "he couldn't have been unhappy in his work."

"Birks's been here almost two years, and all of a sudden, poof, no reason, no nothing, gone."

"Birks Robinson?" I said. "That's the name?"

"Uh-huh."

"Anybody at the Zinnia phone him and ask what's the complaint?"

"Nope."

I leaned over the bar. "Malcolm, have we reached the magic moment where I start paying for names, addresses, details? Is that why you've turned monosyllabic?"

Malcolm smiled and looked less slitty-eyed. "Oh, hell," he said, "on the house this time. Nothing I say's going to help you find Birks, anyway."

"What's so elusive about the guy?"

"In the time he's worked here, I bet he's had a dozen different addresses. Lived with this guy, that guy. He's as gay as a tulip, you know. So, finally, the woman who does the books here got fed up and listed this place as Birks's address. Income tax, health insurance, UIC, any government stuff, the Zinnia is his official place of residence. Otherwise, he has no fixed address."

I turned to Annie.

"Elusive sounds accurate," she said.

Malcolm went away to serve a new arrival at the bar.

I looked at my watch. "Maybe I should take a trip upstairs," I said to Annie. "Let them know we're in the lineup for a table."

"Maybe you should."

I took the inside route to the dining room, and when I came down the stairs, Annie was engaging Malcolm in a cheery exchange.

"Malcolm tells me Birks Robinson is a writing waiter or a waiting writer," she said to me. "Published and everything."

"Not enough to make a living out of," Malcolm said. "He isn't that much of a writer."

"What kind of writer?" I asked.

"Creative," Annie answered. "Short stories."

"And a novel," Malcolm said, "if he ever finishes it. I think he's started two or three of them and given them up and started over on another one."

"Published?" I said. "In what, literary magazines, quarterlies, things like that?"

"I guess," Malcolm said. "He was really proud of one story. It was in a book. A collection with other writers, I guess you'd say. All about being a teenager and being black and gay and having problems, what else? You'd never guess it to talk to Birks that he's got that stuff in him, whatever it is you need to have to be a writer. Know what I mean?"

"Approximately," I said.

"But it's helpful to know Birks is a part-time writer, you agree?" Annie said to me. "Could help in tracing him?"

"A long shot, but yeah."

I turned to Malcolm. "Anything else you can think of about Birks in the way of building a profile?"

"Well, he's very popular, lots of friends. I guess that goes without saying."

Malcolm tapped his fingers on the top of the bar. "What more? Well, he's … uh, he's a very elegant dresser."

"Malcolm, that goes without saying, too," I said. "Most of the gays I know *are* elegant dressers."

Malcolm spoke to Annie. "I'm not gay."

"But you dress elegantly."

"Thanks."

Annie switched topics. "When's dinner?" she asked me.

"After one more aperitif."

"Same again?" Malcolm said.

Annie's glass of wine hadn't dropped to the three-quarters mark.

"Me only," I said to Malcolm.

He brought a fresh vodka on the rocks.

"Stop me if this is pushing your present generous nature, Malcolm," I said. I took out the photograph I'd removed from David Rowbottom's locked drawer from my inside jacket pocket and placed it on the bar. "But has this gentleman crossed your path?"

"The Waxer," Malcolm answered immediately. "Hubert Wax is his name. Where'd you get the picture?"

"Hubert," I repeated, and thought about the name. "Hubert. That's someone Shumacher mentioned in my office. Cleve Shumacher."

"The used car dealer," Annie said.

"Stockbroker," I said. "David Rowbottom knows a Hubert, too. All these Huberts must be the same guy."

"Where'd you get the picture?" Malcolm asked again.

"Best I keep that confidential, Malcolm."

Malcolm's expression went indignant. "Oh, sure, you expect me to blab my brains out. But with you, I ask a simple question, all of a sudden you're Mr. Undercover Agent."

I reached for my money clip and removed a fifty-dollar bill from it.

"For the drinks, Malcolm," I said, "and for all the rest you know about the Waxer, beginning with why he has the dopey moniker."

Malcolm whisked the fifty off the bar top.

"It's his name from his motorcycle gang, and I wouldn't call it dopey if I were you, not if Hubert's in the vicinity."

"He doesn't take kindly to joshing?"

"Hubert can turn on the charm, but what you have to watch about him, you never know which side of the bed he got out of." Malcolm shook his head. "Hubert is the only person who works here that I walk on eggshells around when he comes in. See what Miss Wax's mood is before I speak."

"Hold it, this guy works at the Zinnia?"

"Part-time, two or three shifts a week upstairs. Not tonight, though."

I picked up the photograph. "The shirty waiter the first night I ate here," I said to Annie. "I asked about Ian, and he blew me off."

"That's our Hubert," Malcolm said.

"Didn't remember him from the photograph," I said.

"Malcolm," Annie said, "a *motorcycle gang*?"

"The Gay Desperadoes."

Annie snickered.

"They're for real, I kid you not," Malcolm said. "Tattoos and the leather regalia and big, you know, *choppers*, whatever they're called. Harley-Davidsons."

"But gay," Annie said.

"Takes all kinds." Malcolm shrugged. "There's a guy that comes here who makes his living driving one of those humungous tractor trailers. Another customer's a spot welder. Another's —"

"We grasp your point, Malcolm," I said. "Macho but gay, especially Hubert 'The Waxer' Wax."

Malcolm smiled the practised smile. "Got your fifty's worth?" he asked me.

"As always."

I finished the second vodka, and Annie and I went upstairs. The blackened catfish was off the menu. Annie chose something billed as New Orleans filé gumbo. She pronounced it scrumptious.

CHAPTER NINETEEN

The plastic container of hot coffee slid off the top of the Volks's dashboard, bounced once on the steering wheel, and upended in my lap.

"*Eeyow!*"

I'd jerked the car ahead too quickly, forgetting about the coffee container. It was David Rowbottom's fault. He had rushed out of his condo's front entrance, a stuffed briefcase in one hand, a leather athletic bag in the other, and climbed into the backseat of a black Buick. It was five forty Wednesday morning, and Rowbottom's sudden exit caught me off guard, only two or three minutes after I'd arrived with intentions of waiting for an early-morning confrontation. The black Buick must have been a government perk. Its driver had on a cap and uniform and drove the car with a professional's touch. He guided the Buick east on Front. I followed in the Volks. Steam rose from my crotch.

The Buick turned south at Sherbourne. I wheeled down the window and tossed out the empty coffee container. The Buick went south past the tangle of cross streets at Lake Shore Boulevard and kept on course toward the docks and shipyards at the harbour.

"Goddamn it."

I mopped at my groin with a dirty rag from the glove compartment.

The Buick reached Queens Quay and turned right.

"What in hell?"

There was nothing on that stretch of road except parking lots, barren fields, and restaurants that wouldn't be open for hours.

The Buick hung a surprise left. I slowed down. All I could see where Rowbottom's car had headed was a long one-storey warehouse with dozens of trucks backed up to its bays. I turned in, anyway. Some of the coffee had seeped down the seat. I was sitting in it.

The Buick drove on.

"Ah."

Up ahead, partially hidden from the road by the warehouse and trucks, were two enormous white bubbles. A large sign in stylish script announced the Waterfront Tennis Club. The Buick pulled past several cars parked in a space between the bubbles and deposited Rowbottom at the club's entrance. He sprang up the stairs two at a time and disappeared through the door.

I stopped and got out of the Volks. My movements were gingerly. I walked in little circles and shook loose the coffee that hadn't settled into my flannels to stay. I experimented with my sport jacket, arranging it to cover the big stain. It didn't work.

The hell with it. I let the jacket hang straight and went into the Waterfront Tennis Club.

"Hi there, can I help you? I'm Monica."

The voice, unbelievably vivid for the hour, came from a young woman seated behind a waist-high counter. She had a handsome face and a smile like Marilyn Monroe's.

"Hi, ah, Monica."

The young woman's view was confined to my upper half, but the brilliance of her greeting increased my self-consciousness over the unseemly dark spot.

"Would you like a tour of the courts?" Monica asked me. "There're seven of them. Look over the facilities?"

"Well, yeah, I *play* tennis," I said, "but not much recently. My old club folded."

"The Downtown, right? Okay, you'd love it here. Tons of old Downtown members came to us."

"Great. But at the moment, this morning, I'm waiting to see Mr. Rowbottom."

"David? He's in the Early Bird Clinic. You can wait for him in the dining room," Monica said, standing up and pointing down a short hall. "And help yourself to —" she spotted the stain "— fresh coffee."

Monica turned up her smile to full blast.

"And the men's room's over there," she said. "It has lots of towels."

I slunk into the washroom and applied towels to my flannels. When the wet spot appeared to have returned to a colour approximating the rest of the pants, I walked into the dining room, shoulders back, as confident as a Miss Canada candidate stepping out on centre stage.

People in sweaty tennis clothes sat drinking orange juice and chewing on Danishes. I gathered myself a tray of juice, muffin, and coffee and carried it down some stairs to the dining room's lower level next to the windows. They looked across the harbour to the crescent-shaped grouping of the Toronto Islands. There was a handful of sailboats on the water, and a tubby old ferry plowed its way to Ward's Island. I relaxed.

David Rowbottom caught me an hour and a half later in a daydream by the window.

"I'm told you're waiting to see me," he said.

"Huh? Oh, yeah, thanks."

"I'm pressed for time. What is it?"

"We have mutual concerns," I said. "They need discussing."

Rowbottom looked me over. "Do I know you?" he asked.

"We talked on the phone," I said. "You did the talking. I listened. Monday morning around ten fifteen."

Rowbottom sat down across from me. He was a lanky guy in his mid-forties and had high, hunched-forward shoulders. He had the kind of build no amount of expensive dressing can disguise.

His tailor had tried. The suit Rowbottom had on looked like about two thousand dollars' worth of double-breasted tweed. His face was long, and all the bones in it were prominent — cheekbones, forehead, jaw. The skin over the bones was pulled tight and had a pale shine. The eyes were his best feature, electric Paul Newman blues, and he seemed to know how to use them, raising or lowering the voltage so that all a person noticed about him were the eyes.

"You're the man who broke into my apartment?" Rowbottom asked, incredulous. He was putting a total glare on me. "I could walk over to the phone on Monica's desk and get the police here in two minutes."

"Yeah, but do that, and all of us'll be in a colloquy about embarrassing subjects like murder."

"Look, what's your name?"

"Crang."

"Well, Mr. Crang, I'm not about to let you get the better of me a second time."

"Who's Hubert, apart from a part-time waiter and full-time motorcycle cowboy?"

"No, no, no." Rowbottom made a motion with his right hand like he was rubbing a brush back and forth across a blackboard. "I ask the questions."

"The doorman phoned you? Mikey? Told you two guys had gone up to your apartment?"

"The message went from the receptionist to my secretary to my executive assistant to me. I couldn't understand what the fuss was about."

"You thought it was Hubert? Him and, I guess, another guy?"

"Naturally Hubert has the run of — *Stop* right there. I told you I was asking the questions."

"Good thing for me you called the apartment first. Before you rang the cops, I mean."

Rowbottom revved up the eye voltage. "Who, just *who are* you that you think you can pull off a stunt like this?"

"Who am I? Friend of Ian Argyll. Friend of Alex Corcoran. Both dead. Both connected to you."

A little wind went out of Rowbottom's sails. "You're very sure of yourself for a common burglar," he said.

"Uncommon actually. Only do it in crisis situations. Anyway, not to waste the time of a busy public servant like yourself, there's a photograph of Ian Argyll in that little hidey-hole of yours, and you phoned Alex Corcoran on the Friday night of Ian's funeral. So can we take your connections to them as established, no horsing around?"

"You stole one of my photographs."

"Of the aforesaid Hubert 'The Waxer' Wax, yeah. I'll see you get it back. But let's stick to Ian and Alex."

Rowbottom seemed to be regrouping. His eyes were back on beam. "I knew Ian Argyll socially. Did you expect me to deny it? As for Alex Corcoran, I make many phone calls every day and night. If I rang Alex on a certain evening, it was undoubtedly concerning cabinet business."

"He was in education, you're in culture and communications."

Rowbottom's smile was condescending. "I can see you fail to understand the workings of government, Crang. There is a great deal of cross consultation, if you must know, among ministers and senior members of the civil service, as Alex Corcoran was."

"Okay," I said, "instead of fencing with one another, I'll lay out what I think is a possibility."

"I'm not sure I'm interested in your possibilities, Crang. Correction, I *know* I'm not interested."

"Well, get interested," I said. "Here it is. Some gay guy with AIDS passed on the disease to Ian Argyll. He died, and Alex Corcoran set out to find and kill the gay guy with the AIDS. The guy found Alex first and killed *him*. Until you get off your high horse, Mr. Rowbottom, and prove otherwise, I rank you as a good wager for the role of Alex's killer."

Rowbottom's face passed swiftly through emotions from disbelief to stupefaction to plain old wrath.

"If you repeat in public what you just said to me," he said through clenched teeth, "my lawyers will slap you with a slander action before your eyes can blink twice."

"I take it you're denying my thesis?"

"You have been warned, Crang."

"Somebody else told me the same thing just this Sunday."

"They were right."

Rowbottom stood up.

"I haven't finished," I said.

"I *have*."

"What about your late-night caller?" I asked. "Bart the Bulge?"

"Bartley Santucci? What about him?"

"Is that his last name?"

"What *about* Mr. Santucci?"

"He makes movies," I said. "The department you run dishes out money to moviemakers. My question, assuming Santucci is a receiver of grants, would it warm the electorate's heart to know his movies are porno?"

"Crang," Rowbottom said, his voice restrained and even and simmering with underground storms, "my ministry's grants to filmmakers, poets, sculptors, composers, performance artists, oboe players, and goddamn weavers and potters are a matter of public record."

"Yeah, well, what do you say —"

Rowbottom brought his bony face, with its juts of jaw and forehead and high cheeks, to within a couple of inches of my own face.

"Crang," he said, "fuck off."

Rowbottom turned to the restaurant's inner stairs and trotted up them, two at a time again.

"Hey," I called after him, "we haven't discussed Paulie Ross or Birks Robinson...."

Some of the tennis players looked up from their juice and coffee and glared at me, the noisy intruder in their midst. David Rowbottom continued out the front door.

CHAPTER TWENTY

Two hours later, two hours after I left the Waterfront Tennis Club clutching a membership application that Monica with the smile had pressed on me, I asked John Rose about Birks Robinson.

"Birks Robinson," John repeated. "Help me a little more."

"A short story of his was in an anthology published in the past couple of years."

"That really narrows it down," John said. "To a select five hundred or so."

"It must be a clue that he's a guy. Isn't there a rule about Canadian short story writers? They have to be women."

"True. And he's a Canadian for sure?"

"As far as I know. And black. And gay."

"Gay? You should have said that at the beginning."

John got up from his desk and ambled down an aisle toward the back of the store. John's store, called Bakka, is on Queen a block and a half east of my office. Bakka deals in books, and it's been on the street longer than I have, longer than any of the current establishments except maybe the Legion Hall. The store's specialty is science fiction, but it buys and sells second-hand books in every category. Its smell is necessarily of mildew, old basements, and other people's libraries.

"Right about …" John was in the CanLit section, and his hand was running along the spines of books on a lower shelf. "Here."

He pulled a book out of the line, a large-sized paperback. I read the book's title over John's shoulder. *The Third Sex: New Canadian Stories.*

John flipped to the table of contents. "Birks Robinson, his very self," he said, pointing to the name. The story Birks had written was called "And You Thought James Baldwin Had It Tough."

John held the book so that the spine showed the publisher's name.

"MacPherson Press," he said. "They're one of the good little houses, strictly quality stuff."

"Is that Mr., Mrs., or Ms. MacPherson?"

"It's avenue, as in MacPherson Avenue," John said. "I forget the name of the people who run it, but a clever criminal lawyer like you shouldn't have trouble figuring out the address."

"Okay," I said, "I owe you one, John."

"You owe me six bucks," John said. "The book *is* for sale."

"Oh, yeah."

I took the book to the office and read "And You Thought James Baldwin Had It Tough." If I was any judge, Birks knew how to write. The story was funny and ironic and without a lot of wasted motion.

I looked up MacPherson Press in the phone book and got a woman on the line who said she was the editor-in-chief. I told her I was a literary agent.

"In the market for fresh blood," I said to her. "It's the only thing that keeps an agency vibrant. Foreign sales is what I have in mind."

The woman hesitated on the other end. Maybe I hadn't struck the right note.

"You're actually *looking* for writers?" she said. "All the agents I know are beating them away with a big stick. Too many amateur writers out there and too few agents."

"Well, I'm new in the game, trying to establish an identity, you know."

"You *must* be new. I've never come across your name before," the woman said. "Oh, well, who is it you're interested in?"

"A young fellow from one of your collections. Birks Robinson."

"Oh, *Birks*." The woman's voice brightened. "He's a gem. If I could just pull that novel out of him…. I hope you're not planning to steal him away from me and take him to one of the big houses."

"A *novel*." I raised my brightness to the woman's level. "That really excites me. And no fear, as I said, I'm only looking to develop foreign markets. Wouldn't dream of interfering with your relationship with Robinson. You wouldn't happen to have an address where I might reach the young man?"

"Stay there a minute."

The woman was gone from the line for less than a minute. She came back on with a number on Euclid Avenue.

"If you're sincerely keen on helping new writers," she said, "I've got three women I'm high as a kite on…."

I needed ten more minutes to shake MacPherson Press's editor-in-chief. When she got off the line, I went down the long lists of Robinsons in the phone book and came up with a Robinson, C. at the Euclid address.

I dialed the number.

"Who is it?" A man with a raspy voice answered.

"Yes, hello, is Birks at home by any chance?"

"No."

The raspy-voiced guy hung up.

Euclid Avenue was probably forty minutes by foot from my office. I locked the door, walked west along Queen and angled north until I was above College Street. Euclid was heavy on Portuguese who put chain-link fences around the front yards and painted the bricks of the houses in noisy shades of scarlet and aqua.

At the number I was looking for, there was no fence, and the brick was in its original state. The house had a wooden veranda, and a man was sitting on a sofa that took up half the veranda's width. He was an older black man with long legs and a skinny body that collapsed into the sofa's contours. He had a high forehead and greying hair, and he was listening to music from a tape deck. I recognized the tune. It was a Bud Powell recording of "Polka Dots and Moonbeams."

I walked up the front walk to the veranda stairs and waited for the song to finish.

"Not many piano players left like that," I said.

The man looked at me. He had deep vertical lines in his face and yellowy eyes.

"Not *any* piano players left like Mr. Bud Powell," he said. I recognized the raspy voice from the phone.

"Well, I mean, there were all kinds of wonderful bebop pianists," I said. "Dodo Marmarosa, Al Haig, Duke Jordan. But Bud Powell was the original."

The man didn't respond immediately. He seemed to have a habit of leaving time gaps between the end of my statements and the beginning of his.

"You're too young, young man, to've heard all the piano men you just named so confidently," he said after a bit.

"On records," I said. "I never heard Bud Powell live. In person, I mean. But live, I've heard other people, other instrumentalists who came out of bebop. Frank Morgan, James Moody, Dizzy of course."

"Mr. Dizzy Gillespie, ah, now. You *heard him*, you say?"

"Several times."

"*I played* with Mr. Dizzy Gillespie."

"You did?"

"The month of December 1951 at the Casino Theatre down the street from the old City Hall. Mr. Dizzy Gillespie had Mr. John Coltrane on tenor saxophone, Mr. Milt Jackson at the vibraphone, and sundry others. He came to town with no piano player. A friend of an acquaintance mentioned my name as worthy to Mr. Dizzy Gillespie, and as a consequence, I performed one week, four shows a day at the Casino Theatre."

I looked at the man's hands. They had fingers long enough to drop on a tenth chord.

The man said, "Mr. Dizzy Gillespie was in the custom of calling many tunes at very fast tempos. Chord changes of great complexity, too."

"Hard on the piano player," I said.

"I was twenty years of age," the man said. "I learned more lessons in jazz music in one week with Mr. Dizzy Gillespie than in all the other weeks of my life."

"You were working with one of the gods."

"When I tell you about all the weeks of my life, I refer to before and since."

"So," I said, "you named your son after Dizzy."

The pause was longer.

"Mr. John Birks Gillespie," the man said. He nodded. It was the first time in our talk he'd moved a part of his body except his mouth. "I called my boy Birks, you have it correct."

"Does Birks appreciate the honour, if that's the right way to put it?"

"Birks is more a words man than a music man."

"I read a story of his," I said. "Birks is talented."

"I believe that to be the case."

I stepped up from the bottom of the veranda stairs and leaned against the railing.

"If, as you say, you have read a little story Birks wrote," Mr. Robinson said, "you are aware he is homosexual."

"I'm aware of that."

"That's all the boy writes about. He tells me he will move out of it and discover other subjects for his stories."

"Artistic growth I think that's called."

"Are you homosexual?" Mr. Robinson asked me.

"No. I'm a criminal lawyer. My name's Crang."

"Well, now, a criminal lawyer who listens to Bud Powell records and is standing on my porch in the middle of the morning," Mr. Robinson said. "I wonder why."

"Birks left his job rather abruptly."

"You are not intending to tell me that his employer sent a criminal lawyer around to call on his daddy?"

I shook my head. "I'm here in my own interests. And Birks's."

"Birks is keeping his own counsel at present."

"But you're in touch with him?"

"I'm his daddy."

"Could I ask you to do this?" I said. "Tell Birks I'm the man he spoke to at the Purple Zinnia a week ago last Saturday, the man wanting information about Ian Argyll. Birks helped me that night. Maybe I can repay the favour."

Mr. Robinson didn't say anything. The gap stretched so long this time I might have thought he'd forgotten I was there on his veranda, except that his yellowy eyes never left my face.

"Well, now," he said at last, "it happens that you observed a bar and grill down the street, Pete's Bar and Grill by name?"

"I didn't," I said, "but I'll watch for it on the way back."

"Greek man runs it. At nine o'clock tonight it would be to your advantage to visit Pete's Bar and Grill."

"Thank you," I said.

I pushed off the veranda railing.

"Don't mention it," Mr. Robinson said.

He took the Bud Powell tape out of the player, turned it over and snapped it back into the machine.

"There can't be a whole lot of call for bebop pianists like you these days," I said.

Mr. Robinson took his finger off the tape deck's play button.

"Cocktail piano is my living," he said. "You are familiar with the style?"

"In the background for people drinking martinis."

"Lounges of Holiday Inns, yes, sir, going on twenty years those have been my places of employment. Dressing up in my tuxedo, driving to the job."

Mr. Robinson's eyes seemed almost locked into mine.

He said, "You have any notion the damage it does to a man's mind playing 'Send in the Clowns' four times a night?"

He didn't seem to expect an answer. His finger pushed the play button on the tape machine. I went down the steps and out to the street. It might have been the way the wind was blowing, the drift of sound, but walking along the sidewalk as I was heading back to the office, I could hear from Mr. Robinson's veranda, faintly toward the end, all of Bud Powell's "Parisian Thoroughfare."

CHAPTER TWENTY-ONE

Mary, Mary, Quite Contrary was telling me on the phone that she knew what I was up to. Among criminal defence lawyers like me, Mary was also known as Bloody Mary and Maximum Mary. Her parents called her Mary Kimble. She was the meanest, smartest, ballsiest, nastiest crown attorney in the Toronto court system, and she'd drawn Cleve Shumacher's fraud case.

"All I'm up to," I answered her on the phone, "is getting some kind of fair shake for my client."

"Sid Stern tried the same tactic I'm sure you got in mind, Crang."

"What's a *tactic* about asking for an adjournment," I said. "Mary, think about it, Cleve Shumacher's case only walked into my office last week."

"So why aren't you moving faster on it?"

"Oh, sure," I said. "The charge against the guy, there's *only* two thousand pieces of paper I have to read my way through. How about letting me get up to speed here?"

"No matter how much you delay, Crang," Mary said, "I'll have Shumacher's ass sooner or later."

"Think so?"

"No problem."

"First time up, Mary," I said, "first time I appear in court on this thing, first time the judge hears I've replaced Sid Stern, I'm going to get an adjournment, anyway, whatever I ask for."

From downstairs came the sound of someone opening the door off the street. Footsteps clumped on the stairs. I wasn't expecting a client.

"So," I said to Mary on the phone, "why are you bothering to oppose the adjournment? Only three months, I promise, is all I'll ask."

"Crang," Mary said, "I'm playing this one tough down the line."

Someone was standing in the open door. I looked up. It was Albert, Paulie Ross's young guy with the scar on his chin.

"Got to go, Mary," I said into the phone. "See you in court."

I hung up.

"Mr. Ross wants to see ya," Albert said.

"Aw, Albert, I've *had* the scenic tour up Bathurst."

"This is the warehouse. Only ten minutes inna car."

"You got Annie outside?"

Albert shook his head. "You is all."

The Lincoln was double-parked on Queen, Joey B. at his customary post behind the wheel. He drove us north and west, on St. Clair past Dufferin into the part of the city that people called Little Italy. Now, with the proliferation of pasta restaurants, Italian bakeries, espresso parlours, and three hundred thousand Italian Canadians in the neighbourhood, it was about as little as Naples. Joey B. pulled in back of a pool hall, up a narrow lane, and parked in a wider area outside a two-storey red-brick warehouse. Three other cars filled up the parking space. All were metal-grey Lincoln Town Cars.

"Fleet's in," I said.

Albert turned in the front seat. "Grey's Mr. Ross's favourite —"

Joey B. cut him off. "Don't pay no attention to the asshole," he said to Albert.

We got out of the car and went into the warehouse through

a dented tin door. We were in a small and cluttered reception room. A blond woman at a desk, in a bouffant hairdo out of an old Sandra Dee movie, nodded hello to Joey B. and motioned us toward a door behind her. To get there, we edged past three guys lounging in wooden chairs. The three were cut from the same mould as Joey B. — solid bodies, deadpan expressions, guys who looked like they had short fuses.

The room we entered was large and low-ceilinged and had a long conference table in the middle. Paulie Ross sat isolated at one end, wearing another of his faultless suits in charcoal grey. In front of him, his hands rested lightly on two neat arrangements of papers. There was a silver carafe of water next to the papers and two glasses positioned upside down. Empty chairs lined both sides of the conference table. Ross looked up from the papers and indicated with a slow glance from me to a chair two down from him that I was to sit. I sat. Joey B. stood at the door, his hands crossed in front of him, his gaze focused on something in the middle distance.

"Now what?" I asked Ross.

"Now I read you a bunch of names."

"This is a game? I get a prize if I pick the winner?"

"It's the loser that counts," Ross said. "And you don't needa do the picking."

"Really?"

"I done it for you."

"That's what I like about you, Paulie, always looking after my interests. Practically twenty-four hours a day your guys look after my interests."

"What I tell you the first time we talked? The Sunday out at my house?"

"That I should butt out."

"You didn't. So, okay, I'm taking care of business for you."

"Then you think I'll butt out?"

"Also, you'll thank me."

Ross levelled his eyes of ice on me just long enough to make me think I should thank him in advance. I held my silence. He shifted his attention to the top sheet on one of the arrangements of papers on the table. He picked it up and read from it.

"Daryl Snelgrove. Bartley Santucci. Cleve Shumacher. Andy Elms."

"Paulie," I interrupted, "what's Andy doing on there?"

Ross took his time, studying me, thinking it over. He turned his head to Joey B. by the door.

"What's this guy's story again?" he asked Joey B. "This Elms?"

Joey B. spoke from his position at the door, hands still crossed. "He's the old guy Crang talked to for fuckin' ever that Tuesday night, him and his old lady."

"The old guy's old lady?"

"*My* old lady," I answered. "Annie. You met her."

"Okay," Ross said to me, "now you know why the old guy's on here."

"He's the *doorman*, for Pete's sake."

"Where's it say a doorman can't of been involved?"

"Listen, Paulie, Andy the doorman was just a source of information. He's a bystander, an *innocent* bystander. The only thing you're going to accomplish by having him on that list for whatever cockamamie purpose you think —"

"Watch it," Ross said.

"I withdraw the word cockamamie. But about Andy, if the tenant in his building, the cabinet minister —"

"David Rowbottom," Ross said. "He's on the list, too."

"If he finds out Andy told Annie and me it was him — Rowbottom I'm referring to — who Bart went to visit that night, he might just have Andy's keister fired out of his maroon doorman's uniform. I don't know how widespread this list of yours is going to get. I'm only concerned for Andy's job."

Ross waved me to a halt. "Relax for Chrissake. The reason the name's on the list, I'm trying to show you this is a thorough job I done, you understand?"

I leaned back in the chair. It had a fake leather headrest and fake leather on the arms. "Read on," I said to Ross.

"David Rowbottom, like I said already. Malcolm Switzer —"

"Is that Malcolm the bartender?"

"The place on Carlton."

"Purple Zinnia."

"And two more guys on here, no last names, Larry and Curly."

"*Ah, jeez.*"

"You're pissing me off, Crang."

I leaned forward again. "If the idea is to record the names of everyone who's a possible for Alex Corcoran's murder, you're barking up the wrong tree with those two guys."

"Larry and Curly?"

"Well, let that part go, their names."

"Coupla thieves is what I hear."

"Commission agents."

"Huh?"

"Let that go, too. It's peripheral. On the main issue though, I guarantee —"

"Guarantee, *shit.*" Ross had a sudden stormy look. "I'm the person telling *you* what's the guarantee here."

"Paulie, at the risk of taking your blood pressure into uncharted territory, may I suggest, *humbly* suggest, other possibilities for your little list. Some guy named Hubert Wax, there's one. Birks Robinson, another. And what about Bartley's piece of muscle, Axe?"

"*Bartley's* piece of muscle? You fuckin' out of your mind?"

"You planted Axe with Bartley?"

"Naturally."

"Well, that's one I guessed right."

"You gonna listen up?"

"I'm all ears," I said, "since my mouth isn't getting me far."

"The situation," Ross began, a new note of formality in his voice, "we got one fag died of AIDS and another fag knocked off by the guy that gave the first fag AIDS."

"Eloquently phrased, Paulie."

"Solution to the problem is we finger the guilty party, namely the guy walking around with the dose of AIDS. You with me, Crang?"

"Ian Argyll died of AIDS, Alex Corcoran of foul play, so on, so forth. Right. But I'd challenge you on one or two points, Paulie. First —"

"I'm *solving* the fucking crime, Crang." Ross spoke with much heat. "You oughta be going, 'Hey, nice, Paulie,' instead of this bitching."

"Do I seem ungrateful?"

"Yeah, especially when I got a document that's gonna wrap this up, no question."

Ross put down the sheet of paper with the names on it and picked up a thicker sheaf of documents held in place by a large paper clip. He skimmed over the top page, developed a small smile and passed the documents to me.

"This here's the clincher," he said, pleased with himself.

The papers I held in my hand appeared to be photocopies of reports from the North Central Toronto General Hospital. Most of what was on them fell into the category of medical mumbo jumbo, but a name leaped off the top page.

I looked at Paulie Ross. "Cleve Shumacher?"

Ross flicked his hand in the air. "Read the thing, will ya already," he said.

I ran my eyes down the pages on the lookout for words among the jargon that would confirm what I was afraid the documents were all about. There seemed to be a lot of data concerning blood types, blood analysis, blood infections, and the term HIV came and went with regularity. The key abbreviation wasn't spelled out until the fifth page. I stopped reading.

"How'd you get your paws on this stuff?" I asked Ross.

"I got contacts wherever I needa have contacts," Ross said. "You understand it, what it says there?"

"Sad to say, yeah."

I reached for one of the glasses on the conference table, turned it right side up and poured water into it from the silver carafe. There were ice cubes in the water.

"I'll take some of that," Ross said.

I poured water and ice cubes into the second glass and drank from my own.

"Cleve Shumacher's got AIDS," I said.

"Those copies you're holding there, a guy made them for me right in the hospital itself. That's the real goods, no horsin' around."

"I believe you."

"We got the killer. Cleveland Shumacher. His name's right there, on paper. Says he's got AIDS. He gave the first dead guy AIDS, and he clipped the second dead guy. Case closed. You wanta ask questions, Crang? Last chance you get."

"What're your intentions for the purloined documents?"

"The evidence? You crazy? I'm giving it to the cops. It proves a guy did a murder."

"Which cops?" I asked. "Not a pair of homicide dicks named Mullen and Polaski?"

"Matter of fact, I ate lunch with Jerry Mullen a couple hours ago. Guy's got an appetite like George Foreman."

"Cleve must have known he had AIDS the day he came to see me," I said. I was thinking and talking at the same time. That was probably a mistake. "I should've pressed him on it, whether he had AIDS. I could've helped the guy. Jesus, this is a grim turn of events."

"Grim, my ass," Ross said with some force. "Corcoran had it in for Shumacher on account of what he did to his pal Argyll, gave him the AIDS. So Shumacher aced Corcoran before Corcoran could ace him. Open and fucking shut."

"Did Mullen say he was going to lay a charge against Cleve after he gets these records from you?"

"Said he likes Shumacher for the killer. Gonna have a go-round with him and after, you know, talk to a crown attorney. Jerry thinks it's ninety-nine percent sure."

"Murder, I haven't taken a murder trial in ten years. Maybe I should brief somebody for Cleve, Jack Pinkovsky, a crackerjack like that, somebody —"

"*Crang*, keep your eye on the ball, okay? I mean, you got a hell of a way of telling a person that done you a favour thanks a lot."

"Thanks a lot, Paulie."

"I proved the case, for Chrissake, whatever you lawyers call it, beyond a reasonable doubt."

"Well, now, Paulie, Cleve Shumacher has AIDS. Those documents of yours don't leave much question of that. I'll even concede Cleve could have infected Ian Argyll. But it may not necessarily follow that the guy who infected Ian, Shumacher or whoever, knifed Alex Corcoran."

"You fucking kidding me?" Ross's face showed high annoyance. "That's what all the crapping around's been about, the trouble you been making for me and everybody else."

"I've had second thoughts."

Ross gave me another of his long stares. "Why don't you take your second thoughts on home. Pour yourself a big drink. Know what I'm saying? *Two* big drinks. See if those second thoughts don't go away."

For the first time, I was aware that Joey B. had moved from the door and was standing behind me. He had a tendency to loom.

"Deal's outta your hands, anyway, Crang," Ross said. "The cops, far as you're concerned, they'll handle Shumacher, the murder, all the details. Hey, you should, like, relax."

"Yeah, well," I said. Joey B. was a mouth breather. "Could be some, ah, wisdom in what you say, Paulie."

"Wisdom, yeah, good idea, you should keep on thinking that way."

I drank some more water from the glass and rattled the ice cubes lightly against the glass's sides. "Generous of you to go to all this trouble for little old me, Paulie, gathering evidence, uncovering new facts."

"Not just for you," Ross said. His eyes went narrow.

"Right, to protect your wife, keep her from finding out about Bart's chosen fields of endeavour."

"What, you being sarcastic? You think I don't love my family, my wife, my stepson?"

"Wouldn't question that for a minute, Paulie, though I couldn't help noticing you had Bartley's name on your list of suspects in Alex Corcoran's murder."

"Your ears stuffed up or something? I told you I was tryin' to show I been doing a real job. Thorough. Bartley knows all these guys, the dead guys, other guys. It woulda been unnatural me leaving him off, even if he had nothing to do with the murder. Which he didn't."

"You were leaving no stone unturned?"

"Right."

"All in the interests of seeing justice done?"

"We don't needa talk about this no more."

"Those are your only interests? Shielding your wife and nailing a killer?"

Ross folded his hands on the conference table. It was a slow and deliberate move. He gave me a look that had the same qualities, slow and deliberate.

"What's it matter," Ross said, "as long as nobody's gotta do any more worrying about who killed the Corcoran guy?"

I didn't answer.

Ross unfolded his hands. "You want a ride back to Queen Street?" he asked me.

I twisted my head up and around to Joey B. standing behind me. He had wide nostrils. They may have been flaring.

"Fresh air'll be good for me," I said to Ross. "I'll walk."

CHAPTER TWENTY-TWO

I walked so far east on St. Clair that the ethnic makeup of the street switched — pizza parlours to Carib chicken joints, Italian to Jamaican. It was time for me to think matters through about Paulie Ross and the cabinet minister and about Bart, Axe, the mysterious Hubert Wax, and the rest. I cut south past the TTC barns where streetcars rest between trips up and down the city's streets, and sauntered into Wychwood Park. It isn't a park in the conventional sense — old people sitting on benches, kids tossing a football, nannies walking babies. Wychwood Park is a residential neighbourhood, a slice of rural England dropped into the centre of Toronto. It has houses built like larger versions of Cotswolds cottages with lots of leafy trees, an open green space in the centre, an air of exclusivity. Or is it snobbishness? I wasn't thinking about Paulie and the others. Maybe it was the distraction of Wychwood Park. Maybe talking was better than thinking, anyway.

I found a phone booth on Davenport Road and arranged to meet Annie at a Vietnamese restaurant in Kensington Market. An empty cab came by. I waved it down and got to the restaurant ten minutes before Annie.

"How did you fare with Mr. Rowbottom this morning?" she asked.

"I'm thinking of joining his tennis club."

"Oh, swell move," Annie said. "You can grill him in the shower room. He'll be a captive audience."

"Rowbottom stonewalled when I asked questions," I said. "But something more immediate, I saw Paulie Ross an hour ago, a private audience you might say."

I told Annie about the dialogue in the Ross warehouse.

"Well, well," Annie said.

"Here's the part that's especially 'well, well,'" I said. "The whole deal smelled of a setup."

"Setting up whom?"

"Me."

"You?"

"Yeah," I said. "Consider this, how did Paulie Ross suddenly come up with the explanation that whoever gave Ian AIDS is also the guy who knocked off Alex?"

"That's the explanation you've been touting around."

"Sure," I said, "but I haven't touted it to anyone except you and, as of this morning, David Rowbottom."

Annie lifted her eyebrows. "You think Rowbottom passed it on to Paulie Ross?"

"It occurred to me," I said. "And if he did, Paulie went into high gear and put together the presentation this afternoon that's supposed to make me think Cleve Shumacher is the AIDS carrier and Alex's killer."

"Those hospital documents were authentic?"

"To my eye. Lot of Latin terms, talk about pathologies, funny little symbols, all that. They couldn't have been fake."

"Paulie Ross is a resourceful fellow. Scary but resourceful."

"He might've been sitting on this stuff for a few days, the evidence that Cleve has AIDS. Maybe he did some checking around on Cleve and all other parties as they came into the picture. As soon as he hit pay dirt with Cleve, he saved it up until it was useful."

"Like this afternoon."

"Like then."

"You're speculating."

"As usual," I said. "It doesn't really matter when or how Ross got the medical records. He's *got* them, and they're mucking up the situation in ways I don't fathom."

"Poor Cleve Shumacher," Annie said.

"I thought you didn't like stockbrokers. MPS Technology and so on."

"I don't," Annie said. "But I can abominate a whole profession and still feel sorry for one of its members who has AIDS."

"One thing's certain, you just have to look at the guy, Cleve didn't stick any knife into Alex."

"Who did?" Annie asked. "David Rowbottom? Are you telling me the purpose of the get-together today was to deflect you from Rowbottom, from him as the murderer?"

"Him. Or perhaps someone close to him."

"It's hard to get the mind wrapped around the concept that a cabinet minister could in fact murder someone."

"Yeah," I said. "I'm having trouble with that one."

Annie and I ate spring rolls — ginger chicken, vermicelli, pork, and bamboo sprouts — helped the food along with green tea, and talked in circles about murder and suspects and a possible linkup between Paulie Ross and David Rowbottom. At eight thirty, I kissed Annie on the lips and left for my appointment with Birks Robinson.

The route I picked out, up and down side streets south of College Street, gave me space to examine the traffic in front and behind. None of it included a metal-grey Lincoln Town Car. I strode on.

Pete's Bar and Grill was on the north side of College close to Euclid, two big windows on the street and the name in blinking yellow neon. Birks Robinson, looking a heck of a lot like the young Harry Belafonte to me, was sitting at a table by one of the windows. He had on aviator sunglasses and was drinking a Coke. I went in.

"Thanks for meeting me," I said to him. "I'm Crang."

Birks half rose from his chair and shook hands.

"Clyde told me you'd be okay," he said. "But I probably would've showed up without him approving."

"Clyde?"

"My daddy."

"I admire his taste in music."

"Yeah," Birks said, taking off the aviator glasses. "That'll get him every time."

A small round man with a white apron tied around his middle and a towel draped over one shoulder came up to the table.

"Whatever the gentleman wants, Pete," Birks said to him.

"White wine," I said.

"In *here*? Birks said. "That Greek stuff'll rot your insides."

"Watch your mouth, kid," Pete said. He laughed, snapped the towel at Birks, and went away.

The restaurant had plastic tabletops and photographs of the Parthenon hanging crooked on the walls. It wasn't much for size, and only one other table was occupied. But a dozen short, swarthy guys stood at the bar watching a television set and doing a lot of cheering and high fiving. The set showed an NBA game, the play-offs, Pistons versus Bulls.

"So," I said to Birks, "who is it you're scared of? Paulie Ross?"

"Who's Paulie Ross?"

"If you don't know him, I guess you aren't scared of him."

"What makes you think I'm scared of anyone?"

"Taking off from the Purple Zinnia that way," I said. "Waving bye-bye to a grand a week."

"Hubert Wax. He's gonna *kill me*."

"The Waxer? That's who's frightened you into hiding?"

Birks nodded his head and looked doleful.

"Why?" I asked.

"Because he's already killed one guy, and I figure I'm next."

Pete brought the white wine. It wasn't particularly chilled and it tasted raw.

"I assume," I said to Birks, "the first victim you're speaking of is Alex Corcoran. Wax killed Alex?"

"It's obvious," Birks said. The skin on his face was silky smooth, and he had clear brown eyes. All his features came together in perfect regularity — or maybe it was regular perfection — and the only thing that marred his beauty at that moment was the worried expression.

"What's so obvious about this Wax guy stabbing Alex?" I said. "Not that I'm exactly speaking from a position of great knowledge here. I've only *met* Wax for five or ten unsatisfying seconds."

"You're lucky," Birks said. He rubbed the Coke can between his palms. "Okay, I'll fill you in from the start, and we'll see if there's a way you can help me out of the squeeze I'm in. I mean, I know you were Alex Corcoran's landlord and friend and everything, and you've got a sort of stake in this thing."

"Shoot," I said.

"I was David Rowbottom's lover for —"

"Is *that* what the photographs in his secret drawer are all about?"

"He showed you those?" Birks's eyes registered amazement. "Those are, like, his private treasure."

"He didn't show me. I helped myself."

"Those are photographs of every man he's slept with," Birks said. "Corny, I know, but you have to realize that David only came out of the closet three or four years ago, and he's so proud of it, you know, so kind of stunned and happy and *giddy.* I mean, here's this country guy, from up there south of Peterborough, a high school principal in his town, married and everything, and he finally lets loose. Admits he's gay. He thinks it's so fantastic he can't get over it, like he's the only man it's happened to in the history of the world."

"And that accounts for the rogues' gallery?"

"Well, I wouldn't call it *that* exactly."

"My apologies. His collection of photos."

"Yeah."

"Listen," I said, "on that subject in general, one item I've been chewing over the last week or so. David Rowbottom is gay, new at it as you say, but gay, and I keep running into people who know he's gay. But what about the premier of the province, Rowbottom's boss? What about the opposition politicians? What about the reporters who cover the legislature? Do *they* know? And isn't his gayness some kind of issue?"

Birks looked at me as if I were more than a trifle simple. "Sure, they know," he said. "It's one of those shared secrets. Nobody talks about it, the press and politicians.... Well, they probably *talk* about it, gossip and make jokes behind David's back. But it's sort of an understood thing they don't say anything in public. That'd change if David made some big dramatic announcement about his sexual orientation."

"Like the MP in Ottawa did a few years ago."

"Svend Robinson," Birks said, "but you notice there was no huge fuss about him being gay."

"Same with the congressman in the U.S., Barney Frank."

"But there *would* be a fuss, a real freaking uproar, if word about his AIDS got around."

"Whose?" I said. "Rowbottom's?"

Birks nodded. "David thinks he's cured."

"AIDS and cured? Jeez, this is getting to be information overload."

"Okay," Birks said, "last summer David got diagnosed for something AIDS related, mild, but who knows where these things lead? So he latched on to this clinic in Buffalo that does some kind of special treatments. I don't know the place, it's either way out front medically or it's a bunch of quacks running a con game. But David went for it, and he's convinced the treatments are the real goods. He thinks the clinic made him healthy and clean and red-blooded and all that."

"Well, he plays tennis, and every set of stairs he comes to, he bounds up them."

"And as part of the treatment," Birks said, "one Saturday a month he goes to the clinic for booster shots or something. And those are super hush-hush. The security he lays on is fantastic. Not even his staff knows how to reach him. Leaves no word, pulls out the plug on his phone. It's like he's disappeared from the face of the earth."

"That explains something."

"What?"

"Rowbottom has that answering machine," I said, "but one Saturday afternoon I rang his apartment and got nothing, no human voice, no machine."

"Man, those Saturdays, he is incommunicado."

There was a roar from the short Greek basketball fans at the bar. I looked over. Isiah Thomas had swished a three-pointer from twenty feet out.

"What about you?" I asked Birks. "As far as AIDS, if you were one of Rowbottom's, ah, lovers, aren't you a candidate for something bad?"

"I wasn't just one of his lovers," Birks said. "For a time there, I was *it*, his guy, his *only* guy. And that's why I'm hiding out from Hubert Wax today."

"Leave him for a minute," I said. "Tell me about you and AIDS."

"Hey, me, I'm the poster boy for safe sex," Birks said. His smile was the type that called for adjectives like *beaming* and *radiant*.

"Uh, condoms, you're talking about."

"On every occasion," Birks said. "When I buy my supply, it's like, I back up the truck to the drugstore and load them by the case."

"So you're clear?"

"Get my blood tested every two months."

"Safe sex, condoms and so on, is that the case with the other guys in Rowbottom's photo collection?"

"Well, obviously one of them was careless."

"Ian Argyll?"

"Yeah," Birks said, "and right there, that's where the story starts to make me very nervous, man."

"Go back to the part where you and Rowbottom were, ah, lovers."

Birks gave me a sober look. "Listen, Mr. Crang, if you're having trouble talking about gay relationships, maybe you're not the guy to help me."

"I *shouldn't* have trouble, not after living upstairs from Ian and Alex all those years. Just maybe the terminology needs getting used to."

"'Lover?' That terminology?"

"All right, you were Rowbottom's *lover*. When was that?"

"Last fall," Birks said. "We were tight, a real couple, like it was gonna be a forever thing. That was until David met Hubert Wax and got turned on to that real stud scene, leather and tattoos and the rest of the whole adolescent biker mentality. So David told me to take a hike. He handled it very nicely, I'll give him that. Presented me with a farewell gift, you know, a laptop computer for my writing."

"You do it very nicely, by the way, the writing. I read one of your short stories."

"Thanks," Birks said. "But I don't do it on any laptop computer. Can't stand the tippy-tap noise and that damn little green screen."

"Oh, yeah?"

"Stick to my good old Underwood. Type on it, you really know you got a machine under your fingers."

Another eruption broke out from the fans at the bar. I peeked at the TV set. Michael Jordan had gone back door. Slam dunk.

"Have I got your attention, Mr. Crang?" Birks asked, slightly edgy.

"Rowbottom and Wax became an item," I said. "What next?"

"They still *are* an item, which is the problem."

"How'd you take it after Rowbottom ditched you?"

"I sulked. Man, I was depressed. Went on for months. I think it was my ego. You know, like, I'm always the guy who dumps *other* guys so when I was on the receiving end, I couldn't take what was happening to me inside. One thing's for sure, I wanted to get a shot back at David."

"And, let me make a guess, you saw your chance when Alex Corcoran came around?"

"You got it," Birks said. "Like, I knew the whole background. I knew David and Ian Argyll'd had their little moment. Knew Ian died of AIDS. So when Alex Corcoran walked in the Zinnia asking questions, man, I pointed him right at David."

"When was this?"

"Noon of the same Saturday you were by later for dinner," Birks said. "Alex had lunch. I knew who he was, Ian's companion, and I'm telling you, Mr. Crang, I just grabbed my chance. Told him Ian and David had done their thing. Told him David had this AIDS-related sickness. I gave him stuff that got that man's attention."

"How did Alex react?"

Birks thought for a moment. "Very calm, very steady. Said he was going away a few days, gonna think on it. But I could tell, just something in the aura around him, he had bad notions in mind for David."

"By that Saturday noon," I said, "maybe you aren't aware of this part, Birks, Malcolm the bartender downstairs had already tipped off Alex about Rowbottom being a guy Ian had drinks with at the Zinnia."

"He loves to dish the dirt, that Malcolm."

"And hold his palm out at the same time."

"I never knew that. He charges, huh? The rascal."

"In any event," I said, "what you knew that Malcolm didn't was that Ian and Rowbottom had actually engaged in an affair."

"The nitty-gritty details, yeah." Birks nodded. "I had it in my head for a long time I was gonna shaft David for dropping me. But you know what? I felt lower than a snake from the moment I opened my mouth to that Alex cat. And not because it got Hubert Wax on my case. I hated myself just because it was a lousy thing to do, ratting on David like that."

"How come you steered me on to Malcolm that Saturday night?"

"Well, first off, I knew you weren't gay."

"You did?"

"Hell, a gay guy can *always* tell who's gay and who's straight."

"Really? Always?"

"And I decided you were probably the guy who had the house where Ian and Alex lived. Ian used to do all kinds of jawing at the bar about you, this wild lawyer always getting himself in jackpots, one thing and another, funny stories, and you fit the description. So —"

"Wild? Is that your word or Ian's?"

"His."

"Not distinguished or something similar?"

"Afraid not, man. So, anyway —"

"Hm."

"So, *anyway*, you're in the Zinnia, I thought to myself, you asking about Ian and all, I thought maybe the reason you showed up was you might be looking to keep Alex out of grief."

"You hit it on the nose, Birks."

"But hell, man, look what's happened." Birks's handsomeness crinkled into an alarmed expression. "Hubert Wax killed Alex Corcoran. It has to be him. To protect David, he killed Alex, and that's on my head. It's my *fault*. And now, sure as shit, he's gonna come after *me*."

"Listen, Birks," I said, "it's a considerable leap from wearing leather and riding a motorcycle to actually stabbing a man. You're not, maybe just a little, overrating Mr. Wax?"

"Want to know why he's called 'The Waxer'?"

"A spin off on his surname?"

"Because he polishes guys off. Get it? Like in wax? The Waxer? That's the man's reputation."

I spent a moment on the glass of white plonk and thought about Birks's portrait of Hubert Wax. "Well, okay," I said, "I'll govern myself on the assumption you're right. I'm not saying I agree the Waxer did his waxing on Alex. But I'll assume it, as far as the next step is concerned."

The guys at the bar went into another frenzy. I took a glance. On television, Dennis Rodman had levitated about ten feet in the air to haul in a rebound.

"Mr. Crang," Birks said, "I gather you like basketball."

"Only team sport that makes sense."

"Well, don't let my little trouble keep you from the goddamn game."

"No sweat, Birks," I said. "I'm totally focused on the next step."

"Yeah?"

"I'll have a sit-down with the Waxer."

Birks looked disbelieving. "A man needs to have a ton of nerve to go at Hubert on something like this," he said. "Or else be insane."

"Where can I find the guy?"

"Hubert's mostly at David's apartment or the house up in his riding, real beautiful little place near Peterborough. But neither one of them's right for a meet."

"Uh-uh."

"Not the Zinnia, either. And the only other place I know of that Hubert's a regular at is Tight Buns."

I let out a sigh. "More of the gay netherworld I have to hear about?"

"A bar," Birks said. "You know that part of town down where the parkway ends? Pretty grungy section, factories, stinks of pollution?"

"Tight Buns is in there?"

"A gay biker crowd hangs out at it."

"What address?" I asked. "What street?"

"Oh, man, you can't miss it. Tight Buns is the only place around there open nights."

"And I inquire after Hubert Wax?"

"If you're stupid enough to go asking," Birks said. "I'm grateful enough to wish you luck, man."

Both of us stood up.

"Birks, may I ask you something?" I said. "Who do you think you look like? Me, I say the young Harry Belafonte."

"Ah, *man*."

"Malcolm, on the other hand, the bartender, he votes for a much lighter Denzel Washington."

"You white folks, *goddamn*, always coming up with this shit."

"Which shit is that?" I said. "Hey, wait a sec, you think what I asked is racist?"

"Every good-looking black woman, *she* looks like Whitney Houston."

"I suppose that's true."

"I look like *me*, man."

"Birks," I said. "I retract —"

"Who do you think *you* look like?"

"Me?" I said. "Oh, well, ah, possibly Steve Martin without all the grey?"

"That's rich, man, that's really rich."

Birks turned and went out the door. He was laughing as he left.

I stood where I was for a moment. A younger Jean-Paul Belmondo without the snarl? I gave it up and joined the basketball aficionados at the bar. I was the tallest guy there.

CHAPTER TWENTY-THREE

Tom Catalano looked like steam might come out of both his ears any minute.

"Case?" he said to me. "Don't, for God's sake, introduce a word like *case* into this discussion."

"Well, if you want to look at it strictly speaking, it is a case. Cops think so. A case of murder is what they call it."

"All right, all right." Tom moved his hands in a placating gesture. "I'll grant you the noun. But you understand where I'm coming from, my worry in this."

"Daryl Snelgrove and that he isn't mixed up in the, ah, case."

"You assured me the other night, right there in the SkyDome, damn it, nothing'd get out on this ridiculous episode."

"Nothing *got* out."

"Ridiculous doesn't half describe it. More like maddening."

"Tom, this is mountains and molehills you're talking."

"If my partners knew I was frittering away billable hours on a problem in sexual relationships, shit, *homo*sexual relationships, they'd go around shaking their heads. 'Old Tom's lost it.' Behind my back, they'd do that."

Tom was pacing. I was sitting. We were in his office on a floor high up in the TD Centre. The door to the office was shut. I'd arrived unannounced, and Tom told his secretary to hold his calls.

"On the other hand," Tom said, "if Snelgrove makes the papers for any reason except his goddamn batting average, my partners'll blame me for not servicing the client."

"You always walk back and forth like that?"

"People who sit still when they've got a major problem, it leads to an ulcer. I read that somewhere."

"Sounds like *Reader's Digest*."

"*Psychology Today*, I think."

"It's very disconcerting for the other guy in the room. Feels like I'm at a tennis match."

"Christ, I love that. I didn't *have* a major problem until you walked in the door. This story about meeting some guy in a warehouse yesterday, which you're going to have to make where it fits in much clearer, by the way. That, and you keep talking about a murder, and all I see is Daryl Snelgrove back in the glue."

"Tom, you want to forget about the ulcer possibility? I came here to ask for a favour, and no fooling, good news comes with it."

Tom looked at me over his shoulder, stopped pacing, and faced toward me. "Try out the good news and maybe I'll be in the mood for the favour."

"Daryl Snelgrove definitely didn't murder Alex Corcoran."

"That isn't *good news*. That's *old news*."

"Just a sec, Tom, wait for it."

Tom shifted his weight from one foot to the other. "Explain what I'm waiting for."

"The guy running the meeting at the warehouse, the one with just me and him and a hood of his, this guy came up with evidence he thinks is good enough to point the finger at another gent as the murderer."

"Not at Snelgrove?"

"Gent named Cleve Shumacher."

Tom swung the desk chair around and sat on it. The swivel chair had dark wood and red leather. I was sitting on a matching red leather sofa on the other side of an oriental rug.

"That's nice," Tom said. "Nice that Daryl's off the hook. Not that I ever imagined he was *on* the hook. But listen, buddy, it doesn't *eliminate* my concern because you haven't assured me that in all this fandango Daryl's name isn't going to surface in a public way."

"It shouldn't."

"*Shouldn't* doesn't cut it with me."

"As close to nil as you can get."

"That's a trace better."

I clasped my hands behind my head and leaned back on the leather. On the wall across the office, there was a David Milne watercolour, delicate and buoyant. It must have cost a few hundred of Mcintosh, Brown and Crabtree's billable hours.

"See, Tom," I said, "this is a very complicated set of facts we have on our hands."

"Oh, God, I loathe it when criminal lawyers start off with that phrase."

"Keeps the other side on their toes."

"Crang, one point I thought was crystal clear, we, that is you and I and the Blue Jays, are on the *same* side."

"Facts are still complicated." My hands were going numb clasped behind my head. I unclasped them. "Complication number one, the guy who called the meeting in the warehouse yesterday smells of the mob, guy by the name of Paulie Ross."

"Just what I need."

"Complication number two, also directly or indirectly involved is an Ontario cabinet minister name of —"

"*Wait.* A provincial cabinet minister?"

"Right, guy name of —"

"*Don't* tell me." Tom was sitting very erect in his red leather chair. "If questions are asked later, for any reason at all, I want to be able to deny I heard the name."

"You're leaving me alone on the front lines?"

"Where you've always been, anyway."

"True, but I need you for backup."

Tom started to make noises that I knew would be of objection. I cut him off. "In an information capacity only," I said.

"What kind of information?" Tom asked, his guard still up.

"Keep in mind, before you get snotty on me, pal, I'm the one making sure Daryl Snelgrove's name appears only in the sports section."

"Where it belongs."

"Instead of all over the tabloids."

"Okay, I concede there's a quid pro quo in operation."

"Actually, the papers would probably put it in the lifestyle section, one of those pieces oozing sympathy, you know, the macho athlete revealing his tender side and coming out of the —"

"*Crang.*" Tom slapped his palms together. "What *kind* of information, before I change my *mind.*"

"The kind about —"

"Hold it." Tom interrupted again. "Why does this have to go any further? A minute ago you told me the meeting you attended yesterday ended up with the murderer being unveiled or whatever the expression is."

"Unveiled is good," I said. "The guy unveiled was Cleve Shumacher."

"Well?"

"My instincts tell me Cleve didn't do it," I said. "As a matter of fact, anybody's instincts would tell them Cleve is a guy who'd get squeamish about swatting a mosquito."

"Your instincts?"

"Yeah."

"Well, I'll concede this," Tom said, getting more comfortable in his big chair, "your instincts haven't been much off the mark in the past."

"Thanks."

"A little wingy at times, but basically reliable."

"Okay," I said, "the kind of information I'm looking for is the kind about this guy I mentioned, Paulie Ross."

"Yeah," Tom said, considering. "That name ... something's striking a tiny gong inside." Tom picked up his phone and spoke into it. "Sally, ring me through to Jimmy Crothers, please and thanks."

Tom covered the mouthpiece with his hand. "This is relevant," he said to me. "You met Jimmy Crothers?"

I shook my head.

"His office is two floors up." Tom made an okay sign with his thumb and forefinger. "One guy in the firm's got a steel-trap mind, it's Jimmy. Great corporate lawyer."

Tom went back to the phone. "Jimmy, run this name through your synapses. Paulie Ross. What bounces back?"

Tom listened and hummed appreciatively at regular intervals. I passed the time running my eyes over the rest of the pictures on the walls of Tom's office, and discovered that the first David Milne was no accident. All of the watercolours on the walls were Milnes, six of them, good ones, museum quality. Milne collectors would go bananas in Tom's office.

Tom hung up the phone.

"Get this," he said to me. "This guy Ross's corporate work? It's all done by the Turbide firm."

"I don't get it."

"The Turbide firm *only* acts, or *practically* only acts, for clients who've got some dodge going."

"Like what kind of dodges?"

"Oh, laundering money, setting up dummy corporations offshore. That kind of thing. The Turbide people are notorious on the street."

"So, Paulie Ross is sort of by definition and association bent?"

"I'd say so."

"Well, Tom, I'd already more or less figured out that part."

Tom spread his hands on the desk. "Then what *do* you want from me?"

"Details of Paulie Ross's bentness, for starters."

"Hell, man, you've got to be more specific than that," Tom said, swinging a little back and a little forth in his chair. "Maybe what you're trying to ask me is, could I find out what companies the Turbide firm's incorporated for Ross? Land holdings, any of his corporations big in that area? Any partners in his companies? What're the companies empowered to do? Maybe that's what you had in mind to ask me?"

"Would you believe it?" I said. "You took the words right out of my mouth."

"You can *ask*, pal." Tom had a big grin. "But I'm not about to do all the work involved in what I just suggested."

"You aren't?"

"No, but I'll get one of our articling students on it, some eager beaver."

"Gee," I said, "what are friends for?"

Tom came from behind his desk. I stood up, and Tom slung his arm over my shoulder. He said, "What I see is everybody getting what they want out of this. The Blue Jays get a ball player who has nothing on his mind except his hitting stroke. I get a contented client. And you get … What is it you want out of this again?"

"The murderer. Come on, Tom, my friend's killer."

"Right."

Tom was steering me to the door. "The student's name is Audrey Gostick, the one I'll assign to Paulie Ross. Touch base with her in a couple of days."

We were at the door. I turned back into the room. "This is fantastic, the grouping of paintings you've got here."

"Oh, yeah?" Tom looked around as if he were noticing the Milnes for the first time. "Pretty pictures," he said.

"You kidding? David Milne was a heck of a nifty painter. Minor maybe but nifty."

"Woman comes in every six months. Rotates the paintings in all the offices. The firm has her on retainer. She does the choosing. Impresses the hell out of the clients. Some of the clients, anyway."

I looked around some more. "Listen, Tom, next rotation day, tell the woman you want a room of Paul Youngs."

"Paul Young?"

"Nudes. The guy paints these lush nudes. Think of the impact …"

Tom opened the office door. "Get outta here, Crang."

CHAPTER TWENTY-FOUR

Birks Robinson was wrong about me and Tight Buns. He said I couldn't miss it. The Volks and I criss-crossed the neighbourhood south of the Don Valley Parkway and found only dark buildings and empty streets.

The buildings were elderly and brick and no higher than four storeys. Factories, warehouses, a Canada Post sorting plant, a dumpy little diner with a closed sign hanging in the door. The only traffic seemed to be the occasional speed merchant taking a shortcut from Eastern Avenue to Lake Shore.

I stopped under a streetlight and pondered alternatives. Two motorcycles cruised by. Their rackety motors sent vibrations bouncing off the walls of the buildings. I edged the Volks away from the curb. Wherever the bikes were headed, so was I.

They made a left turn, a right, slowed down, and glided into a line of Harleys and Kawasakis and Suzukis. The drivers lifted off their bikes and swaggered toward a building that had boards over its windows and showed no light apart from a single bulb over a door. We were on a narrow street, no more than a block long, one I'd missed during my criss-crossing. The guys from the bikes disappeared through the door under the single light bulb.

I drove to the end of the block and around the corner. The street showed no signs of human life. I got out of the car and walked back to the building I'd seen the bikers enter. I entered, too.

In design, Tight Buns appeared to take its inspiration from a Dodge City saloon. It was large, over-lit, and high-ceilinged. A wooden stand-up bar filled the wall straight ahead of me. Tables and chairs, also wooden, covered most of the remaining space. At some tables, men played cards. At others and along the bar, they drank and talked. The talk was loud. Maybe years of riding choppers had rendered the guys hearing impaired.

Black was the colour of choice in apparel — black leather pants, black jeans, black T-shirts with cut-off sleeves. But there was nothing particularly menacing about the black or the guys wearing it. They looked less like Hells Angels and more like guests at a theme costume party.

I found a space at the bar, and after a few minutes one of the three bartenders came over to me. He had a shaved head and wore a black tank top. He nodded but didn't say anything.

"Nice night," I said.

The bartender waited in silence. I shuffled through my mental list of icebreakers. Behind the bartender, a photograph of Winston Churchill hung on the wall. It was the one of him laying bricks at his house in the country. I looked around. All the photographs in the place were of Churchill. Flashing the V sign. Smoking a cigar. Flashing a V sign and smoking a cigar. Delivering the 'Some chicken! Some neck!' speech in Ottawa.

"Original decor," I said to the bartender, "the pictures of good old Winnie."

"Gay historical figure of the month," the bartender said.

"Pardon?"

"We hang a different gay historical figure every month."

"Winston, come on, *Churchill*?"

"It's been documented."

"Who by?"

"Our club archivist," the bartender said, impatient. "Little-known historical fact about Churchill. The archivist can prove it, though."

"I hesitate to ask this," I said, "but who's going up on the walls in June?"

"I forget which is which," the bartender said. "Babe Ruth in June and Gary Cooper in July, or the other way around."

"I guess I'd like a drink," I said.

The bartender rested his hands on the bar. "You from another town, Mac?" he asked.

"Beginning to think I'm from another planet."

"Because you probably came to the wrong bar," the bartender said. "The CN Tower, that kinda tourist place, is over west of here."

"I'm looking for Hubert Wax."

"Waxer?" The bartender's respect for me may have zipped up a couple of levels. "He expecting you?"

"He'll be intrigued to see me."

"That's Waxer in the card game in the corner."

I turned in the direction the bartender was pointing. Five men were in the game. All wore short hair, moustaches, and the black gear. But I recognized Hubert Wax. He looked marginally more threatening than anyone else in the room. He was the biggest of the quintet in the card game and he showed a tattoo on his right bicep.

"Vodka on the rocks," I said to the bartender.

"We only serve two drinks: beer and cognac."

"That's novel," I said. "Okay, cognac."

The bartender served the cognac in a shot glass filled to the three-ounce level. It cost ten dollars. I paid and wandered over to Hubert Wax's card game.

The five guys were playing poker. Wax shuffled the cards for a new hand. I stood behind an empty chair opposite Wax. The tattoo on his bicep seemed to be of an erect penis. Wax looked up from the cards. His eyes passed over me and came back. He stopped shuffling.

"Jesus," he said. His face broke into a smirk.

The four other guys at the table glanced up at me, mildly interested.

"Hubert Wax, correct?" I said to Wax. "We haven't been formally introduced. Mind if I take a seat? Crang's the name. Don't let me hold up your deal."

I sat down.

"Crang the troublemaker," Wax said, still smirking. He had tiny front teeth. "The *reformed* troublemaker."

"Trouble wasn't what I'd intended," I said.

"You're out of the picture, fella," Wax said.

The four other guys swung their heads from Wax to me. They were getting more interested.

"David Rowbottom says I'm out of the picture?" I said. I put my shot glass of cognac on the table. "Look, Hubert or Waxer, Wax, whichever you prefer, let me lay my cards on the table."

I grinned at the four guys.

"Little joke there," I said. "Cards? On the table? Poker game?"

The four didn't grin back.

I shrugged. "I'll be blunt," I said to Wax, "and invite you to be blunt in return. It's the only way to get through this in a hurry."

"Some guy named Shumacher killed your pal," Wax said. "That's what I hear."

"There's another school of thought," I said. "This school ... rumour is probably more like it, word on the street, it says that you, Waxer, may have some light to shed on Alex's death. First-hand knowledge, as it were."

Wax's smirk vanished. "Are you out of your mind?" he said to me.

"As I say, only a rumour I'm running down."

"Coming in *here*, and laying this crap on me."

"When I say word on the street, I'm referring to one source only."

"This is my turf, you stunned prick." Wax's upper body tightened in his chair.

"Territorial imperative, sure, I appreciate that, but I'm offering you the chance to counter this source. When did you last see Alex Corcoran? Let's go at it that way."

Wax pushed himself back from the table. "You're looking to get your head cracked open, know that?"

The fascination quotient among the other four guys at the table had stepped up several notches. One of them, the guy in the chair next to mine, a smoker, let the ash on his cigarette burn down to his fingers. He shook them and stubbed out the cigarette.

"Here's an even simpler question, Waxer," I said. "Where were you a week ago last night?"

"I don't believe this." Wax looked like he was getting ready to stand up. "You accusing me of murder?"

"Not accusing. Inquiring."

"Get this, dick face, I never in my life laid eyes on this Alex Corcoran."

"What about your reputation?"

"What reputation?" Waxer was on his feet.

"For polishing guys." I stood up, too. "Polishing them *off*, I believe I was told."

"With my fists, you dumb dick."

"Waxer's got a wonderful right hand," the guy next to me, the smoker, said.

"Crang, you're either the stupidest guy I've ever ran into," Wax said, "or the most offensive."

"Oh, hey," I said. "Kettle calling the pot black. You wearing a tattoo like that, you're telling me *I'm* offensive?"

"That does it."

Wax stretched all the way across the table, grabbed my sweater with his left hand and smacked me across the cheek and temple with his open right hand.

I yanked my sweater out of Wax's grip and fell back into my chair. Wax got tangled in his own chair. I picked up the book of matches the smoker had been using. Wax straightened on the other side of the table. I lit a match. Wax started around the table. I touched the match to the cognac. Flames spurted out of the glass. Wax stopped in his tracks. I tipped the glass at its base, and a narrow line of fire ran across the table. All eyes were on it. I vamoosed out the door.

On the street, I turned right and went pell-mell to the first crossroad. The left side of my face felt numb. I turned the corner and stopped. The smoker hadn't been kidding about Hubert Wax's right hand. Even with just an open palm, it was wonderful.

I looked back down the narrow street. The door to Tight Buns stayed shut. I gave it five minutes. No one stuck a head out the door.

One error I'd made leaving the bar, I realized, was the right turn. The Volks was parked on a street to the left, on the opposite side of Tight Buns from where I was now standing and experiencing facial hot flashes. To reach the car, I could take a long route down the street I was on, around the block, and double back. Or I could go the short way, straight past Tight Buns. I opted for the direct line.

The door to the bar opened when I was within ten paces of it. Two guys emerged.

"There he is," one of them hollered.

I went into reverse in a hurry. The noises from the rear suggested a stampede of guys was pouring out of the bar and into the street.

I hotfooted it around the corner, up one street, juked down an alley, and pointed myself east, the direction I figured would put the most distance between me and the posse from Tight Buns.

Somewhere, reasonably far enough back, assorted shouts and the gunning of motorcycles broke the general calm. I slowed and made a three-hundred-sixty-degree surveillance of the area. No one was hot on my trail. On the other hand, guys riding bikes could overhaul me in swift order. What I needed was a secure hiding place, a safe spot to wait out the search parties.

I found it in an alley across the street. A metal fire escape ran down the side of a four-storey building. I hoped it wouldn't occur to my pursuers to check above ground. The fire escape ended about seven feet up from the dirt of the alley. The first time I jumped for it, I banged the back of my hands on the bottom rung. The second time, my fingers grabbed metal, and I hauled myself up. I clambered to the second level and sat down.

A couple of minutes later, two guys on foot stopped at the mouth of the alley.

"We couldn't have missed him," one guy said. I recognized the voice of the smoker at Hubert Wax's table.

"Listen, Allan," the second guy said, "what are we *doing* out here?"

"What are you talking about? We're supposed to, you know, put the boots to that man."

"Oh, *really*. What is he, a pyromaniac or something?"

"He insulted Waxer."

"Hubert Wax, *God*," the second guy said. "Whenever there's an upset at the club, why is it always Hubert *Wax*?"

"Well, he likes to, you know, kick ass."

"Allan, look at me," the second guy said. "What are we, the two of us? Think about it, we're two queens from Scarborough who like to drive our motorcycles out into the country and have a picnic. Am I right? We do not, ever, kick ass."

"I guess so."

"You know so," the second guy said. "Then what are we doing out here in the middle of the night on some lunatic mission for Hubert Wax, whom I can't abide, anyway?"

"When you put it that way …"

"Allan, both of us have to work in the morning," the second guy said. "Let's walk back to the club, drink one more beer, and go home."

The two guys turned away from the alley.

"Perhaps we should split the one beer," the second guy said.

I waited another quarter hour. Now and then, the backfire of a bike's motor erupted in the empty streets. But soon enough the quiet returned. If there were searchers in the neighbourhood, they were on little cat feet.

I dropped from my perch and landed on the ground flat-footed. It was all clear in every direction. I picked my way through the streets, sticking to the shadows. I was also limping. The balls of my feet felt tender from the flat landing in the alley.

I reached the Volks.

Hubert the Waxer Wax was leaning against the front fender.

"Hey, Hubert, just the guy," I said. "Where had we got in our little discussion?"

The Waxer pushed off the fender and let fly a sweeping round-house right at my head. I ducked and raised both arms. Wax's fist hit muscle somewhere close to my left elbow.

"Is dialogue out of the question, Waxer?" I said. The feeling had fled from the lower half of my arm.

Wax shot a left hook. It caught me on the skull. My vision took on a red tinge. Wax pulled back his right hand to shoulder level. He drove it into my chest. I staggered backward and plunked down on a line of garbage pails against the brick wall of a building.

"Get up," Wax said, an order.

I got up and brought a garbage pail lid with me. Wax cranked up another straight-ahead right. It was on course for my chin. I stuck the garbage pail lid into its path. Wax's clenched fist plowed into the centre of the lid.

For a fraction of a second, I read surprise in Wax's wide open eyes. Then he screamed.

"I'd get that hand looked at, Waxer," I said.

Wax bent way over, his hand clenched to his chest, his feet dancing a little cha-cha-cha of pain.

I stepped around him and walked to the car. My progress was none too steady. I drove to the light at Eastern Avenue and Parliament. My eyes were going through bizarre changes. I couldn't distinguish red from green. A car behind me honked. The light must have been green. I drove through the intersection and kept to a slow and stately pace all the way home.

CHAPTER TWENTY-FIVE

My eyelids hurt.

So I didn't open my eyes.

I knew it was morning because I could hear the rush of cars picking up on Beverley Street. But looking at the day was a prospect I could do without. Every region and tributary of my body was undergoing its own personal ache — every bone, muscle, tissue, fibre, cell, nail, and hair.

I reached my hand for the phone on the table beside my bed. My eyes stayed closed. I found the phone, fumbled, lost my grip. The phone bounced off the floor. The clatter sent new spasms of pain careening to my brain, which announced the onslaught of fresh suffering to the rest of the body.

I tried again for the phone, got it, and dialed Annie. The dialing required open eyes. My pupils hurt, too. I asked Annie what time it was.

"Eight twenty-two exactly," she said.

"What day?"

"Friday," Annie answered. "Was it *that* bad at Hard Buttocks?"

"Tight Buns," I said. "It was worse than bad."

I described my injuries, and Annie said to soak in a hot bath and she'd come over later to play nurse.

The floor wavered when I stood, and I needed assistance from walls, furniture, and other objects I leaned on getting to the bathroom. The splash of water filling the bathtub rattled the interior of my head. But when I climbed into the tub, the heat dulled some of the body's soreness. I submerged to chin level, and for maybe forty-five minutes, I let my mind drift to memories of when I felt whole.

In the mirror, I inspected myself. A bruise just coming to purple above my left elbow. Raw patches on the backs of both hands. A small swelling where the outside of my right thigh climbed toward the hip. And the soles of my feet stung, but there was nothing down there except calluses, scales, and the normal ugly stuff.

I tottered back to bed and lay on my stomach listening to the radio. On *Morningside*, the weekly medical panel came on, and the program's host introduced the topic for this morning's deep thinking: AIDS.

"Oh, *jeez*."

I turned off the radio, dozed, and at noon Annie arrived with a container of chicken soup.

"Homemade," she said.

"Whose home?"

"Nice Polish lady runs a takeout shop around the corner from me."

Annie poured the soup into a bowl and served it to me in bed.

"The bikers did this to you?" she asked. "Laid you low?"

"Not exactly."

"Bikers, the way I hear it, gay or straight, they don't trifle with strangers on their turf."

"Not exactly that, either," I said. "Most of the Tight Buns crowd, probably all of them except Hubert Wax, seem to be in it mainly for the image. Wear the leather, go vroom-vroom on the bikes, fundamentally harmless stuff. On the violence end, I don't see them mixing it up over anything except maybe the poker table."

"Sounds like a bowling league or something."

"About on that level."

"Except for Hubert Wax?"

I took in some more soup and wiped my mouth with a paper napkin. "Yeah, well, there has to be a bully in every group, I suppose. In this case, it's the Waxer, and I got to say he packs a wallop."

"So I noticed, you poor thing."

"Waxer may be the genuine article. A real biker type, I mean, sold on the macho thing."

"The rest of the Tight Buns guys ought to pool resources. Toss Hubert out of the club."

"The timing'd be right," I said. "Waxer's flying on one wing at the moment."

Annie carried my soup bowl to the kitchen and brought back a refill.

"On the subject of Hubert Wax," she said, "how do you size him up in the murder sweepstakes?"

"He denies everything. Says he never met Alex."

"What did you expect from the man? A confession?"

"Wax *could* have killed Alex. I mean in the sense that he's probably capable of killing a person. On the other hand, I didn't get the impression that Wax is as scary a guy as Birks Robinson seems to think."

"You sound like someone who's waffling."

"Might have something to do with my physical state."

"Try it from another angle," Annie said. "What motivation would Wax have for murdering Alex?"

"He's pals with David Rowbottom...."

"More than pals."

"Okay, Rowbottom's lover. He could have killed Alex to protect Rowbottom from something. Protect him from Alex who decided Rowbottom was the one who infected Ian and, ah ..."

"That's not bad," Annie said, "that theory."

"Maybe," I said. "But all returns aren't in yet."

Annie stroked my forehead.

"Get more rest, honey," she said.

Annie left, and I slept off and on until she came back at six thirty. She was carrying a bulky package under each arm. I could identify one package as Chinese food by the smells it gave off. The second package was a large plain white envelope.

"You owe me five dollars and forty cents," Annie said. She tossed the white package on my bed. "The cabbie was in the act of delivering this. I paid him."

I slit open the envelope, and stacks of photocopies and computer printouts spilled around me.

"Hey, action stations," I said. "This is the stuff on Paulie Ross, the stuff Tom Catalano assigned his student to round up."

"Fast service," Annie said. "Where's the five forty?"

"On the dresser."

Annie collected her money and took the Chinese food to the kitchen. I got out of bed, going at it with much regard for my delicate condition. The material about Paulie Ross could wait until my brain started ticking over. I put on the maroon dressing gown Annie had given me one Christmas and shuffled into the living room.

"You want wine with this?" Annie called from the kitchen. "Or shall I brew some tea?"

"Tea."

"That confirms it," Annie said. "You're definitely under the weather."

I turned on the CD player and slid in a set of tunes written by Billy Strayhorn. Duke Ellington sidemen played on all the tracks. The first tune was "Intimacy of the Blues."

Annie carried food and implements from kitchen to living room in relays, containers of moo shu pork, Kung Pao chicken, bean curd, rice soup, tea, plates, cups, and napkins.

"That's lovely," she said, "the music."

"The tune on right now is 'Lotus Blossom.'"

"I sort of recognized it," Annie said. "All the songs are so romantic and gentle and sweet."

"That was the nickname of the guy who wrote them, Swee' Pea."

"What was the rest of his name?"

"Billy Strayhorn," I said. "He was gay."

"No kidding. A gay jazz person."

"Takes all kinds," I said, "as someone was remarking recently."

"Malcolm the bartender."

"Yeah."

We ate the food, listened to the CD, and by eight thirty, Annie was on her way home and I was back in bed.

Next morning, feeling about eighty percent human, up from Friday's fifty percent, I spread the thick wad of documentation on Paulie Ross across the kitchen table and began the process of making sense out of it. It turned out to be not a particularly taxing chore. By the time Annie arrived at noon, I had the papers organized into one tidy pile.

Annie produced an assortment of salads.

"Listen, guy," she said, "Meals on Wheels is supposed to be for senior citizens. You may act like an old fart at times, but age-wise you don't qualify for the service."

"There's progress on the health front," I said. "I'm beginning to feel the blood course through my veins."

"When it reaches your feet, let's step out for a dinner."

"Tomorrow night," I said. "A real blowout, I promise."

Annie lined up the salads on the kitchen counter.

"How's it going with the paper chase?" she asked.

"I'm in need of your assistance."

"My analytical powers? My critical faculties? My natural instinct? What?"

"Your contacts," I said.

"Aw, you really know how to bring a girl back to earth."

"Your input is key, honestly," I said. "Want a drink before we get into it?"

"Do *you*?"

"Maybe a mild Bloody Mary."

Annie made the drinks, light on the Tabasco, heavy on the lemon, and sat at the kitchen table.

"The first piece of information I need," I said, "is subsidiary but useful. Did David Rowbottom's ministry hand out grant money to Bart the Bulge?"

"That's a matter of public record."

"So I'm told."

"Except not on Saturdays. The Ministry of Culture and Communications is closed."

"That's where I hoped one of your contacts might come in," I said. "Someone you can phone who keeps files on such matters?"

Annie dipped a finger in her Bloody Mary and tasted it. "Mm," she said. "Sure, I know two or three people who might be worth a shot. But I doubt if any of them would recognize Bart by his *nom de strip*."

"Tell them to look under Santucci. Bartley Santucci."

"Santucci. Gotcha," Annie said. She started to stand up.

"Before you hit the phones," I said, "there's more."

Annie stayed put.

"Everything you see before you," I said, waving a hand over the stacks of documents on the tables, "this defines the Paulie Ross empire. He presides over twenty-six, I think it is, twenty-six or twenty-seven companies in the same number of commercial areas."

"He isn't just a run-of-the-mill drug overlord, the type I might recognize from reruns of *Hill Street Blues*?"

"Probably got started that way," I said. "Probably made his original stake in cocaine or gambling or prostitution, but now he's more or less legit."

"What are these commercial areas he's more or less legit in?"

"Parking garages, the enclosed kind," I said. "He's got them right across the province. Let's see, a linen supply business. And he rents out video games to bars and restaurants. Distributes magazines. I suspect they're magazines that run to acres of bare female flesh. He's big in hotels, in towns too small for a Ramada or a Best Western. The kind of hotel that sells gallons of beer in the public rooms."

"Okay," Annie said, "that's enough on lists."

"You have the picture?"

"I do," Annie said, "and what I want to know, is there a smoking gun?"

"Not in the enterprises I just described," I said. "But there might be a whiff of gunpowder over here."

I picked up a single sheet of paper. "Paulie Ross's land holdings," I said.

"Apart from the property his hotels sit on, his parking garages, et cetera."

"Oh, right. His *independent* land holdings, more accurately," I said. "Two pieces of real estate."

"The chateau out in the sticks off north Bathurst Street and what else?"

"You're fast off the mark today, lady."

"Get on with it, Crang."

"Six thousand and thirty-three contiguous acres," I said. "All in one parcel, and I gather from the legal description of the property, the township and county and so on, it's located somewhere in the neighbourhood south of Peterborough."

"Where does that get us?" Annie asked.

"Unless I'm mistaken, smack in the middle of David Rowbottom's riding."

"You've been boning up on the fine geographical points of provincial politics?" Annie asked, showing some slight surprise.

"Birks Robinson mentioned where Rowbottom's riding is," I said. "Birks is wrong about some things. Like he's probably overestimated Hubert Wax, being so definite about Hubert as the killer and everything. But I don't think Birks is apt to get confused about a simple fact like the whereabouts of David Rowbottom's riding."

"You'd still like me to verify it with one of my myriad contacts?"

"Please."

"Glad to," Annie said, "but I wasn't aware I *had* a contact in provincial politics."

"The guy on the radio, on *Metro Morning*," I said. "Remember, when you used to do the movie reviews for the program, there was the reporter who had the beat over at the legislature?"

"Jerry. He still has the beat."

"He was kind of sweet on you."

"I never noticed that."

"It's the sort of detail I always notice," I said. "Phone Jerry and talk ridings with him. And while you're at it, while he's on the line, ask if there's anything special cooking around the legislature on garbage."

"Garbage?"

"Yeah," I said. "Any important decisions coming up, maybe a bill going through the voting process, big deal moves of that nature."

"On *garbage*?"

"Sure, you know, the detritus people put out for collection in green plastic bags twice a week."

"I *know* what garbage is."

Annie picked up a pen and a couple of sheets of blank paper from the table and went into the bedroom. I heard her dial the phone and talk into it, not the words, just the murmur of her voice. My system seemed to be absorbing the Bloody Mary without complaint. I examined the salads on the counter. Salmon. Tomato. Green. Chicken. Bean. My stomach didn't seize up at the prospect of digesting them. I cleared the kitchen table of most of the documents, set two places for lunch, and waited.

CHAPTER TWENTY-SIX

Annie came back from the bedroom fifteen minutes later.

"Bartley Santucci a.k.a. the Bulge received an arts and communications grant last spring," she said. "Fifty thousand."

"Lucky Bart," I said. "At the rate he cranks out the movies, that sum ought to finance a dozen features."

Annie consulted what she'd written on one of the sheets of paper. "From Jerry," she said, "I got the exact boundaries of Rowbottom's riding."

She handed me the piece of paper. "What'll you do?" she asked. "See if the description you have of Paulie Ross's property fits inside the riding boundaries?"

"Exactly."

I went back and forth between Annie's notes and the legal description in the title search of the Ross property that the student at Tom Catalano's office had meticulously transcribed. I compared the two, isolated one inside the other.

"Verified," I said.

"Paulie Ross owns a large chunk of David Rowbottom's riding?"

"Six thousand and thirty-three acres of it," I said, "What else from Jerry of *Metro Morning*?"

"He wondered why a movie reviewer was asking questions about a homosexual cabinet minister."

"How curious was Jerry?"

Annie thought for a minute. "Not very," she said. "I passed it off as research. I mean, I *am* a movie person and Rowbottom *is* culture and communications."

"What about the garbage?"

"Jerry acted like me asking about that was more on the suspicious side, but he didn't grill me or anything."

"Good," I said. "Now, would you please tell me if something is brewing at the legislature in the garbage area?"

"Where does garbage come into the picture, anyway?"

I sighed. "Think of what Albert said in the Lincoln the day we were escorted out to the Ross mansion for the tête-à-tête. Albert said, 'Garbage dumps is gonna be big.'"

"Recycling depots. Joey B. corrected Albert. Not garbage dumps. Recycling depots."

"Sweetie, under *either* designation, what did Jerry tell you on the telephone ten minutes ago?"

"His term of choice is garbage dump."

"*Annie.*"

"As opposed to recycling depot."

I folded my arms on the table and rested my forehead on them.

"Just teasing, honey," Annie said. "Jerry had good material. At least, not knowing precisely why I was asking the questions I was asking, I *think* it's good material."

I raised my head.

"May I refer to my notes?" Annie asked. "This is complicated for a simple go-between like myself. A mere researcher."

I shifted around in my chair. "Are you enjoying yourself?" I asked Annie.

"Well, you must admit you were a little peremptory, the way you asked me to do the dirty work on the phone."

"You're right."

"My stalling around, that was just taking a tiny measure of revenge."

"Okay, I apologize for the peremptoriness."

"Well." Annie ran her eyes over the notes she'd made. "It seems there is something going on in the upper minor leagues of garbage in Ontario."

I waited in respectful silence.

"Down in the eastern part of the province," Annie went on, "Brockville, Belleville, about a dozen towns and small cities down that way, they've got a common problem. Too much refuse and no place to stow it. The dumps are overflowing, a stink is in the air. So for the last two, three years, they've been co-operating, these communities, in trying to find one massive dump that'll accommodate all their tons of old chicken bones, orange peels, and eggshells."

"A single locale, right."

"But," Annie said, "politics keeps rearing its homely head. This is all according to Jerry. Every time the city fathers of Brockville, Belleville, and the rest think they've found a site for the big dump, someone locally, some group of concerned citizens, generates their own stink, and the plans get canned."

Annie paused and took a deep breath. "Hence," she said, "with things hitting the crisis stage, garbage piling up by the minute, the issue has been kicked upstairs. A senior body, the guys at the top, *somebody* has to make a decision, designate a site, and enforce the selection. Now then, guess who the body is that's arriving at the choice of dump?"

I opened my mouth to answer.

Annie leaped in first. "Never mind," she said. "You'll just get it right and spoil my fun. The decision maker, the bunch who's going to hand down a verdict any time next month, is ... ta-da ... the provincial cabinet."

"Of which," I said, "David Rowbottom is a member in good standing."

"A guy who may be connected somehow or other to a shady customer named Paulie Ross."

"Who," I picked up, "happens to own a piece of property in Rowbottom's riding large enough to welcome the refuse of practically the whole of eastern Ontario."

Annie leaned across the table and lifted her eyebrows at me. "Interesting, wouldn't you say?"

"Absolutely fascinating."

Annie straightened up. "What use do you see yourself making of this train of coincidences or connections or whatever?"

"Getting a little leverage."

"Who from?" Annie asked. "I hope not Paulie Ross."

"Uh-uh. He's too formidable."

"And has too many henchmen."

"My sentiments precisely," I said. "No, I'll lay it on David Rowbottom's desk."

Annie hesitated. "I was going along swimmingly, following all the twists and turns, but I think I just went off the rails."

"I'm operating on the principle, shake a tree and something might fall out of the branches."

"That's a principle?"

"Well, maybe a modus operandi," I said. "What I'll do, I'll waft a breath of this possible scandal past Rowbottom's nose. Let him know I'm wise to Paulie Ross's six thousand and thirty-three acres in his riding, the cabinet decision upcoming on the garbage dump, all that inside dope, and it might scare a revelation of some sort out of him."

"A revelation about who killed Alex?"

"That's the end we're aiming at. You never know, I could squeeze Rowbottom for a secret."

"I'm beginning to see the light," Annie said. "Rowbottom must know *something* about the murder."

"Or know someone who knows something."

"One thing," Annie said, "the last time you went on one of

these fact-finding missions, you were the guy who ended up getting pounded on."

"This'll be in safer territory," I said. "Rowbottom's own office. First thing Monday morning, I'll beard the lion."

"In his den."

"Right. Confront him boldly."

Annie raised her glass.

"I'll drink to that," she said.

We clinked Bloody Marys.

CHAPTER TWENTY-SEVEN

The Ministry of Culture and Communications was in a building on Bloor near Bay. That put it a leisurely half-hour walk from my place. I left on foot about eight forty Monday morning, north through the university campus and past the Royal Ontario Museum. The sun was warm on my shoulders, and after most of three days in bed, the spring was back in my step.

The building at Bay and Bloor was twenty storeys tall with a postmodern arch outside, revolving doors in a glass archway, and a high lobby that the architect had invested with artsy touches. The floor was terrazzo, partly covered by two enormous Scandinavian-looking rugs. There were round columns running up to the ceiling and cacti in planters along the walls. The information desk, in the middle of the lobby, had a marble face and a slanted silver panel that listed the occupants. Rowbottom's office was on the twelfth floor. The elevators were to the left of the desk. I rode up.

The foyer on twelve was deep in maroon carpeting. Dead ahead, a pretty, dark-haired receptionist sat under a splashy 1950s abstract expressionist painting.

"My name's Crang, to see the minister," I said. "I have no appointment but I'm not a grant seeker or a loony who's wandered in off the street."

"No appointment?" The receptionist maintained her gorgeous smile.

"Pass my name up the line," I said. "It'll catch someone's ear."

The receptionist picked up a white phone and punched a button.

"I have a Mr. Crang here," she said in a low voice. "He'd like to see the minister. No appointment."

She waited, dark head down.

"C-r-a-n-g, I think," she said into the receiver, and looked up at me.

"Right," I said.

She listened and after a few seconds hung up the phone.

"Martha doesn't know who you are," she said to me.

"Makes us even. Who's Martha?"

"In charge of the executive assistant's appointments."

"Aim higher." I twinkled my eyes at the receptionist. "The minister himself. Trust me, he'll recognize the name."

The receptionist was still smiling. "I'll try," she said, "just because it's a slow morning so far."

"Not because of the winning look in my eye?"

"I thought a bug had landed on your pupil for a minute, there."

"That's called a twinkle."

The receptionist tapped her fingers on the phone buttons, and in the low voice again explained my presence on the twelfth floor.

"Really?" she said into the phone. She hung up and looked at me. "Mr. Brander will be right out."

"Mr. Brander?"

"The minister's executive assistant."

A door opened behind the receptionist, and a slightly overweight young guy with slicked-back hair came out.

"Ray Brander, Mr. Crang," he said to me, shaking hands. "Please come in."

I followed Brander through the door and down a long corridor. Brander had a gliding way of walking. We turned right and went straight through an open door into a large office with a large desk. David Rowbottom was sitting behind the desk. He didn't get up.

"I'll see Mr. Crang alone, Ray," he said to Brander.

Brander looked hurt but left the room without whimpering. He shut the door on his way out.

Rowbottom's office had an open, airy feel. It had two large windows, and the rest of the wall space was busy with paintings. I recognized a Harold Town, Louis de Niverville, and Gordon Rayner.

"You got enough pictures in here to open a law firm," I said.

"What sport do you think you're playing, Crang?" Rowbottom said.

"I'm trying to find out who killed Alex Corcoran," I said. "And it's no sport."

"You set fire to a bar last week and assaulted an innocent citizen."

"Oh, hey, good thing Hubert Wax doesn't work for a newspaper," I said. "He'd make a lousy reporter."

I sat down in an armchair.

"What gave you the idea Hubert had anything to do with the murder?" Rowbottom asked. His blue eyes were at peak glare.

"It wasn't a *what* that steered me Waxer's way," I said. "A *who*. Birks Robinson."

"I should have guessed," Rowbottom said. "Birks has an overwrought imagination."

"He's supposed to have one of those," I said. "He's a fiction writer."

"And he's prepared to think the worst of Hubert."

"Yeah, I know, ever since you ditched him in favour of Wax."

Rowbottom gave me another of his death-ray looks.

"If it means anything to you," I said, "I don't share Birks's view that Wax killed Alex."

"Of course he didn't. This person Shumacher is under investigation for the crime."

"Grant me some credit, Rowbottom. Did you expect I'd fall for the charade in Paulie Ross's warehouse?"

Rowbottom gave the impression he was thinking very carefully about the wording of his next remark. "Crang, you're a fool if you don't accept the evidence against Shumacher."

"A fool? Is that the best you can come up with?"

"It's your opportunity to walk away from these events and leave well enough alone."

"I'll take a walk when I know who Alex's murderer is."

Rowbottom smacked a fist on the arm of his chair. "Goddamn it, Crang, haven't you the sense to see the position you're in?"

"Rowbottom," I said, "you're a hotshot cabinet minister. You have a ministry full of people working for you, and you dish out money in impressive bundles. That makes you an important guy. But at the moment, you're not coming close to scaring the living daylights out of me because I know something about you almost nobody else knows."

"That I'm gay? Don't be absurd. Everyone knows and no one cares."

"I know that you're setting up Paulie Ross to make a big money score in the garbage trade."

The combination of Ross's name and the word *garbage* gave Rowbottom a small jolt. He sat back in his chair, and some of the dazzle went out of his baby blues.

"What garbage?" he said.

"The garbage that's going to get dumped into the six thousand and thirty-three acres of land Paulie Ross owns in your riding."

Rowbottom cleared his throat. "There are no laws against an entrepreneur like Mr. Ross accumulating property."

"I'm talking something tougher to get around than laws," I said. "Ethics. Sometime very soon, whenever you and your cabinet buddies talk about the problems the folks down east are having with their garbage disposal, you're going to twist a few arms, whisper in some ears, smooth talk your colleagues into seeing their way clear to settling on your man Paulie Ross's vacant acreage for the new dump. No laws broken, you're right. Just some ethics in tatters."

"Where do you get off —"

"The way I read it, Rowbottom," I said. I had built up a good head of steam. "I'm positive you've already cut corners on Paulie's behalf. Those six thousand acres of his were zoned farmland when he bought them. That's what it shows on the title search, agricultural use. After Paulie scooped up the land, eight or nine different farms, the zoning changed like magic to commercial. *Any* commercial use, not excluding the dumping of garbage. And it wouldn't surprise me a whit if the moving force behind the switch in zoning was the local member of the provincial legislature. Maybe not illegal, Rowbottom, but your hands don't look spotless."

"Crang ..."

Rowbottom stopped. There was a door in the left wall of the office. It opened, and a man stepped into the room. Paulie Ross.

CHAPTER TWENTY-EIGHT

I said, "How's it going, Paulie?"

"Fairly rotten," he said, "but it's gonna get worse for you, asshole."

"You shouldn't be in here," Rowbottom said to Ross. "Not with Crang in the room."

"Shut up," Ross said to Rowbottom, no rancour in his voice.

Ross had on a double-breasted charcoal-grey suit and a tie with a lot of white in it. He sat on a sofa under the Harold Town and crossed his legs.

"I shoulda done what I thoughta doing when you first stuck your nose in my business," Ross said to me.

"Which was?"

"Have you clipped."

"Oh."

"I still might."

"Paulie," Rowbottom said, "please don't use that street talk in front of me."

Ross looked slowly over at Rowbottom and back to me. He jerked a thumb in Rowbottom's direction and said, "It was him that thought up the meeting at my warehouse."

"And I didn't buy it," I said.

"More's the pity for you," Rowbottom said. He sounded weary.

I spoke to Rowbottom. "You knew it was a choice between me accepting Shumacher as the murderer and going quietly away or leaving it up to Paulie to deal with me in his inimitable style?"

"I should have known you were beyond understanding a compromise."

"Nice try, Mr. Minister," I said, "and thanks. But, deep down, Shumacher murder someone? Give me a break."

"Christ, Crang, you're a pain in the ass," Ross said.

"I've heard that refrain before," I said.

"Right now, my opinion is that I should kill you," Ross said. He might have been talking about having a mangy dog put down.

"Paulie," I said, "the garbage scam is what's got you worried, and it's something I don't give a rat's ass about."

"For somebody who says that, you've made yourself very damned up-to-date on the deal I spent the last year working on."

"If you were listening in from next door, you know I told your tame cabinet minister all I want is Alex's killer," I said. "The thing you have going with the dump, to me it's only a tool to pry out of you clunks what you know about the murder. And I won't quit, that's a guarantee. I'll keep on prying."

"Not if you're dead," Ross said.

"You're operating on a false premise, Paulie," I said. "You think I'm the only guy who's hip to your plan for the garbage? Come on, I couldn't have put the details together by myself. A senior guy in a big law firm helped me on this. He knows I got myself pointed at you. His student knows. Half the firm probably knows. You intend to kill all of them?"

Ross recrossed his legs and didn't say anything. Rowbottom sat behind his desk, very still. I sweated in my armpits and wondered how far my exaggerations would carry me.

"What's the name of this big law firm?" Ross asked me.

"Mcintosh, Brown and Crabtree," I answered.

Ross looked over at Rowbottom. Rowbottom nodded his head.

"The garbage dump is a fuckin' gold mine," Ross said to me.

"Paulie," I said, "I couldn't topple the financial universe you've constructed if I wanted to, the hotels and the parking places, the linen supply company. And I don't want to. I don't want to disturb you and your foray into garbage, either, but I think I could. At least I could make a godawful fuss."

"Yeah, probably," Ross said.

"But that's not my purpose."

"No shit."

I switched to Rowbottom. "And I don't want to blow the whistle on you."

Rowbottom stirred himself enough to develop an indignant expression. "You're beneath contempt, Crang," he said. "I haven't made any money out of the garbage dump, and I'll never make a dime out of it in the future."

"Not the dump," I said. "I'm talking about your AIDS."

Rowbottom ran a hand over his forehead. "Oh, dear God."

"Birks Robinson let me in on that secret, too."

"Then he must have told you I'm cured."

"The clinic in Buffalo?" I said. "The point, Rowbottom, whether you had AIDS or still have it, it's the club Paulie's holding over your head, am I right?"

Rowbottom stared at me, not speaking, giving off waves of something compounded of fatigue and resignation.

"Maybe you're cured, maybe not," I said to him. "Either way, you're tainted goods, and your fear is if Paulie spreads the word, the premier'll set speed records kicking you out of the cabinet."

"My party," Rowbottom said slowly, "doesn't have a reputation for turning on its own."

"But it's what you're afraid of, your political career heading into the can. No more grant money to spread around, no more office with the art collection, no more power. It's the reason you're bending to Paulie's blackmail."

"Okay, Crang," Ross said, "you've proved you're a smart guy. Now what?"

"Jeez, don't you guys listen?" I said. "All I'm looking for is Alex Corcoran's murderer."

"That's it?"

I nodded.

"And you'll quit gettin' in my hair?"

"Cross my heart."

Ross stood and straightened his suit jacket.

"Beat it, Crang," he said. "I'll be in touch."

I waved a hand at Rowbottom. He stared straight ahead, dead-eyed, and I went out to the elevators. Downstairs in the lobby, Albert and Axe were standing beside one of the round columns. When they saw me, they moved purposefully in my direction.

"What a coincidence, guys," I said. "I was just talking to your head honcho upstairs."

The two stood on either side of me, not laying a hand on my person but leaving no doubt that I wasn't going anywhere without their permission. Albert wore a guileless smile. Axe smouldered.

"Welcome back to the big leagues, Axe," I said.

"I never left." Axe's voice was a rolling rumble.

"Just on temporary loan from Paulie to Bart?"

"Why don't you save the bullshit until we know what we're gonna do to you."

"Joey B.'s on the phone over there," Albert said politely.

Past Albert's shoulder, I saw Joey B. standing at the information desk. He held a phone to his ear. He was listening and not smiling. The uniformed guy who manned the desk didn't appear happy about having his telephone pre-empted, but he had the good sense not to challenge a guy with a face like Joey B.'s.

The phone conversation at the desk lasted another thirty seconds. Joey B. hung up and crossed the lobby.

"It's your lucky morning, Crang," he said to me.

Joey B. had on his deadpan expression and he was breathing through his mouth. He let a couple of long moments go by before he told me more about my lucky morning. My heart was thumping in a region close to my throat.

"Mr. Ross says to let you go," Joey B. said.

Axe and Albert moved aside. I stepped smartly between them and walked toward the revolving doors. There might have been a shimmy in my stride.

"Hey, Crang," Joey B. called.

I stopped and turned.

Joey B. had a small, crooked smile on his face.

"Mr. Ross says to let you go," he said, "for now."

CHAPTER TWENTY-NINE

Coming up Beverley Street that night, about ten o'clock, after dinner at the Bamboo, Annie and I spotted the grey Lincoln at the same moment. It was parked, lights out, in front of my house.

"What should we do?" Annie asked me. "Run?"

"That'd be undignified."

"Which is better, undignified and still breathing or dignified and maybe a notch in somebody's weapon?"

"They wouldn't try anything violent at my own place of residence."

"Oh, yeah? What about Alex? He probably thought he was safe at home from whoever killed him."

We were ten yards from the Lincoln. Its back door opened, and Paulie Ross stepped out. He had on the same suit and tie he'd been wearing in David Rowbottom's office. He slammed the car door and waited for Annie and me to approach. Joey B. sat at the Lincoln's wheel. No one else was in the car.

"We needa talk," Ross said to me. "A coupla minutes is all."

"That's it? Just talk?"

Ross looked mildly surprised. "What else?"

"How about upstairs?"

"Sure."

Ross glanced at Annie.

"She sits in on the talk," I said. "She already knows everything I know."

Ross shrugged.

The three of us went up to my apartment. I turned on the lamp on the pine table and the floor lamp beside the wing chair.

"A drink?" I asked Ross.

"Don't use the stuff."

"Mineral water? Coffee?"

"Coffee's good."

"I'll make it," Annie said.

"Black and strong if you don't mind," Ross said to her.

He sat on the wing chair and eyed me up and down.

"Your jacket don't hang right," he said.

I was wearing the last of the outfits Annie had picked. Its focal point was a one-button double-breasted dark-grey tweed jacket. The button met the buttonhole at my waist.

"This might be a trifle avant-garde for a man with conservative tastes," I said, "such as yourself."

"You want my opinion, it drapes on you like a blanket."

I sat down on the sofa.

"Now that you bring it up," I said, "my clothes haven't been winning rave notices lately."

Annie carried in a cup and saucer, steam rising out of the cup. She handed it to Ross and went back to the kitchen for two glasses of white wine. She sat beside me on the sofa.

Ross drank some coffee. His face, bent over the cup, was enveloped in the steam. He was quick about the drinking.

"Just how I like it," he said to Annie.

"You're welcome," she said. Her voice sounded tentative.

"Okay, this is all business, you understand," Ross said to me.

"What about the suggestion earlier today that I might be clipped?" I asked.

"That's off."

"I was taking it personally for a while there."

"Listen to this, Crang," Ross said. "If it's smart business to kill a guy, the guy is killed. If it's smarter business to deal with a guy, the deal is made. You following me?"

"I'm off the hit list and on to the deal list?"

"That's what I'm tellin' ya."

Ross finished his coffee and put the cup and saucer on the side table next to the wing chair. He took a handkerchief out of his trouser pocket and touched it to his lips.

"I gave Albert to the cops," he said.

Annie and I looked at one another, she wrinkled her forehead, and we turned to Ross.

"I must've missed a step," I said. "You've given Albert to the police? For what reason?"

"Him and the knife both," Ross said. "Albert's the one that killed the Corcoran guy."

Annie sucked in her breath. I groped for a comment and couldn't find it.

"That's my part of the deal," Ross went on. "Your part, you lay off Rowbottom. Nothing gets out concerning the arrangement I got with him on the dump or concerning him and AIDS. A deal?"

I raised my hand slowly. "Paulie, Paulie, I realize this isn't a board meeting where Robert's Rules apply, but could you take it from where we left off in Rowbottom's office this morning?"

Ross spoke to Annie. "Any more of that coffee?"

Annie picked up the cup and saucer, filled the cup in the kitchen, and brought it to the living room. She didn't say a word. Her concentration, if I could judge, was on not rattling the cup in the saucer.

This time, Ross sipped the coffee, a little at a time, looking at me over the rim of the cup as he sipped. I had the idea he was working at controlling his impatience.

"Since noon," he said, "my lawyers been going round with the guys at the crown prosecutor's office. Eight thirty tonight, they put it on paper. Albert pleads guilty to second degree, and the prosecutors tell the judge their recommendation is Albert only gets ten years. Like I said, we handed them the whole package: Albert, Albert's statement, the knife he done it with. Albert's out at West End Detention right now. He goes to court tomorrow. It's all clean, all wrapped up, and everybody loves it, the cops, the prosecutors, me."

"What about Albert?" I asked.

"Albert?" Ross seemed authentically puzzled. Then it passed. "Hell, Albert's a young guy. He comes outta the slam, he knows he's gonna be permanent with me. I owe him for life. Plus, I'm payin' his mother three thousand a month all the time Albert's gone, and she gets it bumped up seven and a half percent a year on account of inflation. Albert's solid."

Annie shifted on the sofa. "To a businessman like you, Mr. Ross," she said, "this may be a technical detail, but did Albert actually kill Alex Corcoran?"

Ross studied Annie as if he was trying to decide whether she had insulted him. Annie met his gaze with one of her wide-eyed expressions.

"I'll give it to you from the top," Ross said, addressing Annie and me.

"You can omit the final parts," Annie said, letting the acid creep into her tone, "the parts where our friend Alex dies."

Ross didn't blink. "Keep it straight in your heads," he said, "we're still talkin' deal. On your side of it, the two of you, you don't mess up nothin' we got arranged with the prosecutors. What I tell you now's confidential."

"Agreed," I said.

Ross checked with Annie.

"Agreed," she said.

"The Corcoran guy phoned Rowbottom two weeks ago tonight," Ross began. "This was long distance. Corcoran was away somewheres."

"Key West."

"And he said he was gonna kill Rowbottom." Ross interrupted himself. "Corcoran really had a hair up his ass, wouldn't ya say?" he asked me.

"He'd come unhinged," I said. "Wanted to avenge his boyfriend's death."

"I'll give the guy this, he shook up Rowbottom."

"Don't get the idea killing was an everyday event with Alex," I said. "A little time and maybe some counselling, he would have got over the obsession he had about evening the score."

Ross waved his hand. "None of that counts no more. The important thing here is Rowbottom comes to me, not whining or nothin', just telling me that this Corcoran was on his case, and he didn't know what in hell to do about it except maybe take a long holiday, vanish, something lame like that. Rowbottom was okay, tryin' to be a stand-up guy, but I could see he was running scared."

"He'd already tried to head off Alex and failed," I said.

"Yeah?"

"Rowbottom phoned Alex at his apartment the previous Friday night," I said. "My guess is he'd learned Alex had him down as the number-one suspect in the AIDS matter, and he tried to persuade Alex he wasn't the guilty party."

"Ironic," Annie said.

"How's that?" I asked her.

"Maybe Rowbottom was right," Annie said. "It could be he *wasn't* the one who passed on AIDS to Ian."

"You wanta hear the background or what?" Ross said, fidgeting.

"Go ahead, Paulie," I said. "We're merely trying to pull in the loose strands."

"No loose strands as far as I give a shit," Ross said. "Just the stuff that hadda happen and so it happened."

"Rowbottom came to you with Alex's threat," I said. "I take it you swung into action."

"I gotta keep Rowbottom on the ball with the cabinet until they put the okay on my garbage dump," Ross said. He shook his head.

"Jesus, the whole deal's been developin' so sweet I should of known some damn thing'd slip out of gear. Anyways, I told Rowbottom to relax and that I'd take care of the Corcoran guy."

"Truer words have seldom been spoken," I said.

"Don't get wise with me, Crang," Ross said. "I gave Corcoran his chance to lay off. I spoke to the guy personally the night he got back from wherever he was...."

"Key West," I said.

"I laid it out nice, how he shouldn't go around making noises about doin' harm to cabinet ministers. He told me to get lost. He was cool about it, you know, a sophisticated kind of guy. But the message was he didn't plan on co-operatin'."

Ross paused.

"So later that night," he said, "Albert went in."

Ross paused a second time.

"It was strictly business," he said, "what Albert hadda do."

Ross shrugged his shoulders. Beside me, Annie was holding her breath. My own throat felt constricted. I cleared it.

"How ..." My voice sounded unnaturally high. I coughed and began again at a lower register. "How did you get on to Rowbottom in the first place?" I asked Ross. "By way of Bart the Bulge?"

"His name's Bartley," Ross said, anger making a flit across his face.

"Sorry," I said. "Bartley."

"I kinda lucked into that situation," Ross said, matter of fact. "Axe was stickin' with Bartley for me, reporting on the kid so he didn't do nothin' that came at me from left field, you understand?"

"The aim, as you keep saying, was to keep Bartley's mother in the dark about the lad's more gross activities."

"Yeah, but Axe came up with something else that caught my attention."

"The fifty-thousand-dollar grant to Bartley from the Ministry of Culture and Communications?"

"For making a friggin' porno movie." Ross sounded astounded at the improbability of it. "Right away I thought, shit, the government's handin' out this kind of bread, maybe it's an arrangement I should include myself in on. So I gave Axe the word to come back with more on these grants."

"Instead," I said, "Axe reported that Bartley's pipeline to culture and communications was of a personal nature."

"Bartley and Rowbottom were tight, yeah," Ross said. He shook his head again, this time in exasperation. "I don't understand the kid, good bringin' up he had, Upper Canada fuckin' College, and where'd it get him? Hanging out with fruits."

"But a superior brand of fruit, Paulie," I said. "For example, a cabinet minister."

"Rowbottom, okay, Axe brought me the goods on him," Ross said. "This came through Bartley. He told Axe how Rowbottom's a highly placed guy and he's got AIDS and nobody knows. Maybe he's cured, what's it matter? The point is it's a very heavy secret. The only people that know are Bartley and a black guy and some motorcycle asshole."

"And, next in line, Axe."

"That's another thing Bartley needs to be straightened out about," Ross said. "He runs off at the mouth. So all right, it was only Axe he was talking to. The kid was showing off, letting Axe see what an inside guy he is, pals with a cabinet minister. But the first lesson is, clam up practically all the time."

"But he didn't," I said, "and Axe communicated the secret to you."

"Naturally. That was Axe's job."

"And at this point, you put the squeeze on Rowbottom."

"For Chrissake, Crang, who's tellin' the story? You or me?"

"From what I learned on my own hook, Paulie, the rest is easy to deduce."

Ross let out a long stream of air. "I shoulda aced you at the start. You're such a pushy son of a bitch. Always asking the questions, making a fuckin' pest of yourself."

"What you proposed to Rowbottom," I said, speaking over Ross, "was your silence on the AIDS in return for his influence on the garbage disposition."

"Disposition, huh?"

"You provide the dump, the province provides the garbage."

"That's about it."

"With Rowbottom as the facilitator."

"It's a real good opportunity." Ross looked thoughtful, his large silver head cocked to one side. "Y'know something, even before I put the fix in with Rowbottom, I'd been thinking there was a hell of a buck waitin' to be made in garbage. Garbage, honest to God, it was on my mind."

"That seems appropriate," Annie said in a low voice.

Ross straightened out of his reverie and shot a look at Annie. "Lady, there's never a time you should get snotty with me."

He stood up and brushed at something invisible on the front of his jacket.

"We talking a deal?" he asked me.

"All I wanted was Alex Corcoran's killer," I said.

"You got him."

"Yeah," I said to Paulie Ross. "Me and the cops."

"Thanks for the coffee," Ross said and left the apartment.

Annie and I walked over to the front window and watched Ross climb into the back of the grey Lincoln and drive away.

"It's all so sad and bizarre," Annie said.

"I'll settle for those two adjectives."

"Albert killed Alex."

"Yeah."

"He killed Alex and we don't even know Albert's last name."

I put an arm around Annie's waist. "It'll be in the papers tomorrow," I said.

CHAPTER THIRTY

On the Thursday after the lesson in civics and the free-enterprise system from Paulie Ross, Cleve Shumacher showed up at the office close to noon.

"Should your name be on my appointment calendar, Cleve?" I asked.

"I took a chance you'd be in, Mr. Crang."

"Pull up the client's chair."

Shumacher was turned out in his customary dapper style, with the exception that his clothes were casual. He had on a navy-blue Yves Saint Laurent sweater, a button-down blue shirt, pressed jeans, and shiny black tassel loafers. There was something else different about him, but I couldn't put my finger on it.

"The police never charged me with Alex Corcoran's murder," he said. "Someone else confessed, apparently."

"A young guy named Albert Fantini killed Alex, Cleve."

"Well, happy endings for me, at least, but it was a dreadful experience while it lasted. Two police detectives came to my apartment and talked to me. *Grilled* me, I guess you'd call it. One was terribly offensive."

"Probably a guy named Jerry Mullen."

"That's the name. He practically *reeked* of offensiveness."

Shumacher had a touch of snap to his voice.

"Was Jack Pinkovsky in touch with you?" I asked. "Before the two cops came calling?"

"That's one of the reasons I'm here, Mr. Crang. To thank you for asking Mr. Pinkovsky to contact me."

"Part of the service, Cleve. I don't do murders. Jack does."

"Smart as a whip, that man. He had me so prepared for the detectives their heads were spinning."

"Good for you, Cleve."

"Maybe not *spinning*, but they could tell I wasn't the pushover they expected."

"The cops were equipped with some documents? Your medical records?"

"That part infuriated me. Having a person's private history … it must be a violation of my civil rights or something."

"Probably," I said. "Are the records accurate? You've got AIDS?"

"I apologize, Mr. Crang." Shumacher's voice was faint but steady. "I lied to you when I first came here. I knew I had AIDS."

"The lying doesn't matter now."

"I realize a client should tell the lawyer all the facts."

"Water under the bridge, Cleve."

Shumacher looked into his lap.

"So, Cleve," I said, "what else is up?"

"I want you to defend the fraud charge against me, Mr. Crang."

"I'm already embarked on that enterprise."

"No, you are not, Mr. Crang," Shumacher said. "What you're doing is stalling the case. That's how you described the strategy last time. And I'm sure it's a clever tactic. But now I'm asking you to *really* contest the case. On its merits, I mean. I want my day in court."

I recognized what else was different about Cleve Shumacher. He'd cast off his nervous mannerisms. He was no longer a walking museum of winks, blinks, and tics.

"Those are fighting words, Cleve," I said.

"I absolutely know I didn't commit a crime, Mr. Crang," Shumacher said, "and I'd like a judge or jury or whoever to agree with me."

"Okay."

Shumacher wore a wry little smile. "That's what I want if it's the last thing I get."

"How much time are we talking about?"

"I have about two years," Shumacher said. "Maybe a few months after that, according to the doctors, but I'll probably be a basket case toward the end."

"We could waive the preliminary hearing and go straight to trial," I said. "That'll shave off a few months."

"Wonderful," Shumacher said. "And, something else, I'm thinking of suing Arthur Mortimer. The son I told you about? The one who brought this foolish charge against me?"

"Sue him for what?"

"For slandering my name. Accusing me of being a crook."

"Libel's another branch of litigation that isn't up my alley," I said. "But, sure, I know a specialist we can bring in, guy named Porter. You'll like him."

"Excellent, Mr. Crang. Just excellent."

I tilted back in my chair. "I got to say, Cleve, you're in particularly feisty form."

"For a man with AIDS, you mean?"

"Actually I was judging you against the feistiness index established by my regular stable of clients," I said. "But on the subject of health and whatnot, how are you doing?"

"Mostly good days, some not so good."

"Lot of time with doctors, I imagine."

"Time is what I've got plenty of," Shumacher said. "I left my brokers job so all I'm doing is thinking about the fraud case and just, well, smelling the flowers."

"You're living with whom, your old mum? I think you mentioned a mum."

"Whose money I used to invest," Shumacher said. "No, I don't live with anyone. Mother died a few years ago, and I'm all the Shumacher family that's left."

"How about a companion? A friend?"

Shumacher shook his head. "That's why I appreciated the relationship with Ian Argyll. I've never been much for making friends."

"Listen, Cleve, don't answer this if you don't care to," I said, "but do you have a view on who might've infected Ian?"

"With AIDS?"

"What else?"

"Perhaps myself."

"Just perhaps?"

"Just that, Mr. Crang," Shumacher said. His voice and looks had a neutral quality, as if he'd reached a point beyond remorse and regret. "The thing is, Ian led quite an active sex life, as you must have discovered, and any one of us, anyone not taking precautions, we could have given it to Ian or he to us."

"That's a depressing thought, Cleve."

"If you want to know who gave what to whom, all that's left is to wait around for people to die and try to discover a pattern. Where the AIDS started and where it ends."

"Even more depressing."

"Isn't it, though?"

I cleared my throat. "Let me make a suggestion, Cleve. I know from the months when Ian had AIDS that there are support groups, guys with the disease who get together and talk about it and give one another a boost. Maybe one of those groups is the ticket for you."

Shumacher didn't answer.

"Just a thought, Cleve."

"Was it Groucho Marx who had that funny line?" Shumacher said.

"He had many funny lines."

"About clubs."

"Sure," I said. "'I'd never join a club that would have me for a member.'"

"That's me, Mr. Crang. I'm more of the loner type."

Somebody came up the office stairs, taking them at a good clip.

"What's happening, guys?" It was Murph, the aging hippie bartender from the Lasso Lounge. He was carrying, with plenty of finesse, a tray that held two drinks.

I said, "I don't recall placing an order, Murph."

"This is on my man Cleve," Murph said.

"I stopped by the Lasso before coming here, Mr. Crang," Shumacher said.

"Very classy gesture, Cleve," I said.

Murph served the drinks with a flourish. "Double Wyborowa on the rocks for Mr. Crang, double Harvey's Shooting Sherry, straight up, for Mr. Shumacher."

"How about a taste for yourself, Murph?" I asked.

"No time, man," Murph said. "I got a dude at the bar says his old lady partied with Jim Morrison in the summer of '69."

"A landmark event in the counterculture, Murph," I said.

"Later, guys," Murph said, and went lickety-split down the stairs.

"Well, Cleve," I said, raising my glass, "what'll we drink to?"

Shumacher raised his glass. "The future," he said.

"Okay, the future."

Shumacher's smile was small and rueful. "Limited as it may be for some of us," he said.

CHAPTER THIRTY-ONE

Later in the day, a little before six, Annie and I were sitting in the white wicker chairs in front of the television set in her living room. I had vodka on the rocks, she had white wine.

"Did the woman specify which channel we're supposed to tune to?" Annie asked.

"All she told me on the phone was not to miss the six o'clock news," I said. "'The minister requests that you specifically watch the local news at six,' were her words. Which minister? I asked, not that I've met more than one. 'Mr. Rowbottom,' she said, 'the Minister of Culture and Communications.'"

"That's all?"

"The woman had a tremor in her voice."

"Let's go with CFTO," Annie said.

"Their people have plastic faces and hard hair," I said.

"We can always switch."

The top item on the CFTO news was about two Middle Eastern countries whacking one another, next a domestic murder in the suburbs, then a report on a separatist group in the Maritimes threatening to split Cape Breton into a sovereign state.

"Variety is the spice of life," I said.

"In a surprise announcement at Queen's Park this afternoon," the anchor person on the TV screen said, a woman with pads in the shoulders of her jacket that came up to ear level, "the Minister of Culture and Communications, David Rowbottom, said that he was stepping down. Mr. Rowbottom, citing personal reasons, handed in his resignation to the premier, who said he accepted it with regret."

"Holy cow," Annie said.

"My sentiments exactly," I said.

"For more on the story," the woman with the shoulders said, "we go live to our Queen's Park correspondent, Wayne Wickin. Wayne?"

Wayne looked about nineteen years old, and the camera showed him standing on the steps outside the Ontario legislative building. A light wind ruffled his jacket, his hair, and the paper he held in his hand.

"Well, Debbie," he said, "the news of the Rowbottom resignation didn't come as a complete surprise here in the corridors at Queen's Park...."

"Little communication problem within the ranks at CFTO news," I said to Annie.

"Shh."

"Surprise or no surprise?" I whispered.

"Unconfirmed rumours about Rowbottom's difficulties have circulated for some months. But there was no hint of them in the brief statement that Mr. Rowbottom issued."

Wayne held up to the camera the piece of paper in his hand. The breeze wafted it out of his grip. Wayne grinned boyishly.

"Gone with the wind," he said, "just like David Rowbottom."

Annie switched to Citytv. Its Queen's Park man was standing, mike in hand, in a wide hallway inside the legislative building. He had grey hair, looked about a half century older than Wayne Wickin, and radiated the air of a guy who'd inhabited many political back rooms.

"It's significant," the man said into the camera, "that while Rowbottom has given up his cabinet post, he's hanging on to his seat in the legislature. In a conversation I had with Rowbottom an hour ago, he said he had no quarrel with his party or with his treatment at culture and communications. None of us in the press gallery ever thought he did. No, in my view, for the explanation behind this sudden resignation, we have to look to Mr. Rowbottom's sexual orientation...."

"Wow," Annie said softly.

"... It's little known outside these halls, but David Rowbottom is gay and my guess, for what it's worth, is that he has decided to leave the cabinet and assess the reaction of the province's voters, especially those in his own constituency, to his homosexuality. Rowbottom is out of the cabinet and possibly into the hot seat. Back to you in the studio, Peter."

"Before you go, Avery." Citytv's anchor came on screen, a lanky guy with spectacles, in shirt sleeves, top button undone, tie hanging loose. "Correct me if I'm wrong, but I don't believe I've come across anything about Mr. Rowbottom's sexual preference in the Toronto media until this minute, Avery."

"Peter, it's a Citytv exclusive," Avery intoned, "and we'll have film at ten on this dramatic story."

"Thanks, Avery."

"Do they really say that?" I asked Annie. "'Film at ten'?"

"They also say, 'This just in.'"

Annie got up, snapped off the TV set, and turned to face me. She had her hands on her hips.

"Well," she said, "Rowbottom's jumped ship as a minister so he doesn't have to do Paulie Ross's dirty work inside the cabinet."

"It looks that way to me."

"What other way could it look?"

"It might be he quit because he has AIDS," I said. "But I doubt that's the reason."

"Me, too."

"If he has AIDS, if he's going to actually die," I said, "he'd take it public in a big way. Just a guess, but that's how I size the guy up."

The buzzer to Annie's apartment sounded, from the street entrance three floors down.

"You expecting company?" I asked.

"It's the cocktail hour," Annie said. "Favourite calling time for Jehovah's Witnesses."

She went downstairs. I poured another drink in the kitchen and arrived in the living room as Annie came through the apartment door. She was ushering in David Rowbottom.

"Hey," I said, "in person, the fourth item on CFTO's nightly news."

"I led off on Global," Rowbottom said. He had a half smile, and his blue eyes were giving plenty of gleam.

I made a show of looking behind Rowbottom into the hall. "Anybody accompanying you?" I asked.

"Entirely on my own, Mr. Crang," Rowbottom answered. "I'm even driving my own car."

"No more limo to the Early Bird at the Waterfront Tennis Club?"

"Not in the immediate future."

Annie shut the apartment door. "Would you care for a glass of wine, Mr. Rowbottom?" she asked.

"Something stronger, if I may," Rowbottom said. He was on his best behaviour. "Is that vodka Mr. Crang's drinking?"

"Polish," I said. "On the rocks."

"Perfect."

Annie went out to the kitchen. I pulled up a third wicker chair for Rowbottom.

"How'd you get Annie's address?" I asked.

"Her name is on the ministry's mailing list."

"Let me rephrase the question," I said. "How'd you know I'd be at the address you got for Annie on the ministry's mailing list?"

"You weren't home, and it seemed logical to look for you here."

"Because sometime over the past couple of weeks, Paulie Ross mentioned I was a twosome with a TV star named Annie B. Cooke?"

"Exactly."

"Just wondering."

"I've apologized to Ms. Cooke for coming here unannounced," Rowbottom said to me. "There is some reassurance I'm seeking from you, if you're inclined to give it."

"That I'll keep my mouth shut?" I said. "That I'll stick to the promise I made to you and Paulie Ross the other day? That I'll observe the promise even though you've bailed out from Paulie? That kind of reassurance?"

"That kind," Rowbottom said. He sat with his knees together and looked almost prim in the chair. "You see, Mr. Crang, about myself and my alleged AIDS ..."

"You want to hold that thought, Rowbottom," I said. "Annie should hear this, too."

"Of course."

We waited in semi-awkward silence. Annie brought Rowbottom's drink and curled up on her chair.

"Mr. Rowbottom was about to discuss AIDS," I said to Annie.

She looked at Rowbottom. "The man on Citytv announced you're gay," she said. "Did you know that he spoke about it on TV?"

Rowbottom got back his half smile. "Avery, yes, he had the courtesy to advise me earlier this afternoon he intended to break the story. He said someone was bound to, and he wanted it to be him. They're very scoop-conscious at Citytv."

"But he didn't mention AIDS," Annie said.

Rowbottom sipped his vodka. "There are two reasons Avery said nothing on that subject."

"For one," I said, "you've managed to keep it a deep dark secret. Even from scoop-conscious guys like Avery."

"The security I've erected," Rowbottom said, a touch pompous, "has been close to impenetrable."

"Except Birks Robinson knows whatever there is to know about you and AIDS," I said. "And Bart the Bulge knows. And Hubert Wax must be privy to everything."

Rowbottom made a small dismissive gesture with the hand that wasn't holding his drink. "Well, of course, friends …"

"As long as Malcolm the bartender doesn't get wind of anything," I said, "you're home and dry."

Annie said, "What's the second reason, Mr. Rowbottom, that Avery didn't mention AIDS?"

"Because I don't *have* AIDS," Rowbottom said, his voice emphatic, beams leaping from his eyes. "What I do have, without getting into medical complexities, is rather akin to HIV."

"The virus that leads to AIDS," Annie said.

"The condition I have can develop into AIDS," Rowbottom went on. "I emphasize the *can*. But the treatments I continue to receive from a remarkable group of doctors in Buffalo are holding it in check."

"That's possible?" I asked.

"Firmly in check, Mr. Crang," Rowbottom said. "Permanently in check. I'm a committed believer in what these people are accomplishing."

All of us busied ourselves with our drinks and with Rowbottom's ringing endorsement of the Buffalo clinic.

"But," I said, "your condition, whatever it is, and the clandestine trips to Buffalo, the possibility of AIDS, even if it is as remote as you say, all of those elements taken together were enough to make you toe the line for Paulie Ross when he came around with his blackmail."

"I'm ashamed to say so," Rowbottom said, hanging his head ever so slightly.

"Ross had you in a terrible bind," Annie said. "That's nothing to be ashamed of."

Rowbottom took a deep breath. "One point I want to emphasize, I had no idea Ross would do what he did to Alex Corcoran."

"Kill him," I said.

"I was horrified."

"But not sufficiently horrified to confide in the cops?"

"Ross didn't tell me in so many words his man murdered Alex Corcoran," Rowbottom said. "I guessed as much, eventually, but was a mere guess something I could take to the authorities?"

Rowbottom looked at me as if he was asking for a pat on the head. I didn't say anything. And I didn't pat him on the head.

"But now that you *have* taken action," Annie said, "resigned from the cabinet and everything, left Ross in the lurch, without anybody to steer the garbage his way, aren't you in jeopardy? From Paulie Ross, I mean?"

Rowbottom laughed. "Oddly, it seems not," he said. "I telephoned Mr. Ross last night to let him know my resignation was coming. He was angry at first, a lot of yelling and cursing. But by the time he hung up, it seemed he'd quite lost interest in me."

"It figures," I said.

"It does?" Annie said.

"Think of this," I said to her, "think of what it is that motivates Paulie Ross."

"Oh, being mean to people, stealing, killing, pillaging, your ordinary crooked-person pursuits."

"Besides those," I said. "More than those."

"*More* than those?"

"Business."

"Oh, yeah, how could I forget?"

"Paulie does what's best for business," I said. "As long as Rowbottom here was a cabinet minister, it was good business to blackmail him with the AIDS story. Now that Rowbottom's out of the cabinet and can't affect the decision on the dump, it's no longer good business, bad business, *any* kind of business to bother with Rowbottom or AIDS or blackmail."

Annie turned to Rowbottom. "Is that how you read things?"

Rowbottom gave a small nod. "Mr. Crang and I are completely in agreement."

"Right now," I said, "Paulie'll be casting around for a Rowbottom replacement, another minister he can bribe or coerce —"

"Oh, now, just a moment, Mr. Crang."

"Hold a gun to a guy's head or dangle a carrot in front of his nose."

"I definitely do not share your cynicism, Mr. Crang," Rowbottom said.

I shrugged. "It happened once. Twice shouldn't shock anyone."

"Uh, everybody's drink okay?" Annie said, coming in quickly.

Rowbottom said his was, and I raised my glass to show Annie it was half full.

"What about your political career?" Annie asked Rowbottom. "Is it sort of in disarray?"

"I've retained my seat in the legislature, of course," Rowbottom said.

"Avery on Citytv seemed to find that a big deal," Annie said. "Significant, I think he called it."

"Wayne Wickin ought to hang out with Avery," I said. "Pick up tips on covering the political beat."

"Maybe I should, too," Annie said, speaking to Rowbottom, "because I don't get the significance of it, either, of you not resigning your seat."

I answered. "It means Mr. Rowbottom can lie low awhile, sit on the back benches until Paulie Ross and the garbage dump are just a memory, and later on, it could be the premier'll invite him back into the cabinet."

"If it isn't immodest of me to blow my own horn," Rowbottom said, getting a touch smug again, "it's fair to say I established at culture and communications that I'm capable of administering a cabinet portfolio."

"What about Avery's scoop?" Annie asked. "You being gay? How'll that go over?"

"The premier has assured me my homosexuality won't affect his continuing support," Rowbottom answered.

"You've spoken to him already?" Annie said. "The premier himself?"

"As soon as Avery spoke to me," Rowbottom said. "The president of my riding association pledged his backing as well."

"Lovely," I said, and swallowed most of the rest of my drink.

Rowbottom was close to buoyant. "Before I left the legislature to drive here, four of my fellow cabinet ministers — pardon, *former* fellow ministers — called to say they were one hundred percent with me."

"Swell."

"And the phone messages were running in my favour."

I sat and smiled.

"What's the joke?" Annie asked me.

"Politics," I said.

"Yes?"

"They make strange bedfellows."

CHAPTER THIRTY-TWO

After David Rowbottom left, taking with him the reassurance he'd come looking for, that I'd stay mum on all the past transgressions by all parties, I went out to the kitchen and organized another vodka on the rocks. In the living room, Annie sat with her elbows on her knees, her hands under her chin, a frown across her forehead.

"It's a depressing situation," she said.

"What?"

"I don't mind Rowbottom coming out more or less unscathed," she said. "Not really. He's been through a load of grief, and he did an honourable thing in the end."

"He probably has more grief to come."

"If those Buffalo doctors are quacks."

"What *do* you mind?" I asked. "What's depressing?"

"Paulie Ross walking around loose, the baddest guy of all."

"It'd take a lot to bring down a man like that, all the years he's been in operation, all the money and muscle."

"I realize that. Doesn't make me feel any better realizing it, though."

"Come on, kiddo," I said. "We made a few yards. We got Alex's killer and kicked a dent in Paulie Ross's machine."

Annie stood up and walked over to the front window.

"What about Ian?" she said. "We'll never know who gave him AIDS. In one sense, it doesn't matter. Ian's dead regardless of who infected him. Still ..."

"I was discussing that very topic this afternoon."

"Who with?" Annie asked. She had her back to me, looking out at the trees and the street.

"Cleve Shumacher. He thinks he might've been the one who passed the AIDS to Ian."

"But he isn't sure?"

"Not under the circumstances of Ian's apparent promiscuity," I said. "It could be the other way around, that Ian infected Shumacher."

Annie was silent for a moment. "Poor Cleve Shumacher," she said after a while.

"That was your line once before."

"I mean it. Poor Cleve Shumacher."

"You've never met the guy."

"With everything that's happened," Annie said, still at the window, looking out, "I *feel* like I know him."

I got up from my chair, the drink in my hand.

"Cleve's showing new spunk these days," I said.

Annie turned around. "A man's dying and he's showing spunk?"

"Grace under pressure or whatever the quote is."

"What's he got, a strong support system, family rallying around?"

"His old mum's dead, and there isn't anyone else in the family sense."

"Friends?"

"Didn't get the idea there's much going on there, either," I said. "I suggested to Cleve he should look into an AIDS therapy group."

"And?"

"He didn't precisely rush out of my office and sign up."

"Where the heck's the spunk coming from?"

I shrugged. "Spunk. Well, by that, I mean he wants me to fight his fraud case in court. I'd call that spunky given the alternative, and in general, he just transmits more in the nerve line than he did the first time I dealt with him."

"Doing it all alone?"

"That's my impression."

"Crang." Annie took a few steps into the centre of the room. She hooked one hand on her hip and ran a finger on the other hand across her chin.

"Yeah?"

"Listen, what I'm thinking isn't as crazy as it may sound at first," she said.

"Give me your definition of crazy."

"You've got an empty downstairs apartment."

"Hey ..."

Annie held a hand up. "You'll charge rent, of course."

"Cleve *Shumacher*?" I put my glass on the table and moved closer to Annie.

"It's eerie down there with nobody in the apartment," she said.

"Yeah, but —"

"You don't have to be best buddies with the man," Annie said, her voice coming alive. "Just be there, and he won't be alone with his AIDS, and you'll have him at close hand to consult about the fraud case, and now and then I'll cook something for the three of us, or maybe he's got some dish he specializes in, or we can just have cocktails."

"Well, yeah, Cleve likes his Harvey's Shooting Sherry."

"It could be a wonderful arrangement for everyone."

"This is assuming Cleve's open to the wonderful arrangement."

Annie spread her arms. "All you have to do is ask."

"Ha, hm, sure, that's easy enough."

"I bet he says yes," Annie said. She was smiling.

I took a deep breath. "Okay," I said, "I'll give Cleve a ring tonight."

"Do that," Annie said.

She wrapped her arms around me, and we hugged for a long time.